Writing Effective Employment Application Statements
有效撰寫求職英文自傳

By Ted Knoy
柯泰德

Illustrated by Wang Min-Chia
插圖: 王敏嘉

Ted Knoy is also the author of the following books in the Chinese Technical Writers' Series（科技英文寫作系列叢書）*and the Chinese Professional Writers' Series*（應用英文寫作系列叢書）：

An English Style Approach for Chinese Technical Writers
精通科技論文（報告）寫作之捷徑

English Oral Presentations for Chinese Technical Writers-A Case Study Approach
作好英文會議簡報

A Correspondence Manual for Chinese Technical Writers
英文信函參考手冊

An Editing Workbook for Chinese Technical Writers.
科技英文編修訓練手冊

Advanced Copyediting Practice for Chinese Technical Writers
科技英文編修訓練手冊──進階篇

Writing Effective Study Pans
有效撰寫英文讀書計畫

Writing Effective Work Proposals
有效撰寫英文工作提案

This book is dedicated to my wife, Hwang Li Wen.

　　我國加入WTO後，國際化的腳步日益加快；而企業人員之英文寫作能力更形重要。它不僅可促進國際合作夥伴間的溝通，同時也增加了國際客戶的信任。因此國際企業在求才時無不特別注意其員工的英文表達能力。

　　柯泰德先生著作《有效撰寫求職英文自傳》即希望幫助求職者能以英文有系統的介紹其能力、經驗與抱負。這本書是柯先生有關英文寫作的第八本專書，柯先生教學與編書十分專注，我相信這本書對求職者是甚佳的參考書籍。

國立交通大學管理學院 院長

黎漢林

Table of Contents

Foreword

Professional writing is essential to the international recognition of Taiwan's commercial and technological achievements. "The Chinese Professional Writers' Series" seeks to provide a sound English writing curriculum and, on a more practical level, to provide Chinese speaking professionals with valuable reference guides. The series supports professional writers in the following areas:

Writing style

The books seek to transform old ways of writing into a more active and direct writing style that better conveys an author's main ideas.

Structure

The series addresses the organization and content of reports and other common forms of writing.

Quality

Inevitably, writers prepare reports to meet the expectations of editors and referees/reviewers, as well as to satisfy the requirements of journals. The books in this series are prepared with these specific needs in mind.

Writing Effective Employment Application Statements is the third book in The Chinese Professional Writers' Series.

Writing Effective Employment Application Statements《有效撰寫求職英文自傳》為「應用英文寫作系列（The Chinese Professional Writers' Series）」之第三本書，本書中練習題部分主要是幫助國人進階學習的申請及避免，糾正常犯寫作格式上錯誤，由反覆練習中，進而熟能生巧提升寫作及編修能力。

　　「應用英文寫作系列」將針對以下內容逐步協助國人解決在英文寫作上所遭遇之各項問題：

A.寫作型式：把往昔普通常習於抄襲的寫作方法轉換成更積極主動的寫作方式，俾使讀者所欲表達的主題意念更加清楚。更進一步糾正國人寫作口語習慣。

B. 方法型式：指出國內寫作者從事英文寫作或英文翻譯時常遇到的文法問題。

C.內容結構：將寫作的內容以下面的方式結構化：目標、一般動機、個人動機。並了解不同的目的和動機可以影響報告的結構，由此，獲得最適當的報告內容。

D.內容品質：以編輯、審查委員的要求來寫作此一系列之書籍，以滿足讀者的英文要求。

Introduction

This writing workbook aims to instruct students in writing a well-structured employment application statement. The following elements of an effective employment application statement are introduced: expressing interest in a profession; describing the field or industry to which one's profession belongs; describing participation in a project that reflects interest in a profession; describing academic background and achievements relevant to employment; introducing research and professional experiences relevant to employment and, finally, describing extracurricular activities relevant to employment.

Rather than merely listing one's personal information and previous achievements (which are often found in a resume), an effective employment application statement reflects an applicant's ability to demonstrate his or her language capabilities within a confined space. More importantly, an effective employment application statement can elucidate the way in which one's academic and professional interests would benefit the company at which one is seeking employment; one's anticipated contribution to a company if employed there, and one's acquired knowledge, skills or leaderships qualities that are relevant to employment.

Each unit begins with three visually represented situations that provide essential information to help students to write a specific part of an employment application statement. Additional writing activities, relating to those three situations, help students to understand how the visual representation relates to the ultimate goal of writing an effective employment application statement. An Answer Key makes this book ideal for classroom use. For instance, to test a student's listening comprehension, a teacher can first read the text that describes the situations for a particular unit. Either individually or in small groups, students can work through the exercises to produce a well-structured employment application statement.

簡 介

　　本書主要教導讀者如何建構良好的求職英文自傳。書中內容包括: 1. 表達工作相關興趣 2. 興趣相關產業描寫 3. 描述所參與方案裡專業興趣的表現 4. 描述學歷背景及已獲成就　5. 介紹研究及工作經驗 6. 描述與求職相關的課外活動 7.綜合上述寫成精確求職英文自傳。

　　有效的求職英文自傳不僅必須能讓求職者在企業主限定的字數內精準的描述自身的背景資訊及先前成就，更關鍵性的因素是有效的求職英文自傳更能讓企業主快速明瞭求職者如何應用相關知識技能或其特殊領導特質來貢獻企業主。

　　書中的每個單元呈現三個視覺化的情境，提供國人英文工作自傳寫作實質訊息，而相關附加的寫作練習讓讀者做實際的訊息運用。此外，本書也非常適合在課堂上使用，教師可以先描述單元情境而讓學生藉由書中練習循序完成具有良好架構的工作自傳。

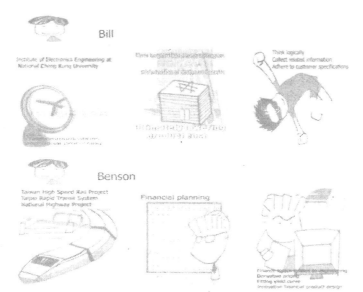

Bill

Institute of Electronics Engineering at
National Cheng Kung University

Think logically
Collect related information
Adhere to customer specifications

Benson

Taiwan High Speed Rail Project
Taipei Rapid Transit System
National Highway Project

Financial planning

Elements of a successful employment
application statement

Look at an example of an effective employment application statement:

The prospects of a looming global economic recession have negatively impacted industrial productivity in Taiwan, posing a great challenge for me as I enter the tight employment market as a recent graduate from National Chiao Tung University (NCTU). The competition for employment among individuals with an engineering graduate degree is indeed fierce.

While some view the volatile economic fluctuations with great alarm, I view them as the beginning of a journey. Employment at your company would allow me to nurture my brainstorming skills in a production-intensive environment. I have chosen your company for employment because of its global reputation as an incubator of technological innovation.

As a graduate student of Industrial Engineering at NCTU, I constantly focused on acquiring analytical skills and knowledge that are necessary in the workplace. In addition to meeting the core curricular requirements, I took courses such as Finance and Supply Chains to understand more about commercial operations. Professors within the department provided especially valuable instruction on IC manufacturing management.

The research process not only clarified concepts taught in class, but also allowed me to obtain advanced professional knowledge by operating relevant software and interviewing the upper-level management of real enterprises. Such practical experience will facilitate my transition from university life to the workplace. Moreover, in my Master's thesis, I not only learned the method of writing a research paper, but also strengthened my ability to design a study, evaluate data, and orally communicate results.

In addition to being diligent in my course work (as evidenced by my solid academic record in the accompanying manuscripts), I participated in several extracurricular activities and took part-time jobs to ensure the necessary balance between academic and social development. Through such activities, I broadened my perspective of how to handle routine tasks systematically and efficiently. Moreover, my calm nature and objective frame of mind allows me to communicate with others when preparing, planning, and coordinating numerous activities.

In sum, my personal traits such as gregariousness, seriousness, responsible nature, humility, enthusiasm, and perseverance are conducive to your company's working environment. Reflecting upon my academic career until now, I am anxious to find out the extent to which this knowledge will provide a blueprint for my career. Continually learning and absorbing new information appear to be the only means of remaining abreast of the latest trends and maintaining one's core value.

Despite the volatility of financial markets and economic uncertainty, I look forward to the future. I am also confident of my ability to perform tasks efficiently, and to adjust to your company's organizational culture. Moreover, as a member of your corporation, I would wholeheartedly contribute to your company's goals.

Not necessarily in the following order or that of the above example, a successful employment application statement comprises the following elements:

A Expressing interest in a profession 表達工作相關興趣

1. Stating how long one has been interested in a particular field or topic 描述專業興趣所延續的時間

Consider the following examples:

- My interest in environmental protection stems from my conviction, developed while I was an undergraduate, that economic development, while improving our lives, should not deplete non-renewable resources.
- When I was at high school, a book by a leading authority on Internet-based technologies aroused my desire to obtain more information about network applications.
- Biology has fascinated me ever since I participated in a university-sponsored summer camp. My interest eventually led to my decision to acquire a Bachelor's degree in this field.
- An article I read in The Journal of Engineering Advances during my junior year in university on the latest biotechnological applications aroused my interest in this rapidly developing area, eventually leading to my pursuit and successful completion of a Master's degree in this field.

2. Describing the relevance of one's interest to industry or society 描述興趣與產業及社會的相關性

Consider the following examples:

- Taiwan has become a member of the World Trade Organization, and solid design and manufacturing capability aside, financial expertise in global markets will be a necessity for Taiwanese companies. I am especially interested in the financial aspects of how companies will become globally competitive.

- Biotechnology is one of the world's fastest growing industries. Taiwan is widely anticipated to fuel this growth, and to become a hub of development in this rapidly evolving sector.

- In the information era, learning is a lifelong adventure that allows individuals continuously to upgrade their knowledge and skills, to remain competitive in the tight labor market and avoid redundancy in the workplace.

- The Taiwanese government has restructured local financial markets in recent years. Numerous opportunities for personal growth explain my interest in investment within the hi-tech sector.

3. Stating how one has pursued that interest until now 描述興趣形成過程

Consider the following examples:

- Success in my field of interest depends on developing a truly interdisciplinary approach, which I tried to nurture during undergraduate and graduate studies by exposing myself to a diverse array of seemingly polar topics and searching for their possible relationships in a practical context.

- A solid academic background and abundant research experience in materials science make me confident of becoming an accomplished scientist. I believe that these two ingredients are crucial to my fully realizing my career aspirations, hopefully at your company.

- My dream of becoming a widely respected engineer who will design innovative products has motivated me to pursue a Ph.D in Electrical Engineering at National Taiwan University to prepare for a career in research - hopefully at your institute.

· The strong departmental curricula at National Chung Hsing University instilled in me the academic fundamentals necessary for advanced research. Biotechnology has captured my interest because of its complexity and diverse applications.

4. Stating how finding employment related to one's interest would benefit the applicant and/or the company 描述興趣與工作的配合對勞資方都有利

Consider the following examples:

· The opportunity to work at your company would allow me fully to realize my career aspirations. The environmental engineering group in your company is the undisputed leader in environmental engineering in Taiwan. Renowned for its strong organizational culture and management structure, your company offers professional training that can enhance my work. Moreover, I am strongly attracted to your company's willingness to provide solid on-the-job training.

· Your excellent research environment and abundant academic resources will enhance my research capabilities and equip me with the competence to realize fully my career aspirations.

· I am impressed with your company's commitment to nurturing professionals in the hi-tech sector through your comprehensive six-month training program for all new employees, from which I will definitely benefit.

· The stringent six-month training program offered by your company's Human Resources Department will equip me with the skills to adjust to your corporate culture and to contribute significantly to your company's excellence in IC design.

B Describing the field or industry to which one's profession belongs 興趣相關產業描寫

1. Introducing a topic relevant to one's profession 介紹業界所關心的相關主題

Consider the following examples:

· Following its rapid industrial development in recent decades, Taiwan is now striving to become the 'Green Silicon Island' by simultaneously pursuing environmentalism and developing high-tech industries.

· Taiwan severely lacks technology professionals with a background in biotechnology and business administration, preventing the island's economy from keeping up with recently emerging trends in global R&D.

· Given the island's recent entry into the World Trade Organization and the eradication of many trade barriers to the local market economy, Taiwanese must continually upgrade their professional skills and linguistic abilities to remain competitive in the global workplace.

· Despite political differences, China and Taiwan share many common economic interests, as evidenced by their increasingly strong economic ties in the Asia-Pacific region. I am interested in a profession that would contribute further to strengthening these ties.

2. Describing the importance of the topic within one's profession 強調主題的專業性

Consider the following examples:

· Bioinformatics attests to the potential for integrating seemingly polar disciplines to create new technical and market opportunities.

- Integrating computers and biological science into the recently emerging bio-informatics sector in Taiwan has tremendous commercial and societal implications for the island.
- Taiwan's pivotal role in the industrial development of Greater China necessitates that local investors remain attuned to the latest technological and developmental trends on both sides of the Taiwan Strait.

3. Complimenting the company on its commitment to excellence in this area of expertise 讚美公司對專業的自我期許

Consider the following examples:

- As a leading IC manufacturer, your company has distinguished itself in its commitment to in-house research projects, as evidenced by your excellence in product innovation.
- In your company, the diversity of research projects and departments committed to implementing them is quite impressive.
- The great working environment, combined with the impressive number and diversity of training courses to maintain the competitiveness of your employees in the market place, would definitely benefit my professional development.

4. Stating anticipated contribution to company in this area of expertise if employed there 所期望對公司的專業貢獻

Consider the following examples:

- Rather than confining myself to my technical skills as an engineer, I hope to contribute to your company as a technology professional with management proficiency. I firmly believe that engineering and management expertise are essential in the intensely competitive hi tech sector.

8

- Following my development of particular expertise in graduate school, I believe that employment at your company will expose me to new fields as long as I remain open and do not restrict myself to the range of my previous academic training.

- If I am successful in securing employment at your company, my strong academic and practical knowledge, curricular and otherwise, will enable me to contribute positively to your corporation.

- As a member of your corporation, I hope to upgrade continuously my knowledge and skills so that I remain competent within my profession. The work experience I have gained so far has enticed me to further understand system-level electrical simulation for IC and electromagnetic phenomena-related research. Such in-depth investigation will hopefully equip me with the advanced professional knowledge to make me better placed to undertake IC package design.

C Describing participation in a project that reflects interest in a profession 描述所參與方案裡專業興趣的表現

1. Introducing the objectives of a project in which one has participated 介紹此方案的目標

Consider the following examples:

- As evidence of my commitment to this profession, I collaborated with other statisticians in developing an efficient evaluation model capable of selecting brands of natural gas buses.

- Owing to my deep interest in this profession, I actively participated in a project to develop an efficient response surface method for optimizing ordered categorical data process parameters.

· My strong commitment to this profession is demonstrated by my recent collaboration with colleagues in constructing an effective performance index (PCI) and developing an objective hypothesis testing procedure for PCIs, capable of assessing the operational cycle time (OCT) and delivery time (DT) for VLSI.

· My active participation in several projects in this field attests to my determination to pursue this career. For instance, I participated in a collaborative effort to develop a deterministic and stochastic model of groundwater flow to assess alternative monitoring networks.

2. Summarizing the main results of that project 概述該方案的成果

Consider the following examples:

· The results of that project confirmed the ability of our model not only to evaluate precisely the relationship between the cost and effectiveness of all viable alternatives to bus systems, but also to generate evaluations that provide economic information on all viable alternatives to bus systems.

· The method developed in our laboratory accurately estimates the location and dispersion effects. It can be easily implemented and clearly distinguishes these effects.

· According to our results, the hypothesis testing procedure that we developed allows firms to assess operation cycle time (OCT) and delivery time (DT) performance indices of VLSI, increasing the competitiveness of suppliers.

· The scheme developed in our research can help IC design engineers to minimize die size, optimize design and achieve an appropriate type of package, best package trace and excellent thermal / electrical performance. The scheme can also reduce the need to use trial-and-error, to 30% less than that required in the previous stage.

3. Highlighting the contribution of that project to the company or the sector to which it belongs 強調該方案對公司或部門的貢獻

Consider the following examples:

· The scheme developed in that project can shorten the design flow and dramatically reduce the time to market. The IC product's excellent characteristics can elevate a company's technical and market positions.

· Following that research effort, the enhanced carrier recovery on a digital receiver can outperform conventional models with respect to tracking, thus improving the competitiveness of communication products.

· Incorporating macroeconomic factors into the neural network structure developed in that research project can increase its accuracy of prediction, facilitating related assessments of a mixture of investments. Investment planners can adopt the neural network structure to include bankruptcy prediction in evaluating a company's financial solvency.

· In addition to providing a valuable reference for government when selecting brands of bus systems, the model that we developed includes a ranking methodology that provides a more objective outcome, with weights of related decision groups, than provided by other methodologies.

4. Complimenting the company or organization, at which one is seeking employment, on its efforts in this area 讚美公司對業界的專業努力

Consider the following examples:

· Your company offers a competitive work environment and is home to highly skilled professionals: these ingredients are essential to my continually upgrading my knowledge, skills and expertise in the above area.

· As a leading manufacturer, your company has distinguished itself in its commitment to in-house research projects, which match my professional interests, as evidenced by your commitment to excellence in product innovation.

· After carefully reading your company's on-line promotional material, I am especially interested in your innovative product development strategy and the abundant resources that you have devoted to IC design projects.

· Your company offers comprehensive and challenging training for those undertaking research in innovative IC product development programs.

D Describing academic background and achievements relevant to employment 描述學歷背景及已獲成就

1. Summarizing one's educational attainment 總括個人的學術成就

Consider the following examples:

· While my Master's degree in Biochemistry prepared me for the rigorous demands of conducting original research in this field and publication of those findings in international journals, doctoral study in the same field equipped me with the required knowledge, skills and professional expertise to excel in the biotechnology profession.

· Widely recognized as one of Taiwan's leading institutes of learning, the Experimental High School in Hsinchu Science-based Industrial Park from which I graduated, is renowned for its mathematics and physics departments, which provide special science education programs that include visits by well-known academics who conduct workshops and seminars for students.

· I received my undergraduate and graduate training in Industrial Engineering at National Chiao Tung University and National Tsing Hua University, respectively. Both are higher institutions of learning in which many staff at the Hsinchu Science-based Industrial Park developed their professional skills.

- Immediately following four years of highly theoretical study and intellectual rigor at National Taiwan University in successful pursuit of a Bachelor's degree in Chemistry, I gained entry to the highly prestigious doctoral program in the same field at National Tsing Hua University.

2. Describing knowledge, skills and/or leadership qualities gained through academic training 描述學術訓練所獲得的技能及（或）領導特質

Consider the following examples:

- My diverse academic interests reflect my ability to see beyond the conventional limits of a discipline and fully comprehend how a field relates to other fields. Solid training at a prestigious institute of higher learning equipped me with strong analytical skills and research fundamentals.

- Undergraduate and graduate courses in mechanical engineering often involved term projects that allowed me to apply theoretical concepts in a practical context and to develop my problem-solving skills.

- In the accompanying academic transcripts, high marks in those courses that equipped me with a solid theoretical background in electrical engineering reflect my commitment to acquiring knowledge and skills that will not only make me competent, but also allow me to thrive in the workplace.

- Critical thinking skills developed during undergraduate and graduate studies have enabled me not only to explore beyond the first appearances of finance-related issues and delve into the underlying issues, but also to conceptualize problems in different ways.

3. Emphasizing a highlight of academic training 強調一個學術訓練的特定領域

Consider the following examples:

· Studying at National Tsing Hua University, one of Taiwan's premier institutes of higher learning, strongly motivated me to acquire the latest knowledge, skills and technical information. More specifically, I learned how to analyze problems, find solutions, and implement those solutions according to the concepts taught in class.

· I also participated in a research project during my senior year, learning how to be a contributing member of a team and developing a thorough understanding of teamwork. I also attended several international conferences that addressed issues in biotechnology to broaden my perspective on potential applications of biology and computers- these areas are now my main areas of interest.

· Heavily emphasizing self-learning and development aimed at contributing to collaborative research efforts, graduate school ignited within me a strong desire to diversify my knowledge and skills, and thus adopt multi-disciplinary approaches in an industrial setting.

· My curiosity and determination to adopt unconventional or multi-disciplinary approaches to solve networking problems not only distinguished me from other graduate research students, but also led to my developing a software program that has already been commercialized.

4. Stressing how academic background will benefit future employment 強調學術背景對未來求職的利處

Consider the following examples:

· Graduate school has equipped me with much knowledge and competence in logic, to address effectively problems in the workplace, even though I may lack experience of a particular topic. After clarifying a problem at hand and identifying its components, I divide it into individual questions, clarify all the variables, their effects and possible consequences. After careful consideration, I then make a logical conclusion based on available information and propose available options for further research. I believe that your company will find in this approach a valuable asset.

· I am absolutely confident that my academic background, experimental and working experience in materials science, desire for knowledge, and love of challenges will enable me to succeed in your company's highly demanding product development projects.

· Extensive laboratory training improved my ability to define specific situations, think logically, collect related information and analyze problems independently. These qualities will prove to be valuable in any collaborative effort in which I am involved in your company.

E Introducing research and professional experiences relevant to employment 介紹研究及工作經驗

1. Introducing one's position and/or job responsibilities, beginning with the earliest position and ending with the most recent one 介紹個人歷年至今所任工作職位及職責

Consider the following examples:

· My enclosed curriculum vitae reflects extensive management experience in the semiconductor industry, acquired over more than a decade, made possible by graduate training at one of Taiwan's finest institutes of higher learning, and by collaboration with many globally renowned industrial partners.

· After serving for five years as an administrative assistant to the general manager, in which role I balanced personal goals and departmental progress, I was promoted to assistant manager of the procurement department, becoming adept in gathering information, evaluating data, negotiating prices and reviewing budgets.

· After receiving a Master's degree in Power Mechanical Engineering from National Tsing Hua University and completing our country's compulsory military service immediately thereafter, I began working at ABC Corporation, a leading manufacturer of chipsets and a designer of graphic ICs.

· I still felt somewhat unprepared for the rapid emergence of new technologies in the work place, particularly in electromagnetics, explaining why I returned to university for doctoral study. I will shortly complete my doctoral degree and look forward to applying my newly acquired knowledge and skills as an employee of a globally renowned corporation such as yours.

2. Describing acquired knowledge skills and/or leadership qualities 描述個人所獲得的知識、技能及（或）領導特質

Consider the following examples:

· The occasional frustrations of slow progress in research strengthened my resolve to excel in the laboratory, making me more tenacious. Extensive laboratory work also exposed me to advanced experimental techniques and significantly improved my analytical skills and data collection capabilities.

· By assuming such responsibilities, I acquired a breadth of experience in dealing with complex environmental issues. In addition to refining my ability to coordinate related activities, these experiences enabled me to examine an array of issues in economic, social, political and public financial contexts.

· Responsible for coordinating inter-departmental activities to utilize effectively the company's manpower and resources, I learned how to incorporate the seemingly polar approaches of different departments to solve particular problems in a cohesive framework that drew upon the strengths of the departments involved.

- Doing so involved not only absorbing other colleagues' perspectives, but also learning how to negotiate carefully with others so that the dignity of each collaborator is maintained.

F Describing extracurricular activities relevant to employment 描述與求職相關的課外活動

1. Introducing an extracurricular activity that one has participated in 曾參加的相關課外活動介紹

Consider the following examples:

- An outstanding manager must balance academic and social skills. Therefore, I actively participated in our university's student union, the most reputable student organization on campus, to apply systematically my knowledge and skills and broaden my horizons. After several years of participation, I served as a vice-president of the association, in which role I was responsible for various tasks such as coordinating student welfare and communicating students' needs to pertinent school authorities; holding campus events, and contacting student unions of other universities to set up collaborative events.

- As an undergraduate, I organized a private consulting group of university students who tutored junior high school students in an array of subjects. Despite initial difficulties in establishing this group, I was able to recruit several tutors, rent a location, purchase teaching materials, and design a daily study schedule so that the students could keep up with the curriculum. The community response was overwhelming, as evidenced by the large number of students who enrolled in our tutorial courses.

- As a volunteer for the Society of Chemical Engineers at graduate school, I was responsible for organizing academic workshops; managing departmental publications; performing various administrative tasks, and organizing book exhibitions. This experience instilled in me the importance of synergy and efficiency when collaborating with others.

· During my life on campus, I spent time developing my own interests and focusing on personal growth beyond academia.

2. Highlighting the acquired knowledge, skills or leadership qualities that are relevant to employment 強調和求職相關的已有知識技能或領導特質

Consider the following examples:

· Extensive global travel for business and recreation has made me more receptive to the sometimes opposing values of different countries. Closely observing and comparing different societies, rather than making sweeping generalizations about a particular country or group of people, has allowed me to understand various management practices in different cultures.

· My participation in numerous extracurricular activities at university, taught me how to organize activities competently; express my opinions clearly; communicate with others effectively; transform conflicts into constructive situations that promote collaboration, and cope with failure by analyzing the underlying problems that prevent success.

· Participating in the university Heart club, a social service organization, helped me to nurture leadership and collaborative skills as an organizer and coordinator of many activities. ALE, an acronym for "Actual Living English", not only strengthened my listening, speaking, reading and writing skills, but also allowed me to make new friends from different cultures and express my feelings in another language, which is challenging for me. Experiences gained through my participation in extracurricular activities have greatly enriched my life by enabling me to achieve the necessary balance of academic and social skills.

· While leading the campus orchestral group, I learned how to motivate group members to hone their individual talents for a common goal. Dealing with the occasional frustrations of fiercely individualistic orchestral members when trying to reach a consensus has made me a strong leader. I was able to listen patiently to individual concerns and tried to incorporate them in a group consensus. I believe that that role was good training for the workplace.

Unit One

Bob

Allen

Expressing interest in a profession

表達工作相關興趣

Vocabulary and related expressions　相關字詞

solid background　強有力的學術背景	quality control　品質控管
financial analysis　財務分析	determination 決心
collaborative　合作的	invaluable 珍貴的
exposure　接觸	a logical choice　明智的抉擇
upon graduation　即將畢業	eager 熱切的
organizational culture　組織文化	semiconductor industry 半導體產業
intensely competitive　激烈競爭	driven by　被驅動
dynamic environment　動態環境	intrigued by　被吸引
ancient　古代的	richness and color of　豐富內涵
anthropology　人類學	advent of　出現
knowledge economy　知識經濟	pure capital　純資本
profoundly　深切地	invaluable　珍貴的

A Write down the key points of the situations on the preceding page, while the instructor reads aloud the script from the Answer Key.

Situation 1

_____

_____

_____

Situation 2

_____

_____

_____

Situation 3

_____

_____

_____

B Based on the three situations in this unit, write three questions beginning with **What**, and answer them. The questions do not need to come directly from these situations.

Examples

What is Bob determined to become professionally?

A successful manager

What department at National Central University does Allen hope to secure employment?

Human Resources

1. _____

   _____

2. _____

   _____

3. _____

   _____

C Based on the three situations in this unit, write three questions beginning with *Which*, and answer them. The questions do not need to come directly from these situations.

Examples

Which industry has Bob been preparing to enter for several years?

The semiconductor industry

Which organization is a leading core logic and graphics supplier?

DEF Corporation

1. _____

   _____

2. _____

   _____

3. _____

   _____

D   Based on the three situations in this unit, write three questions beginning with **Why**, and answer them. The questions do not need to come directly from these situations.

Why does Bob consider ABC Corporation to be a logical choice for his first employment upon graduation?

Because of its active role among global enterprises

Why did Tom take a Master's degree in Electrical Engineering from National Tsing Hua University?

To acquire advanced academic training

1. _____

    _____

2. _____

    _____

3. _____

    _____

E. Write questions that match the answers provided.

Example

Which organization is a leading core logic and graphics supplier?

DEF Corporation

How long have telecommunications and related consumer products intrigued Tom?

Since high school

1. _____

   _____

   One of Taiwan's premier institutes of higher learning

2. _____

   _____

   A successful manager

3. _____

   _____

   Human relationships

Unit One

Express inerest in a profession
表達工作相關興趣

1. Stating how long one has been interested in a particular field or topic.
描述專業興趣所延續的時間

2. Describing the relevance of one's interest to industry or society.
描述興趣與產業及社會的相關性

3. Stating how one has pursued that interest until now.
描述興趣形成過程

4. Stating how finding employment related to one's interest would benefit the applicant and/or the company.
描述興趣與工作的配合對勞資方都有利

Common elements in expressing interest in a profession include:

1. Stating how long one has been interested in a particular field or topic 描述專業興趣所延續的時間

◎ Consider the following examples:

◎ I remember my fascination with science as a child.

◎ My fascination with physics can be traced to my childhood when I often attempted to understand complex phenomena commonly found in nature.

◎ My interest in environmental protection stems from my conviction, developed while I was an undergraduate, that economic development, while improving our lives, should not deplete non-renewable resources.

◎ When I was at high school, a book by a leading authority on Internet-based technologies aroused my desire to obtain more information about network applications.

Biology has fascinated me ever since I participated in a university-sponsored summer camp. My interest eventually led to my decision to acquire a Bachelor's degree in this field.

◎Of all the science courses in which I enrolled during university, I most enjoyed biology and chemistry , impelling me to broaden my knowledge of biochemistry.

◎ Visual effects created using computer graphics in motion pictures have always fascinated me, causing me not only to ponder how such effects were created but also to develop a love for computer science.

◎ An article I read in The Journal of Engineering Advances during my junior year in university on the latest biotechnology applications aroused my interest in this rapidly developing area, eventually leading to my pursuit and successful completion of a Master's degree in the same field.

◎ My interest in the veterinarian profession dates back to high school.

◎ I still clearly recall my excitement when coding my first program, a turning point in my career, when I ultimately decided to pursue studies in preparation for work as a programmer.

◎ The explosion of wireless technologies to make communication accessible at an ever-falling price never ceases to amaze me.

◎ Biology has long intrigued me, as evidenced by my high marks in related courses at high school.

◎ Immersing myself early on in my undergraduate studies, in issues related to technology law , I came into contact with actual enterprises . Nothing can prevent me from acquiring in-depth knowledge of this rapidly emerging field in Taiwan.

◎ My intrigue in veterinary science stems from early in my life, and has led to my near completion of a Master's degree in this field from National Chung Hsing University, with a concentration in animal physiology.

◎ I have dreamt of becoming a widely respected scientist for as long as I can remember.

◎ Astronomy has enthralled me since high school.

◎ I have been fascinated for quite some time with how the Internet has pervaded nearly every aspect of our daily lives, as evidenced by common buzzwords such as high-speed connections, broad bandwidth and ADSL.

◎ I have dreamt of becoming an inventor since childhood, wanting to design and patent a device that would revolutionize daily life.

◎ Since childhood, I have enjoyed playing charades. Guessing someone's intended meaning, although not apparent at the time, has always been fascinating for me, which fact explains why I became interested in cryptology during my undergraduate studies.

◎ I remember, as a child, taking apart and reassembling our family's radio and other home appliances to understand how they operated.

◎ As a child, I day-dreamed of patenting inventions that would transform our lives, which fact explains why, following a rigorous nationwide university examination, I gained entry into National Taiwan University of Science and Technology and majored in Construction Engineering.

◎ Politics has fascinated me since childhood even though I didn't understand its underlying principles at the time. A Bachelor's degree in Political Science at National Cheng Chi University allowed me to understand more fully how politics functions at different levels.

◎ Innovations in product technology, especially those contributing significantly to quality of life, have enthralled me since childhood.

◎ I have enthusiastically enrolled in accounting and finance courses since junior college, which fact explains why, with such a strong analytical background, I acquired a Master's degree in Economics from National Central Tung University.

◎ My inquisitive nature during childhood often surfaced in the detailed and unconventional questions that I posed to my parents about different technological concepts that were a mystery to me.

◎ From an early age, I became fascinated with Taiwan's natural surroundings, which fact explains why I chose Biology as my preference during our country's highly competitive university entrance examination.

◎ I remember the curiosity, which overcame me as a child, about how the electrical appliances in our home were assembled.

◎ From an early age, I often asked my parents about nature-related topics, especially biology.

◎ High school sparked my interest in engineering, and led to my acquiring a Master'ss degree in Electrical Engineering at National Cheng Kung University, which is widely respected in Taiwan for its technical-oriented curricula.

◎ Art history has captivated me for as long as I can remember. It is an interest that I developed by avidly reading biographies of renowned painters and sculptors.

◎ The way in which computers have made individual's lives more flexible and efficient, has intrigued me for quite some time.

◎ The human anatomy has fascinated me since childhood, to the point that I dreamt of becoming a widely respected physician someday. This dream culminated in my completion of a bachelor's degree in Physiology from National Yang Ming University, a leading medical institution of higher learning in Taiwan.

◎ I have been drawn to electronics since junior high school, and now I am determined to become an engineer in a globally renowned corporation such as yours.

◎ By adopting different perspectives, I enjoy the thrill of solving a difficult programming problem or deriving a complex mathematical formula after spending much effort on it.

◎ After working for several years as a quality control engineer, I became more interested in management issues than in the purely technical aspects of product development.

◎ Clarifying my career direction has allowed me to see clearly not only my professional interests, but also the knowledge and skills tat I must attain to rise to the challenges of a tight labor market.

◎ Long before entering college, I felt an affinity for politics, evidenced by my sensitivity to those around me, and my concern for their welfare.

2. Describing the relevance of one's interest to industry or society 描述興趣與產業及社會的相關性

Consider the following examples:

◎ Traditional industries that fail either to develop advanced manufacturing procedures or to lower their production costs face a bleak future in the global economy.

◎ While many Taiwanese companies have invested in the Chinese market, governmental authorities are wary of the potential detriment to local industry if the rate of capital transfer is left unchecked.

◎ Despite Taiwan's well-established semiconductor fabs, IC design firms and PC industry, the island's telecommunications sector is still in its infant stage.

◎ Taiwan has become a member of the World Trade Organization, and, solid design and manufacturing capability aside, financial expertise in global markets will be a necessity for Taiwanese companies. I am especially interested in the financial aspect of how those companies will become globally competitive.

◎ Biotechnology is one of the world's fastest growing industries. Taiwan is widely anticipated to fuel this growth, and to become a hub of development in this rapidly evolving sector.

◎ Trends in the Internet and globalization have exacerbated the global dissemination of information, computing power and network applications.

◎ Advanced knowledge of biotechnology is essential for me to confront the future challenges of this sector that is evolving rapidly in Taiwan. Previously, I never associated biology with technological development. The full potential of biotechnology can only be harnessed by integrating biology with seemingly unrelated fields such as computer science and engineering.

◎ Urban planners in Taiwan have the valuable opportunity to work with their counterparts on the mainland to integrate management and engineering practices.

◎ As the Internet demands the rapid transformation of conventional types of legal regulation, the field of intellectual property rights aims not only to protect the ownership of ideas in cyberspace, but also to understand how existing law governs the flow of information on-line.

◎ Advances in information technology and global commerce have inspired me to broaden my horizons beyond Taiwan, explaining why I majored in Computer Science with a minor in Business Administration during university.

◎ In the information era, learning is a lifelong adventure that allows individuals continuously to upgrade their knowledge skills to remain competitive in the tight labor market and avoid redundancy in the workplace.

◎ The increasing amount of information exchanged among Internet users has created strong consumer demand for greater bandwidth and higher frequency signals.

◎ Flexible communication has become a vital part of daily life, as evidenced by the widespread use of mobile phones.

◎ Network applications have dramatically risen in status within the hi tech sector, as evidenced by society's increasing reliance on the Internet . This fact explains my great interest in the field.

◎ Given the global interest in developing renewable alternative sources of energy, the commercial possibilities for this hi tech sector appear limitless.

◎ Biotechnology has recently emerged as one of the most extensively researched topics worldwide, explaining why many Taiwanese companies have ventured in this area.

◎ The banking sector in Taiwan has undergone a tremendous transformation in recent years, especially in the area of auditing practices. Such a transformation has drawn me into studying this field, and particularly in the area of reform within local financial institutions.

◎ The Taiwanese government has restructured local financial markets in recent years. Numerous opportunities are available for expansion, explaining my interest in investment opportunities within the hi-tech sector.

◎ As biotechnology emerges as a major industrial sector in Taiwan, related developments will impact society in ways previously unimaginable. I hope that by joining your company, I can significantly contribute to this increasingly important field.

◎ Researchers worldwide are fascinated by the implications of merging biotechnology with computer science, which fact explains why I majored in Bioinformatics at National Taiwan University of Science and Technology.

◎ Instead of discouraging me, uncertain economic times challenge me to acquire the necessary knowledge and skills to thrive in the intensely competitive labor market.

◎ Disciplined scientists contribute to society by solving problems to elevate human living standards. The nobility of this profession explains why I majored in Chemistry at National Chung Cheng University.

◎ The Taiwanese government has earmarked bioinformatics as an area of priority for national technological development. The field will require skilled professionals with relevant knowledge and skills.

◎ DNA research in Taiwan has received much attention lately, making Chang Gung University, a hotbed of related study, my preferred choice for a Master's degree in this field.

◎ My interest in biotechnology is related to its recent emergence as a global trend that will significantly impact our lives in unimaginable ways.

◎ This recently emerging trend reveals the vital role of biology in paving the way for future technological developments.

◎ The increasing number of biological applications of technology has motivated me to understand underlying natural scientific concepts.

◎ In addition to creating a more flexible classroom, distance learning allows students not only to acquire information efficiently, but also to learn anytime and anywhere with few constraints.

◎ Despite an island-wide recession, the biotechnology sector has witnessed modest growth, as evidenced by continued investment in this recently emergent area of development. This sustained growth motivates my interest in pursuing a career in this sector, hopefully at your company.

◎ With the easy access it provides, and its rapidly advancing technologies, mobile communications has dramatically changed our daily lives. However, current applications have not matured in terms of satisfying consumer demand.

◎ With the rapid global expansion of the Internet and information technologies, I am drawn to a career as a software engineer in the hi tech sector.

◎ Governmental authorities are increasingly concerned with how to develop biotechnology-based solutions to meet the needs of Taiwan's aging population. This development will require highly qualified professionals with relevant expertise.

35

◎ Moreover, my inquisitiveness and perceptiveness towards nature have remained with me since childhood and allowed me to expand my academic interests to graduate level research in biology.

◎ The Internet allows humans to connect with each other even from remote locations more flexibly, efficiently, and economically than before. Developing technologies that bring people closer is a logical career direction for me.

◎ Taiwan's recent entry into the World Trade Organization will, in the short term, adversely impact the local currency market and certain industrial sectors. Devising strategies in which local companies can remain competitive in the face of increasingly open domestic markets, hopefully at a securities investment firm such as yours, is a worthwhile career direction for me.

◎ The way in which mobile communication devices have become common-place in daily life attests to the accelerated development of information technologies in recent years, and explains why I have decided to pursue a career in this rapidly expanding field.

◎ The Information Age has accelerated the almost dizzying pace of technical invention, as evidenced by the widespread commercialization of telecommunication products and services.

◎ With an increasing number of individuals' accessing information on-line, the narrow bandwidth of a company's network can severely limit corporate communication and profits.

◎ Chemical engineering has played an instrumental role in Taiwan's industrial development from an agricultural-based economy into a manufacturing-based one; it is a profession to which I am proud to belong.

◎ In addition to significantly elevating living standards, computer science has created a technological revolution, which I want to join as a software engineer and, in a small way, push even further.

◎ Continuous advances in network applications have accelerated progress in the information technology sector to an unprecedented rate.

3. Stating how one has pursued that interest until now　描述興趣形成過程

Consider the following examples:

◎ Having spent considerable time researching and organizing data on information science applications in medicine, I have developed a particular interest in integrating concepts from these two fields and applying them to the recently emerging field of bioinformatics, an emerging hi-tech sector in Taiwan.

◎ In addition to exposing me to the latest trends in IC design, your company would also nurture my managerial skills as I strive to find a practical context for the strong academic fundamentals acquired in graduate school.

◎ Success in my field of interest depends on developing a truly interdisciplinary approach, a skill which I tried to nurture during undergraduate and graduate studies by exposing myself to a diverse array of seemingly polar topics and searching for their possible correlation in a practical context.

◎ During university, I pursued my interest in biotechnology by enrolling in several departmental courses that introduced practical and theoretical applications. Successfully completing these courses depended on the concentrated efforts of various classmates, instilling in me the importance of collaboration to fully grasp technical concepts. From these courses, I realized the need to attain a graduate degree in this field to make a meaningful contribution in the workplace.

◎ The solid departmental curricula at National Taiwan University included courses such as Network Applications, Integrated Systems, and E-Commerce, which provided me with advanced knowledge necessary for this highly competitive profession.

◎ This curiosity about electrical appliances led to my pursuit of electronics-related knowledge and intrigue with the diversity of their application in our daily lives.I have delved into electronic engineering to understand further the growing number of applications and the ways in which they will dramatically change our lives in the future

◎ University fostered my interest in distance learning, leading to my current pursuit of a Master's degree in Computer Science with a concentration in educational technology. Following completion of this degree and employment at your company for an extended period, I hope to continue with this line of research and acquire a Ph.D in this field, which is a recently emerging sector in Taiwan.

◎ Not particularly drawn to pure theory, I tend to search for practical applications in industry. This fact explains why I acquired a Bachelor's degree in Computer Science from National Cheng Kung University. Computer Science not only combines science and related applications, but also boosts Taiwan's competitiveness globally.

◎ Motivated by my fascination with this exciting field, I received a Master's degree in Information Management at National Cheng Kung University, one of Taiwan's prestigious institutes of higher learning.

◎ During my academically challenging undergraduate work at National Chung Hsing University, I was exposed to several seemingly polar yet increasingly integrated disciplines, such as biology, information science and statistics.

◎ The strong research fundamentals acquired during my undergraduate years at National Central University have prepared me for a career in the constantly evolving IC design sector.

◎ A solid academic background and abundant research experience in materials science make me confident of becoming an accomplished scientist. I believe that these two ingredients are the only means of fully realizing my career aspirations, hopefully at your company.

◎ This aspiration has resulted in my nearly completing a Master's degree in Business Administration from National Cheng Chi University.

◎ This hobby led to an active interest in product design, resulting in my completion of a Bachelor's degree in Mechanical Engineering from National Chiao Tung University.

◎ Studying Finance at Tamkang University furthered my lifelong interest in commerce, which fact explains why I eventually pursued a Master's degree in Business Administration with a concentration in Accounting from National Cheng Chi University, one of Taiwan's leading institutes of higher learning.

◎ My dream of becoming a widely respected engineer who would design innovative products has motivated me to pursue and successfully complete a Ph.D in Electrical Engineering at National Taiwan University to prepare for a research career, hopefully at your institute.

◎ To satisfy my intellectual curiosity, I acquired a Bachelor's degree in Environmental Science from National Taiwan Ocean University to understand the practical context of marine life sciences in an island economy.

◎ Owing to my diligent preparation and avid interest in natural sciences, I scored highly enough to gain entry into the prestigious Department of Biology at National Taiwan University.

◎ This curiosity led to my avid interest in the latest electronic innovations and logical decision to major in Electrical Engineering at Feng Chia University.

◎ During graduate school, I focused on network applications in asynchronous environments. Despite the daunting challenges it poses, this research is in an intriguing field with many potential applications in the hi tech sector.

◎ To foster my interest in this rapidly emerging field in Taiwan, I took the unique opportunity to undertake biotechnology research, allowing me to obtain both a theoretical and practical understanding of the field in a laboratory environment.

◎ The semiconductor industry in Taiwan has helped transform Taiwan's economy into a hi-tech-oriented one, inspiring me to acquire a Master's degree in Industrial Engineering at Feng Chia University.

◎ To further understand how humans impact the environment, I enrolled in several biology and ecology courses during high school, which motivated me even further to acquire a Master's degree in Biochemistry from Fu Jen Catholic University.

◎ While the strong departmental curricula at National Chung Hsing University instilled in me academic fundamentals necessary for advanced research, biotechnology captivated my interest owing to its complexity and diverse applications.

◎ Owing to my strong interest in machinery and strong desire for advanced study, I acquired a Bachelor's degree in Mechanical Engineering from Tung Hai University and successfully met the degree requirements for a Master's in Control Engineering at National Chiao University.

◎ As a child, my fascination with new inventions and their underlying concepts allowed me to foster my critical thinking skills and strive to complete challenging tasks systematically.

◎ Immersing myself in pertinent literature on the latest developments in semiconductor manufacturing, I focused on equipping myself with the knowledge, skills and expertise to achieve my aspiration eventually to become a project manager.

◎ As widely anticipated, the recently emerging biotechnology industry will revitalize Taiwan's economy, explaining why I concentrated on this field while acquiring a Bachelor's degree in Biology at National Sun Yat Sen University.

◎ With my fascination in computers since childhood, I have received extensive training not only to excel in programming, but also to remain abreast of the latest trends.

◎ This fascination with outer space inspired me to dream of becoming an astronaut, explaining why I successfully completed a Master's degree in Aeronautical Engineering from National Cheng Kung University, one of Taiwan's leading institutes of higher learning.

◎ Driven by a strong desire to refocus my career from a technical-oriented one to a management-oriented one, I resigned my current position and returned to academia in pursuit of a Master's degree in Business Administration.

◎ By pursuing a career path that diverges from my previous academic training, I have not only had to adjust to a more competitive working environment, but also had to acquire new knowledge and skills and continuously upgrade them to keep pace with the latest technological trends. Renowned for its state-of-the art research facilities and the ability to attract highly qualified professionals, your company is the logical choice for me to launch my career as an electrical engineer.

4. Stating how finding employment related to one's interest would benefit the applicant and/or the company 描述興趣與工作的配合對勞資方都有利

Consider the following examples:

◎ Interacting with the highly skilled professionals in your company will undoubtedly provide me with a practical context for the academic training that I have received so far.

◎ Your excellent research environment and abundant academic resources will enhance my research capabilities and equip me with the competence to realize fully my career aspirations.

◎ I am impressed with your company's commitment to nurturing professionals for the hi-tech sector through your comprehensive six-month training program for all new employees, a program that I will definitely benefit from.

◎ The stringent six-month training program offered by your company's Human Resources Department will equip me with the skills to adjust to your corporate climate and to contribute more significantly to your company's excellence in IC design.

◎ What attracts me most to your company is the wide spectrum of product development projects, highly qualified and seasoned professionals and state-of-the art facilities.

◎ I am very much looking forward to interacting with the highly skilled, multi-disciplinary professionals in your company.

◎ Eager to devote myself to the electrical engineering profession, I believe that your company would be the ideal starting point for this career path, equipping me with the knowledge and skills to succeed in this highly competitive technology sector.

◎ Your company's vast resources and highly skilled professionals can greatly facilitate my quest to grasp more fully the latest technological applications in software design.

◎ Your company would provide the ideal environment for me to contribute fully to this sphere of technology.

◎ Securing employment at your company would allow me to develop further my knowledge and skills, and to realize more fully my aspiration to become an accomplished IC designer.

◎ Your company will prepare me for a successful and challenging career in the IC sector by building upon the strong academic skills I acquired in graduate school.

◎ Your company will offer me with a competitive environment to integrate further my knowledge, skills and work experiences to predict accurately market trends in the hi tech sector.

◎ The multi-cultural environment of your company would help me better to appreciate diversity in the world's managerial and commercial practices, and hone my knowledge and skills in the global market place.

◎ With a solid background in economics, I would like to join your company as a financial planner in one of your many undergoing development projects.

◎ I would like to build on my solid background in accounting and acquire more practical experience by joining your CPA firm.

◎ Access to cutting-edge resources and quality professionals within your company will greatly facilitate my reaching my career aspiration to become a respected quality engineer.

◎ I strongly believe that working in your company will allow me to excel as a graphics designer by providing a practical context for my rich academic background.

◎ I look forward to taking full advantage of the many resources that your company offers, such as state-of-the-art facilities and equipment, diversity of research activities and numerous training opportunities.

◎ The opportunity to work at your company is the logical choice for me to achieve my career aspirations. The environmental engineering group in your company is the undisputed leader in the field in Taiwan. Renowned for its strong organizational culture and management structure, your company offers professional training that can enhance my work performance. Moreover, I am highly attracted to your company's willingness to provide solid on-the-job training.

◎ I believe that your company's working environment will support me in acquiring the necessary expertise to succeed in this intensely competitive profession.

◎ Securing employment at a renowned manufacturer such as your company, devoted to product excellence, is my next step towards advancing my expertise in IC design.

◎ Your company would provide an ideal working environment in which I can apply my research experience and theoretical knowledge gained in graduate school to a practical industrial setting.

◎ Working in the vibrant corporate climate of your company would build on my strong academic foundation, making me better equipped for a career in global finance.

◎ Working at your prestigious firm would sharpen my communication and presentation skills, give me unparalleled access to highly skilled professionals and state-of-the-art facilities that would greatly facilitate my aspiration to become an expert in this rapidly evolving field.

◎ The training opportunities that your company offers in the area of wafer chip design are unparalleled among other firms in the IC industry.

◎ From your web site, I learned of your company's commitment to excellence in manufacturing, on which your highly skilled workforce draws to undertake innovative product technology development programs. I believe that such a a conducive workplace environment is ideal for me.

◎ The unique environment that your company offers would allow me to attain my personal goals and contribute to your organization's technical and market positions.

◎ I believe that SIS, a leading core logic and graphics supplier, provides an excellent environment in which I can further refine my knowledge and skills. I firmly believe that my creativity and industrious attitude will prove invaluable to any collaborative effort to which I belong in developing powerful wafer chips.

◎ Acquiring invaluable work experience at an IDM company, which designs, manufactures, and markets products, is the most effective way for me to realize what this vibrant industry can offer.

◎ I would like to apply my solid academic background and proven research skills at SiS, a leading IC design company in Taiwan. I am especially interested in your company's developments in DCVD (Dielectrics Chemistry Vapor Deposition), including related process applications and developments in deep sub-micro generation.

◎ My strong academic performance and solid background in Industrial Engineering have prepared me to meet the challenges of the intensely competitive semiconductor industry.

◎ Becoming a member of the SiS family would also allow me to apply my strong research fundamentals to this exciting industrial field of integrated circuit design.

◎ With its excellent design facilities and seemingly unlimited resources, SIS provides a conducive working environment that would allow me to put my solid academic training into practice.

◎ I believe that your company provides a unique working environment in which I can fully develop my professional interests.

◎ Your company thrives among tough competition in the constantly changing computer technology field. This seemingly unlimited change would provide an exciting environment in which I can strive to advance my professional skills.

◎ My strong background in Electrical Engineering, with a particular focus on IC design, will not only be a valuable asset of your company's research and development team, but also allow me to develop professional skills in a leading multinational company.

◎ I believe that my solid academic background will compensate for my lack of professional experience in IC design and, allowing me to contribute to the SIS family.

◎ As a proud member of this distinguished profession, I hope to contribute significantly to advancing computer design and creating more reliable devices.

◎ Upon completing my Master's degree, I hope to bring my solid academic skills in these areas to your company.

◎ I believe that your renowned company will provide not only a dynamic environment in which I can apply my academic skills but also invaluable training in becoming an effective manager.

◎ Having developed an interest in this dynamic field, I look forward to joining your company so that I can more fully understand related industrial applications and become an accomplished engineer capable of effectively responding to the continuous demands upon the water supply in Taiwan.

◎ I believe that your company provides a unique environment in which I could build on a solid academic background to hone my professional skills.

◎ I firmly believe that the research fundamentals acquired during graduate school will give me a competitive edge in the workplace, hopefully at your company.

◎ Having successfully completed a Master's degree in Electrical Engineering at National Sun Yat Sen University, I feel that my solid background in this field will allow me to rise to the challenges of this intensely competitive hi-tech sector.

◎ Upon completing this degree, I hope to join your company to match the strong knowledge skills acquired during graduate school to a practical context that your working environment would provide.

◎ Taiwan lacks researchers with abundant work experience in bioinformatics. Joining your company would allow me to begin a career in this rapidly emerging research discipline so that, in addition to contributing to company profits, I can also contribute to the island's expertise in this area.

◎ The solid academic fundamentals I acquired during graduate school will hopefully contribute to the organizational culture of your globally renowned company.

◎ I believe that the theoretical and professional knowledge and skills acquired at graduate school will allow me to excel as an engineer in your IC design firm.

◎ After I submit my Master's thesis at the end of this semester, the solid academic skills nurtured at university will be a valuable asset to any company to which I belong. I hope this company will be yours.

◎ I believe that my solid academic foundation and advanced research expertise will prove invaluable for any project team that I belong to at your company.

◎ As a researcher in this intensely competitive hi-tech sector, I believe that I can contribute to our country's efforts to develop biotechnology-related product technologies.

◎ I hope that employment at your company will allow me to realize more fully the practical applications of these important disciplines in the workplace.

◎ I feel most comfortable working in a professional environment, surrounded by state-of-the-art equipment and highly trained personnel. Your company (provides OR offers) such an environment, which would allow me to be highly productive.

◎ These exciting industrial trends have increased my interest in communications, fueling my aspiration to become a respected engineer in my field of expertise, hopefully at your company.

◎ Your company's rich pool of highly skilled professionals and state-of-the-art facilities will allow me to enhance my knowledge, skills and expertise in the topics that I researched during graduate school.

◎ Securing employment at your renowned company would allow me to build upon my solid mechanical engineering background and relevant work experiences.

◎ My rare combination of graduate-level research in Industrial Engineering and Business Administration will prove invaluable in the intensely competitive hi tech sector, and hopefully to your company.

◎ I hope that, through thoroughly developing PDA software at your telecommunications firm, I can contribute not only to company profits but also to efforts to make daily communications more flexible and efficient.

◎ Continuously developing knowledge and skills will largely determine my success as a software engineer. I believe your company will provide the opportunity for me to develop them.

◎ Employment at your company will provide ample opportunity for me to rise to the challenges of this intensely competitive profession.

F In the space below, express your interest in a profession.

_____

_____

_____

_____

_____

_____

_____

_____

_____

_____

_____

_____

_____

G Look at the following examples of expressing interest in a profession.

Stating how long one has been interested in a particular field or topic 描述專業興趣所延續的時間 The way in which nature operates has fascinated me since high school, explaining why I majored in Chemistry at university to understand the theoretical basis of nature's diversity. **Stating how one has pursued that interest until now** 描述興趣形成過程 Upon graduation, I extended that interest to my current employment at the Chemistry Vapor Deposition (CVD) Department of SiS Corporation. **Describing the relevance of one's interest to industry or society** 描述興趣與產業及社會的相關性 As a chemical application, the CVD process plays an instrumental role in semiconductor technology. In the integration and applications of the CVD process, Taiwan's technological advances parallel those of Japan and the United States. However, the island lags behind in manufacturing CVD production machines owing to its overall absence of basic research in CVD and material development. Other semiconductor processes, not just CVD process, face similar constraints. **Stating how finding employment related to one's interest would benefit the applicant and/or the company** 描述興趣與工作的配合對勞資方都有利 As a chemical engineer in this intensely competitive hi-tech sector, I believe that I can contribute to our country's efforts to manufacture quality CVD production machines, hopefully at your company.

*

Stating how long one has been interested in a particular field or topic 描述專業興趣所延續的時間 My interest in computers stems from childhood, when I played computer games, read computer HW/SW magazines and wrote programs. I instinctively knew that I would someday be software engineer. **Stating how one has pursued that interest until now** 描述興趣形成過程 While math and computer programming were among my favorite courses in university, I knew that to prepare for employment in this highly competitive field, I should hone my research skills, which explains why I went on to complete a Master's degree in Electrical Engineering before entering the workforce. **Stating how finding employment related to one's interest would benefit the applicant and/or the company** 描述興趣與工作的配合對勞資方都有利 Despite my lack of professional experience, I believe that my solid academic background and knowledge base can contribute positively to your company.

*

Describing the relevance of one's interest to industry or society 描述興趣與產業及社會的相關性 Computers, telecommunications and related consumer products have markedly elevated living standards for quite some time. While some products entertain and offer convenience as well as comfort, others save time and reduce workload. **Stating how long one has been interested in a particular field or topic** 描述專業興趣所延續的時間 Such diversified products have intrigued me since high school. **Stating how one has pursued that interest until now** 描述興趣形成過程 This fascination explains why I completed my undergraduate studies in Electrical Engineering at National Tsing Hua University, one of Taiwan's premier institutes of higher learning. To acquire advanced academic training, I also took a Master's degree in this field at this university. **Stating how finding employment related to one's interest would benefit the applicant and/or the company** 描述興趣與工作的配合對勞資方都有利 Offering a unique workplace in which I can put my academic skills into practice, SIS, a leading core logic and graphics supplier can provide me an excellent opportunity to foster my professional skills. I believe that my solid academic foundation and advanced research expertise will prove invaluable to any project team to which I belong at SIS.

*

Stating how long one has been interested in a particular field or topic 描述專業興趣所延續的時間 I've devoted myself to research in computer graphics since entering the Multimedia Products Division at SIS. **Stating how one has pursued that interest until now** 描述興趣形成過程 I am especially interested in developing fast computation algorithms and computer architectures. More specifically, I am constructing a vertex shader-based architecture that computes vertices' attributes instead of fixed functions.

*

Stating how long one has been interested in a particular field or topic 描述專業興趣所延續的時間 I remember falling in love with computers back in junior high school when I would occasionally practice on my classmate's PC. **Stating how one has pursued that interest until now** 描述興趣形成過程 Its deep impact is evidenced not only by my participation in the high school computer club, but also by my successful completion of Bachelor's and Master's degree in Computer and Information Science at National Chiao Tung University. As my graduate school research focused on Computer Aided Design, I hope to secure employment related to design automation.

*

Stating how long one has been interested in a particular field or topic 描述專業興趣所延續的時間 University sparked my fascination with multimedia applications, my desire to enter this exciting field and my eventual success in securing employment. **Stating how one has pursued that interest until now** 描述興趣形成過程 While progressing in my work, I increasingly immersed myself in software and hardware development, particularly because of the difficulty in ensuring the compatibility of architecture in computer hardware. **Stating how finding employment related to one's interest would benefit the applicant and/or**

the company 描述興趣與工作的配合對勞資方都有利 The unique environment that your company offers would allow me to meet my own personal goals as well as contribute to society.

*

Stating how long one has been interested in a particular field or topic 描述專業興趣所延續的時間 Computer games, and especially the techniques involved in programming them, have enthralled me since I started playing them in high school. **Stating how one has pursued that interest until now** 描述興趣形成過程 This fact explains why I majored in computer science in university and later received a Master's in the same field from National Cheng Kung University. I am now an engineer at SiS Corporation.

*

Stating how one has pursued that interest until now 描述興趣形成過程 Owing to my interest in information technologies, I received a Master's degree in Computer Science from National Chiao Tung University, with a concentration in computer architecture. Despite my academic training, I am not particularly interested in hardware design. Instead, I prefer to create organizational and architectural designs and then write programs to simulate their effectiveness. I then proceed to analyze the simulation results and modify the design accordingly to improve performance. IC design houses increasingly emphasize time to market for products to increase profits. However, in light of such constraints, implementing physical-ware and optimizing it is extremely difficult. Therefore, simulation and analysis are necessary to achieve a balance between time to market and product quality. I am especially interested in this area of research.

*

Describing the relevance of one's interest to industry or society 描述興趣與產業及社會的相關性 Stereo 3D displays play an increasingly important role in computer graphics, visualization and virtual-reality systems. However, owing to their complex geometrical computations, conventional methods of deriving stereoscopic images are computationally inefficient. For example, the two view-point stereo display takes more than twice as much time to compute geometry as the non-stereo 3D display. Thus, the inability to resolve the inefficiency problem makes high-quality and real-time stereo 3D applications impossible. **Stating how one has pursued that interest until now** 描述興趣形成過程 I am interested in investigating topics related to this very important problem in the IC design field.

*

Stating how long one has been interested in a particular field or topic 描述專業興趣所延續的時間 Computers have intrigued me since childhood. **Describing the relevance of one's interest to industry or society** 描述興趣與產業及社會的相關性 Their innovation and magic have revolutionized our daily lives, explaining why I have decided to devote myself to the further development of this constantly evolving field of technology. **Stating how finding employment related to one's interest would benefit the applicant and/or the company** 描述興趣與工作的配合對勞資雙方都有利 In particular, I hope to contribute to advancing computer design and creating more flexible and advanced devices.

*

Stating how one has pursued that interest until now 描述興趣形成過程 I received a Bachelor's degree in Organic/Analytical Chemistry from National Tsing Hua University. In addition to loving laboratory work, I am interested in quality control. At my work in the quality assurance department of our company, I focus on statistical process control (SPC) and measurement systems analysis (MSA), occasionally performing MASK inspections. **Describing the relevance of one's interest to industry or society** 描述興趣與產業及社會的相關性 As well known, an unstable or inaccurate measurement system yields errors in process control and

judgment. I am especially concerned with how determine whether a measurement system is stable; how to ensure the repeatability, the reproducibility and the matching of a measurement system, and the criteria by which judgments are made.
*

Describing the relevance of one's interest to industry or society 描述興趣與產業及社會的相關性 Logic designers play a vital role in the semiconductor industry. Customers demand high-performance, low-cost chips. Additionally, the rapid growth of communication products in recent years has ushered in the need to combine strong communication background with logic design experience in designing a wafer chip to customer specifications. **Stating how long one has been interested in a particular field or topic** 描述專業興趣所延續的時間 As a graduate student, I was fascinated by many communication theories, especially those related to digital signal processes, digital communications and coding. This fundamental knowledge has allowed me to undertake telecommunications-related research. However, using my research experience to develop a commercial product has necessitated that I acquire a significant amount of logic design experience. **Stating how one has pursued that interest until now** 描述興趣形成過程 This fact explains why I joined SIS, which has allowed me to obtain this much -needed experience. This advanced professional knowledge, in combination with my already strong research fundamentals, has equipped me to accept rigorous challenges in the workplace. Moreover, language training courses within the company allow me to communicate easily with others. I feel that I am heading in the right direction.
*

Describing the relevance of one's interest to industry or society 描述興趣與產業及社會的相關性 Computers, telecommunications and related consumer products have dramatically enriched our lives, for example by increasing worker productivity, strengthening relationships with families or friends, or simply entertaining us.

Stating how one has pursued that interest until now 描述興趣形成過程 Our increasing dependence on these commercial products explains why, following a rigorous nationwide entrance examination, I entered National Tsing Hua University and majored in Electrical Engineering. Equipped with solid academic fundamentals and determined to enhance my professional knowledge of telecommunications, I later received a Master's degree in Electronic Engineering from National Chiao Tung University. Many research opportunities within this constantly evolving field have equipped me with advanced professional skills in telecommunications that have enabled me to rise to the challenges of a career within this industry. **Stating how finding employment related to one's interest would benefit the applicant and/or the company** 描述興趣與工作的配合對勞資方都有利 With my desire to acquire logic design-related knowledge, I hope to build upon my solid background to design telecommunication-related chips. I believe that SIS, a leading core logic and graphics supplier, provides an excellent environment in which I can further refine my knowledge and skills. I firmly believe that my creativity and industrious attitude will prove invaluable to any collaborative effort to which I belong, in developing powerful wafer chips.

*

Stating how long one has been interested in a particular field or topic 描述專業興趣所延續的時間 I have studied Electrical Engineering since attending a local institute of technology. **Stating how one has pursued that interest until now** 描述興趣形成過程 I continued my studies and later acquired a Bachelor's degree at ISU University. I am especially interested in drawing schematics, measuring digital signals using a scope, and solving EMI-related issues.

*

Stating how long one has been interested in a particular field or topic 描述專業興趣所延續的時間 Materials science has intrigued me since childhood. For instance, learning how to compound a composite material, such as plastic, in my hand fascinated me. **Stating how one has pursued that interest until now** 描述興趣形成過程 I enjoyed conducting chemistry experiments in high school and university. I went on to acquire a Master's degree in Applied Chemistry from National Chiao Tung University, researching topics related to light and electric polymer materials. After performing military service, as is compulsory in our country, I began working at Mosel Electronics Corporation in May 1987 as a process engineer. I was responsible for developing furnace and wet cleaning processes, marking my introduction to the semiconductor industry. Two years later, I joined SiS, in charge of developing the DCVD process, which I still am. The semiconductor field is as challenging and rewarding as performing chemistry experiments in a laboratory. So far, I have been granted more than six patents in the United States for inventions related to the Diff process. I enjoy my profession immensely.

*

Stating how long one has been interested in a particular field or topic 描述專業興趣所延續的時間 As an art, cooking significantly impacts our lives. As a child, I watched my mother cooking for hours, maybe because life was much simpler then or because I always liked to eat as a child. My mother often let me snack while she was cooking, explaining the strength of my interest. **Stating how one has pursued that interest until now** 描述興趣形成過程 Consequently, cooking has become my favorite daily activity. When cooking for my friends, I love to see the satisfaction in their eyes, which is the greatest complement to me. Cooking is a vital skill during rough economic times.

*

Describing the relevance of one's interest to industry or society 描述興趣與產業及社會的相關性 Significantly contributing to the global economy, the semiconductor industry ushers in many commercial trends and elevates living standards. **Stating how long one has been interested in a particular field or topic** 描述專業興趣所延續的時間 My interest in this industry was sparked in related courses while pursuing a Bachelor's degree in Civil Engineering. **Stating how one has pursued that interest until now** 描述興趣形成過程 I began my career at SiS, a renowned IDM company. Acquiring invaluable work experience at another IDM company, which designs, manufactures, and markets products, is the most effective way for me to realize what this vibrant industry can offer.

*

Stating how long one has been interested in a particular field or topic 描述專業興趣所延續的時間 Since childhood, I have long been intrigued by natural phenomena and enthusiastically sought relevant information. **Stating how one has pursued that interest until now** 描述興趣形成過程 This inquisitiveness led to my completion of a Master's degree in Power Mechanical Engineering with a concentration in semiconductor process applications, from National Tsing Hua University, one of Taiwan's renowned institutes of higher learning. I am currently engaged in simulating reactive gases in a chamber. I am also collaborating with a high tech company to develop a more advanced heat dissipation model of the removal of residual heat from a wafer chip. **Stating how finding employment related to one's interest would benefit the applicant and/or the company** 描述興趣與工作的配合對勞資方都有利 Therefore, I would like to apply my solid academic background and proven research skills to SiS, a leading IC design company in Taiwan. I am especially interested in your company's developments in DCVD (Dielectrics Chemistry Vapor Deposition), including related process applications and developments in deep sub-micro generation.

*

Stating how long one has been interested in a particular field or topic 描述專業興趣所延續的時間 Electrical engineering has fascinated me from an early age, and

I have studied related courses since university. **Stating how one has pursued that interest until now** 描述興趣形成過程 Having just received a Master's degree in Electrical Engineering from National Chiao Tung University, I focused on discrete signal process, digital control and VLSI. Graduate school taught me innovative ways of solving problems logically and independently. **Stating how finding employment related to one's interest would benefit the applicant and/or the company** 描述興趣與工作的配合對勞資方都有利 With my fascination with how integrated circuit technologies have dramatically impacted our lives, I believe that SiS would provide the ideal working environment in which I can further pursue my professional interests. Becoming a member of the SiS family would also allow me to apply my strong research fundamentals to this exciting industrial field of integrated circuit design.

*

Stating how long one has been interested in a particular field or topic 描述專業興趣所延續的時間 Electrical engineering has enthralled me since university, and I have devoted myself to researching related topics such as semiconductors and electrical circuit design. **Describing the relevance of one's interest to industry or society** 描述興趣與產業及社會的相關性 The invention of the first transistor undoubtedly ushered in much technological progress over the past century. I am especially interested in furthering my knowledge of electrical engineering by advanced study in computer-aided design, which is a field of increasing important as designed circuits are equipped with an increasing number of devices.

*

Stating how long one has been interested in a particular field or topic 描述專業興趣所延續的時間 I have been mesmerized by computers ever since owning my first one in high school, explaining why my decision to major in Electronics Engineering at university was a logical one. **Stating how one has pursued that**

interest until now 描述興趣形成過程 During undergraduate studies, electronics and computer science-related courses attracted me the most and also made me fully aware of the importance of computer applications in designing integrated circuits. Graduate studies in this field, with a particular emphasis on computer-aided design, further strengthened my solid academic background. **Stating how finding employment related to one's interest would benefit the applicant and/or the company**描述興趣與工作的配合對勞資方都有利 System Integrated System Corporation is globally renowned as a leading IC design house owing to its design capabilities and scale. With its excellent design facilities and seemingly unlimited resources, SIS provides a conducive working environment that would allow me to put my solid academic training into practice.

*

Stating how long one has been interested in a particular field or topic 描述專業興趣所延續的時間 I have long been intrigued by science and technology. This interest culminated in my successful completion of a Master's degree in Electrical Engineering from National Taiwan University, one of Taiwan's renowned universities. I then entered the high-tech IC design industry, with a particular interest in logic design, communications and computer networks. **Stating how one has pursued that interest until now** 描述興趣形成過程 In graduate school, I participated in a project in which I simulated an Ethernet protocol. My first assignment at SiS was to develop an Ethernet MAC controller. I am now developing an Serial ATA controller, a computer network product. I am glad that I have been able to apply my practical laboratory experience from graduate school to the highly competitive working environment that SiS offers.

*

Describing the relevance of one's interest to industry or society 描述興趣與產業及社會的相關性Technological advances have realized things which were considered impossible only a few years ago. This is especially true in computer science. For instance, evolution in architecture and manufacturing has advanced rapidly. **Stating how one has pursued that interest until now** 描述興趣形成過程 My deep interest in this area explains why I have focused my research on VLSI chip design. I want more fully to understand all related processes, from chip design to chip production. **Stating how finding employment related to one's interest would benefit the applicant and/or the company** 描述興趣與工作的配合對勞資方都有利 I believe that your company provides a unique working environment in which I can fully develop my professional interests.

*

Stating how long one has been interested in a particular field or topic 描述專業興趣所延續的時間 Since entering the workforce, I've been fascinated by investment-related issues, such as the fair value pricing of financial services and arbitrage in different markets. **Stating how one has pursued that interest until now** 描述興趣形成過程 Therefore, following six years of work as an engineer, I returned to National Taiwan University where I am pursuing a Master's degree in Finance with a particular emphasis on Financial Engineering. This area addresses how to determine the fair value of financial services by developing related mathematic models.

*

Describing the relevance of one's interest to industry or society 描述興趣與產業及社會的相關性 Knowledge management aims to enhance organizational performance by supplying the right people with sufficient knowledge in a timely manner for proper implementation. **Stating how finding employment related to one's interest would benefit the applicant and/or the company** 描述興趣與工作的配合對勞資方都有利 As an information specialist in a high-tech company, I realize the importance of information exchange. I believe that my solid background in knowledge management will prove to be a valuable asset to your company.

*

Stating how long one has been interested in a particular field or topic 描述專業興趣所延續的時間 Since childhood, I have dreamt of becoming an engineer who can design and repair machines efficiently. I remember enthusiastically taking apart and repairing electrical appliances at home. **Stating how one has pursued that interest until now** 描述興趣形成過程 My interest in mechanical engineering-related topics such as static and dynamic construction has led to my successful completion of Bachelor's and Master's degrees in Power Mechanical Engineering from National Tsing Hua University, a leader among Taiwan's institutes of higher learning.

*

Stating how long one has been interested in a particular field or topic 描述專業興趣所延續的時間 Electrical equipment has fascinated me since high school, explaining why I decided to immerse myself in related research at the graduate level. **Stating how one has pursued that interest until now** 描述興趣形成過程 After acquiring a Master's degree in Electrical Engineering with a concentration in semiconductor technology from National Cheng Kung University, a renowned university in Taiwan, I became intrigued by the recently emerging IC design sector and joined SiS, a distinguished high tech company in Hsinchu Science-based Park. **Stating how finding employment related to one's interest would benefit the applicant and/or the company** 描述興趣與工作的配合對勞資方都有利 My strong academic background enables me to tackle and solve work-related problems logically. SiS thrives among tough competition in the constantly changing computer technology field. This seemingly unlimited change provides an exciting environment in which I can strive to advance my professional skills.

*

Striving to be an excellent design engineer, I hope to acquire the necessary knowledge and skills to be a successful manager in the future. **Stating how finding employment related to one's interest would benefit the applicant and/or the company** 描述興趣與工作的配合對勞資方都有利 My strong background in Electrical Engineering, with a particular focus on IC design, will not only be a valuable asset to your company's research and development team, but also allow me to develop professional skills in a leading multinational company.

*

Stating how long one has been interested in a particular field or topic 描述專業興趣所延續的時間 My inquisitive tendency to discover new things has persisted since childhood. I am especially enthralled by rapid technological growth in computers and telecommunications. **Stating how one has pursued that interest until now** 描述興趣形成過程 This fact explains why I successfully gained entry into the Electrical Engineering Department at National Taiwan University where I received a Master's degree in 2000. **Stating how finding employment related to one's interest would benefit the applicant and/or the company** 描述興趣與工作的配合對勞資方都有利 I believe that my solid academic background will compensate for my lack of professional experience in IC design, allowing me to contribute to the SIS family.

*

Stating how long one has been interested in a particular field or topic 描述專業興趣所延續的時間 Computers have intrigued me since childhood. These innovative and seemingly magical machines have revolutionized the world, explaining why I have decided to devote myself to a career in this constantly evolving technology field. **Stating how finding employment related to one's interest would benefit the applicant and/or the company** 描述興趣與工作的配合對勞資方都有利 As a proud member of this distinguished profession, I hope to contribute significantly to advancing computer design and creating more reliable devices. I would like to do so as an employee at your company.

*

Describing the relevance of one's interest to industry or society 描述興趣與產業及社會的相關性 As computers have revolutionized society, a seemingly unlimited number of products and applications enhance the quality of our lives. Consumers heavily prioritize flexibility and time when using related products and applications. Notable examples include video conferencing, video on demand, and embedded as well as distance learning systems. Such systems require a high quality of service (QoS). Therefore, developing a real-time system ranks high among computer science-related research topics. In particular, information appliances (IA) and embedded systems have received considerable interest recently. **Stating how one has pursued that interest until now** 描述興趣形成過程 To foster my interest in this area, I took a Master's degree in Computer Science from the Institute of Computer Science and Information Engineering at National Taiwan University, one of Taiwan's premier institutes of higher learning, in 1997. Graduate school provided me with a solid academic foundation and advanced research skills to undertake real-time systems-related research. This combination of practical and theoretical training has prepared me for a career in industry-related research. As a software engineer at SiS, a leadership skill chipset design house, I am responsible for creating device drivers and system testing devices. This responsibility necessitates that I am familiar with many operating systems and the latest technological developments.

*

Stating how long one has been interested in a particular field or topic 描述專業興趣所延續的時間 I have been interested in science and management since high school. My congenial personality makes it easy for me to get along with others and understand their perspectives. **Stating how one has pursued that interest until now** 描述興趣形成過程 My interest in technology explains why I majored in Industrial Engineering and Management at National Chiao Tung University, where I am pursuing a Master's degree with a particular emphasis on operations management and quality management. Upon completing my Master's degree, I hope to bring my solid academic skills in these areas to your company.

*

Stating how finding employment related to one's interest would benefit the applicant and/or the company 描述興趣與工作的配合對勞資方都有利 After completing a Master's degree in Civil Engineering from National Chiao Tung university, I plan to work as an environmental engineer, preferably in investigating and remedying soil and water pollution. This work will enable me to acquire knowledge of the perpetual knowledge of environmental and natural resources. Additionally, by working on-site, I hope to understand advanced technologies for remedying environmental pollution by serving as a cooperative professional consultant. Beyond accumulating sufficient work experience and professional knowledge, I hope to preside over environmental pollution remediation projects.

*

Stating how long one has been interested in a particular field or topic 描述專業興趣所延續的時間 Management science has interested me ever since high school. I am also interested in how individuals interact efficiently within an organizational framework, explaining why I majored in industrial engineering and management at university. **Stating how one has pursued that interest until now** 描述興趣形成過程 Immersing myself in operations management and quality management-related issues, I am now undertaking graduate school research in these areas. **Stating how finding employment related to one's interest would benefit the applicant and/or the company** 描述興趣與工作的配合對勞資方都有利 I hope that employment at your company will allow me to realize more fully the practical applications of these important disciplines in the workplace.

*

Stating how long one has been interested in a particular field or topic 描述專業興趣所延續的時間 A solid background in quality control, financial analysis, and industrial management at National Chiao Tung University explains why I am driven to become a successful manager. **Stating how one has pursued that interest until now** 描述興趣形成過程 During graduate school, I participated in many collaborative projects that involved industrial organizations such as ITRI, AMAT and Chailease Finance. This invaluable exposure made UMC a logical choice for my first employment upon graduation, owing to its active role among global enterprises. Eager to contribute to the strengthening of UMC's organizational culture, I have been preparing for several years to enter the challenging semiconductor industry. **Stating how finding employment related to one's interest would benefit the applicant and/or the company** 描述興趣與工作的配合對勞資方都有利 As is well known, the intensely competitive global market is driven by customers who demand the highest quality products. With this in mind, I believe that employment at your renowned company will provide not only a dynamic environment in which I can apply my academic skills but also invaluable training to become an effective manager.

*

Stating how long one has been interested in a particular field or topic 描述專業興趣所延續的時間 As a child, I was fascinated with flowing water. This fascination ultimately led to my interest in fluid mechanics and hydraulic engineering. **Stating how one has pursued that interest until now** 描述興趣形成過程 After taking a Bachelor's degree in Civil Engineering, I attained a Master's degree in the same field from National Chiao Tung University, with a particular emphasis on groundwater.

Stating how finding employment related to one's interest would benefit the applicant and/or the company 描述興趣與工作的配合對勞資方都有利 Having developed an interest in this dynamic field, I look forward to joining your company so that I can more fully understand related industrial applications and become an accomplished engineer capable of effectively responding to the continuous demands upon the water supply in Taiwan.

*

Describing the relevance of one's interest to industry or society 描述興趣與產業及社會的相關性 Semiconductor technologies have ushered in innovative products that significantly impact our lives. ABC Corporation continues to lead the semiconductor industry by significantly contributing to the global supply of semiconductors. This fact explains why ABC Corporation represents an exciting employment opportunity for me. **Stating how finding employment related to one's interest would benefit the applicant and/or the company** 描述興趣與工作的配合對勞資方都有利 While my undergraduate studies in Industrial Engineering at National Chiao Tung University instilled in me the importance of how an enterprise should strive to maximize output and minimize related costs simultaneously, I believe that ABC Corporation would provide a unique environment in which I could build on a solid academic background to hone my professional skills.

*

Stating how long one has been interested in a particular field or topic 描述專業興趣所延續的時間 Flood control has fascinated me from an early age. **Stating how one has pursued that interest until now** 描述興趣形成過程 This fascination has led to my studies in this field during undergraduate studies and graduate school, culminating in my Master's thesis on flood forecasting using an artificially intelligent method that I developed during my research. **Stating how finding employment related to one's interest would benefit the applicant and/or the**

company 描述興趣與工作的配合對勞資方都有利 My evidenced commitment and solid academic foundation in this area would prove to be an invaluable asset for flood control projects within your company. Thus, I wish to seek employment at your company to enhance my own abilities in solving real flood-related problems.

*

Stating how long one has been interested in a particular field or topic 描述專業 興趣所延續的時間 Management literature has intrigued me since childhood. I have dreamt of becoming an entrepreneur who actively participates in various industrial projects and reaps considerable profits. **Stating how one has pursued that interest until now** 描述興趣形成過程 This aspiration explains why I successfully gained admission into the graduate program at Department of Industrial Engineering and Management of National Chiao Tung University, one of Taiwan's premier institutions of higher learning. Graduate school has provided me with a solid academic foundation, particularly in Quality Control-related research, which will prove to be an invaluable asset to any management team to which I belong in the future. **Stating how finding employment related to one's interest would benefit the applicant and/or the company** 描述興趣與工作的配合對勞資方都有利 I firmly believe that the research fundamentals acquired during graduate school will give me a competitive edge in the workplace, hopefully at your company.

*

Stating how long one has been interested in a particular field or topic 描述專業 興趣所延續的時間 As a child, I was enthralled by all aspects of civil engineering, especially hydrology and environmental science. **Stating how one has pursued that interest until now** 描述興趣形成過程 This fascination has resulted in my near completion of a Master's degree in Hydrology with a concentration in ground water contaminants, from National Central University, one of Taiwan's premier institutes of higher learning. **Stating how finding employment related to one's interest**

would benefit the applicant and/or the company 描述興趣與工作的配合對勞資方都有利 My solid academic training and practical laboratory experience will definitely contribute to any research team to which I belong, hopefully at your renowned company.

*

Stating how long one has been interested in a particular field or topic 描述專業興趣所延續的時間 I have long been intrigued by materials science and engineering, especially the response of metals to forces or loads. **Describing the relevance of one's interest to industry or society** 描述興趣與產業及社會的相關性 This field requires knowledge not only of the limiting forces that can be withstood without failure, but also of the temperature and rate of loading which minimize the forces required to convert a cast ingot into a more useful shape, such as a flat plate. Therefore, carefully selecting methods and actions to ensure that the best decision is made will make me a successful materials engineer. **Stating how finding employment related to one's interest would benefit the applicant and/or the company** 描述興趣與工作的配合對勞資方都有利 If employed in your company's research division, I would bring to your laboratory theoretical and practical knowledge magnesium alloys, including related issues of extraction, melting, casting, welding, heat treatment and processing thereof. This topic is becoming increasingly important given the recent emergence of the magnesium industry in Taiwan. This fact also explains why I chose your company for employment. In addition to its distinguished metallic materials research, your company's research in ceramic materials and polymeric materials is widely recognized. I am also eager to gain a broader understanding of all materials. I believe my strong academic performance and solid background in materials science and engineering will prove invaluable to any research team to which I belong.

*

Stating how long one has been interested in a particular field or topic 描述專業 興趣所延續的時間 The way in which nature operates has fascinated me since high school, especially in the fields of physical science and chemistry. **Stating how one has pursued that interest until now** 描述興趣形成過程 This fascination explains why I majored in Chemistry at university and now work in the semiconductor industry. My career has so far focused on attempting to understand more fully how physical and chemical theories are applied in industry.

H. Select the correct answers to the following questions about the three stories in this unit.

1. In what does Bob have a solid background, besides quality control and financial analysis?

   A. industrial organizations

   B. industrial productivity

   C. industrial management

2. What are some of the industrial organizations in which Bob has been involved in collaborative projects?

   A. ITRI, AMEX and Chailease Finance

   B. ITRI, AMAT and Chailease Finance

   C. ITRI, AMAT and Charles Swab

3. How long has Bob been preparing to enter the challenging semiconductor industry?

A. several years

B. many years

C. in recent years

4. How does Bob describe the global market?

A. as a dynamic environment

B. as intensely competitive

C. as challenging

5. What does Bob believe the global market is driven by?

A. industrial managers

B. global enterprises

C. customers

6. Why did Allen complete a Master's degree in Social Anthropology from National
Tsing Hua University?

A. He is always striving to understand human relationships

B. He is especially fascinated by the richness and color of human relationships

C. He is interested in stimulating creativity and increasing work productivity

7. What does Allen believe is essential?

A. skilled manpower

B. management theory and practices

C. organizational culture and leadership

8. What do both Human Resources Management and Anthropology focus on?

A. organizational culture and leadership

B. humans and culture

C. humans and their knowledge

9. What is Allen interested in adopting to stimulate creativity and increase work productivity?

A. salary structure design and performance management

B. intellectual property law and employee law

C. different strategies and problem-solving measures

10. What is one of the things that Allen believes profoundly determines an enterprise's success?

A. leadership

B. the new knowledge economy

C. salary structure design

11. What allowed Tom to acquire advanced academic training?

A. his undergraduate studies in Electrical Engineering at National Tsing Hua University

B. the Master's degree program in Electrical Engineering at National Tsing Hua University

C. DEF Corporation

12. What is one of the things that Tom believes that DEF Corporation can provide?

A. the ability to save time and reduce workload

B. an excellent opportunity to acquire advanced academic training

C. an excellent opportunity to foster his professional skills

13. What kind of workplace environment can DEF Corporation offer Tom?

    A. a unique one

    B. an excellent one

    C. a comfortable one

14. Which word is similar in meaning to "foster"?

    A. acquire

    B. entertain

    C. nurture

15. Which word is similar in meaning to "premier"?

    A. cooperative

    B. renowned

    C. undistinguished

I Select the correct answers to the following questions about one's interest in a profession.

1. What ___ you determined to become professionally?

    A. will

    B. are

    C. have

2. What department at National Central University do you hope ___ secure employment?

    A. to

    B. for

    C. at

3. What have you been preparing ___ several years to do?

   A. as

   B. at

   C. for

4. What ___ you especially fascinated by?

   A. have

   B. are

   C. had

5. What ___ DEF Corporation offer you?

   A. does

   B. do

   C. is

6. What ____ you believe drives the intensely competitive global market?

   A. do

   B. does

   C. are

7. What sort ____ background did your undergraduate studies in Electrical

   Engineering at National Chiao Tung University provide you with?

   A. in

   B. of

   C. on

8. What company will offer invaluable training ____ you to become an effective

   manager?

   A. to

   B. of

   C. for

9. What collaborative projects with industry did you participate in _____ your graduate studies?

    A. by

    B. during

    C. of

10. Which organization is a leading supplier _____ pharmaceutical drugs and hospital products?

    A. of

    B. in

    C. for

11. Which industry have you been preparing to enter _____ several years?

    A. on

    B. in

    C. for

12. Which industrial organizations were involved _____ the many collaborative projects in which you participated during graduate school?

    A. by

    B. in

    C. to

13 In which company _____ you seeking employment?

    A. do

    B. have

    C. are

14. From which university _____ you receive a Master's degree in Social Anthropology?

    A. were

    B. do

C. did

15. At which department at National Central University _____ you hope to secure employment?

A. do

B. does

C. are

16. Which line _____ work do you hope to find after completing your Bachelor's degree?

A. for

B. of

C. to

17. Which strategies and problem-solving measures do you hope _____ adopt to stimulate creativity and increase work productivity?

A. to

B. on

C. for

18. In which profession are you interested _____ entering after you complete your undergraduate studies?

A. with

B. for

C. in

19. Why do you consider ABC Corporation to _____ a logical choice for your first employment upon graduation?

A. in

B. be

C. for

20. Why did you take a Master's degree _____ Electrical Engineering from National

Tsing Hua University?

A. for

B. at

C. in

21. Why did you complete a Masters degree in Social Anthropology _____ National Tsing Hua University?

A. from

B. by

C. as

22. Why do you believe that you will be invaluable to any project team _____ with which you are involved at DEF Corporation ?

A. from

B. by

C. in

23. Why are you interested _____ adopting different strategies and problem-solving measures?

A. in

B. for

C. to

24. Why do you believe that DEF Corporation offers a unique workplace environment in which _____ put your academic skills into practice?

A. on

B. for

C. to

25. Why have you decided to enter the biotechnology profession _____ completing your Bachelor's degree?

A. during

B. after

C. when

26. Why have you chosen DEF Corporation _____ employment in the biotech industry?

    A. in

    B. to

    C. for

27. Why are you impressed _____ DEF Corporation's line of products and services?

    A. on

    B. with

    C. for

Unit Two

Matt

Deregulation and globalization

Interest rate derivatives
Currency derivatives
Liberalization Option
Mortgage securities
Swap

Taiwan's financial markets

Jack

...cs industry

An increasing number of Taiwanese companies have extended their product lines to telecommunications

Telecommunications industry

IC design research

Describing the field or industry to which one's profession belongs

興趣相關產業描寫

Vocabulary and related expressions　相關字詞

World Trade Organization　世界貿易組織	intense competition 激烈競爭
accelerate　加速	deregulation　撤銷管制
liberalization　自由化	interest rate derivatives　利率金融商品
options　選擇權	swaps　互換
mortgage securities　抵押擔保品	currency derivatives　貨幣金融商品
expert capabilities　專家才能	innovation　創新
Financial Engineering　金融工程	implemented　實行的
electronics industry　電子產業	a decade ago　十年前
globally competitive　全球性競爭	assembling　裝配
product components　產品零件	dominated　支配的
vital　重要的	CPU　中央處理器
chipset　晶片組	devoted itself to　專心致力於
complex　複雜的	generate 產生
a sizable share　相當大的部分	extended their product lines　延伸他們的產品線
high added value　高附加價值	IC design research　積體電路設計研究
moving in the right direction　走對方向	exploded　爆炸性發展
emergence　出現	computer graphics displays　電腦圖形顯示
implications　涉入	figures　圖形
integrate　結合	graphics　圖形
audio　聽覺的	semiconductor manufacturing　半導體製造工業
embedding　內嵌	graphics accelerator　圖形加速器
chipset　晶片組	processing recourse　加速方法
CPU　中央處理器	positioned itself to be　定位在
commitment to product excellence 產品優質保證	corporate family　公司大家庭

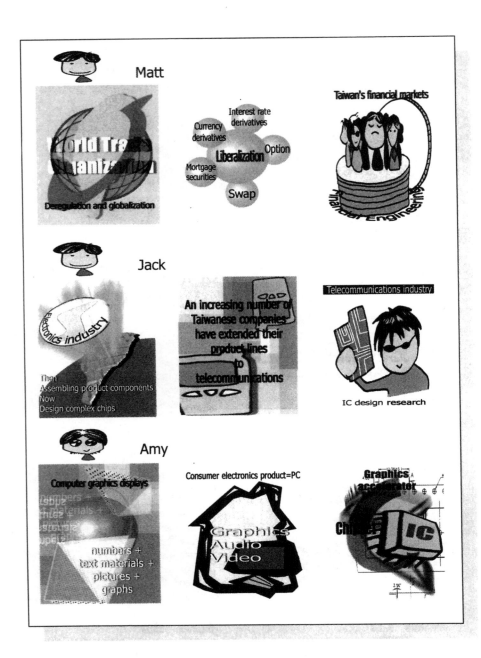

A Write down the key points of the situations on the preceding page, while the instructor reads aloud the script from the Answer Key.

Situation 1

_____

_____

_____

Situation 2

_____

_____

_____

Situation 3

_____

_____

_____

> **B** Based on the three situations in this unit, write three
> questions beginning with *Which*, and answer them.
> The questions do not need to come directly from
> these situations.

Examples

Which company is Matt interested in joining?

ABC Company

*Which company has positioned itself to be a leading manufacturer of systems-
on-chips (SoCs)?*

ABC Corporation

1. _____

_____

2. _____

_____

3. _____

_____

C Based on the three situations in this unit, write three questions beginning with **What**, and answer them. The questions do not need to come directly from these situations.

Examples

What have an increasing number of Taiwanese companies extended their product lines to include?

Telecommunications, especially wireless communications

What companies have captured a sizable share of the global market?

Taiwanese electronics companies that design complex chips

1. _____

   _____

2. _____

   _____

3. _____

   _____

D Based on the three situations in this unit, write three questions beginning with *Why*, and answer them. The questions do not need to come directly from these situations.

Examples

Why will Taiwan encounter intense competition from global financial markets?

Because of its recent entry into the World Trade Organization

Why have local electronics firms been able to generate considerable product revenues and capture a sizable share of the global market?

Because the Taiwanese government has devoted itself to developing the electronics industry so that many Taiwanese corporations can now design complex chips

1. _____

_____

2. _____

_____

3. _____

_____

E Write questions that match the answers provided.

Examples

What is Amy eager to join?

The corporate family

Which products are widely anticipated to have a high added value in the near future?

Telecommunication products, especially those related to wireless communications

1. _____

   _____

   ABC's commitment to product excellence

2. _____

   _____

   In the right direction

3. _____

   _____

   Graphics, audio and video features

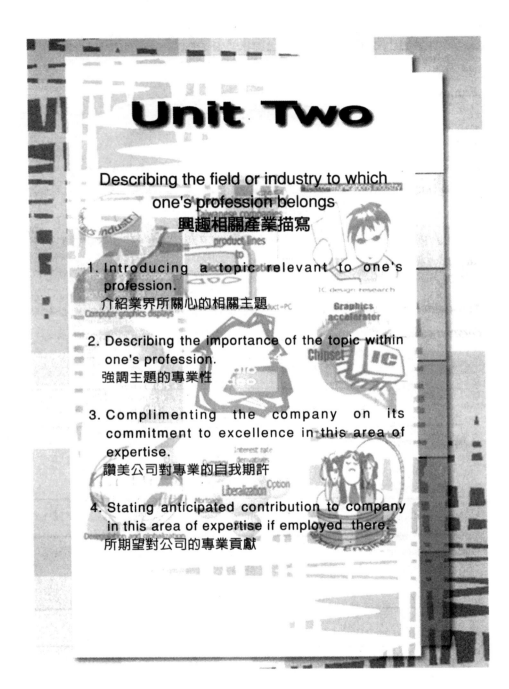

Unit Two

Describing the field or industry to which one's profession belongs
興趣相關產業描寫

1. Introducing a topic relevant to one's profession.
   介紹業界所關心的相關主題

2. Describing the importance of the topic within one's profession.
   強調主題的專業性

3. Complimenting the company on its commitment to excellence in this area of expertise.
   讚美公司對專業的自我期許

4. Stating anticipated contribution to company in this area of expertise if employed there.
   所期望對公司的專業貢獻

Common elements in describing a field or industry to which one's profession belongs include:

1. Introducing a topic relevant to one's profession 介紹業界所關心的相關主題

◎ With its rapid industrial development in recent decades, Taiwan is now striving to become the 'Green Silicon Island' by simultaneously pursuing environmentalism and developing high-tech industries.

◎ Recently, Taiwan has significantly contributed to the global high-tech sector, especially in microchip fabrication, electronic packaging and IC design.

◎ Taiwan severely lacks technology professionals with a background in biotechnology and business administration, preventing the island economy from keeping pace with this recently emerging trend in global R&D.

◎ The island's recent entry into the World Trade Organization has eradicated many trade barriers to the local market economy, so Taiwanese must continuously upgrade their professional skills and linguistic abilities to remain competitive in the global workplace.

◎ Pursuing economic growth while protecting the environment is a careful balancing act performed by most industrialized economies.

◎ Although Taiwan's hardware industry has already matured, its software industry lags behind that of many other developing economies.

◎ Electronic commerce presents numerous growth opportunities for all types of industry.

◎ Tourism is a growth sector in Taiwan. The island is characterized by its array of awe-inspiring scenery, extremely hospitable inhabitants and splendid cuisine. Regardless of your budget, you can dine on a variety of exquisite dishes at restaurants, night markets or food stalls all over the island. Hsin Chu City is renowned for its rice noodles known as mi fuhn and meat meatballs known as gong wan. Even inside Chung Hwa Temple, you can eat in the company of Taipei's ruling deity. You won't be disappointed with Taiwan's diverse cuisine.

◎ The global trend of the reduction of the amount of paper used in offices is spreading rapidly. For instance, many companies use their own intranets and document management systems to control effectively the circulation of security documents. However, encouraging employees to view materials on-line instead of on paper is difficult. Additionally, the use of paper requires too much time to be spent in acquiring necessary signatures on a particular document.

◎ Designing a quality wafer chip for the semiconductor industry is a complex task with many components.

◎ As a member of an exciting and challenging profession, an investment planner not only performs daily equity analysis, but must also assesses potential start-ups in terms of their competitive advantages.

◎ The human anatomy is more sophisticated than the most advanced computer, as evidenced by its miraculous ability to keep its complex systems functioning normally.

◎ Financial planners in Taiwan constantly focus on how to adjust the island economy's investment strategies and enhance global competitiveness.

◎ Quality assessment engineers analyze processes and design various products to ensure that our lives comfortable and convenient.

◎ The biotech industry in Taiwan is rapidly expanding though, unfortunately, this expansion is in the quantity of work produced, rather than the quality.

◎ Providing state-of-the-art computers that satisfy consumer demand depends on the ability to integrate computer science with knowledge from other fields.

◎ The explosive pace at which innovative wire technologies appear in the marketplace never ceases to amaze me, and I am eager to join the field .

◎ Language teaching in Taiwan is slowly moving from a grammatical-translation approach, in which students memorize vocabulary, sentences and grammatical rules, to a more practice-based approach.

◎ Despite political differences, China and Taiwan share many common economic interests, as evidenced by their increasingly strong economic ties in the Asia-Pacific region. I am interested in a profession that would contribute further to strengthening these ties.

◎ Merely a tool when used alone, a computer becomes most effective when facilitating processes in other fields, such as business administration. This fact explains my interest in information management over computer science.

◎ Financial planners attempt to equip companies with the necessary tools to utilize effectively their resources to remain competitive in the marketplace.

◎ A company's financial strength depends on its ability to survive economic turmoil.

◎ Corporate success depends largely on a company's ability to integrate and allocate resources in different areas efficiently.

◎ In an intensely competitive global environment, enterprises must decide whether to expand commercial activities continuously or adopt a conservative attitude.

2. Describing the importance of the topic within one's profession 強調主題的專業性

◎ Taiwan's pivotal role in contributing to the industrial development of Greater China necessitates that local investors remain attuned to the latest technological and developmental trends on both sides of the Taiwan Strait.

◎ The global focus on commercial opportunities in China is intensifying as the country, in addition to achieving an annual economic growth of 7% despite a global recession, has recently entered the World Trade Organization and prepares to host the 2008 Olympics.

◎ Bioinformatics attests to the potential for integrating seemingly polar disciplines in order to create new technical and market opportunities.

◎ The past decade has seen Taiwan experience a great metamorphosis in both its industry and its place in the global community. It has also made strides towards a more democratic society. Consequently, the journalistic practices in Taiwan must be comparable to those found elsewhere. Moreover, journalism professionals must handle responsibly such practices as gathering and reporting information.

◎ Integrating computers and biological science into the recently emerging bio-informatics sector in Taiwan has tremendous commercial and societal implications for the island's economy.

◎ During tough economic times, financial planners are increasingly important as they help many Taiwanese manufacturers to resolve problems such as the retail prices of products' falling below variable cost, inventory pile-up, and large capital expenditures on production equipment and facilities.

3. Complimenting the company on its commitment to excellence in this area of expertise 讚美公司對專業的自我期許

◎ As a leading IC manufacturer, your company has distinguished itself in its commitment to in-house research projects, as evidenced by your commitment to excellence in product innovation.

◎ In your company, the diversity of research projects and departments committed to implementing them is quite impressive

◎ The great working environment, combined with the impressive number and diversity of training courses to keep your employees competitive in the market place, would definitely benefit my professional development.

4. Stating anticipated contribution to company in this area of expertise if employed there 所期望對公司的專業貢獻

◎ With a solid background in electrical engineering, proficiency in three languages and specialized knowledge and skills in IC design, I am confident that I will fit your corporate family closely and significantly contribute to the company's innovative product technologies.

◎ Rather than confining myself merely to my technical skills as an engineer, I also hope to contribute to your company as a technology professional with proficient management capabilities. I firmly believe that engineering and management expertise is essential in the intensely competitive hi tech sector.

◎ Drawing not only on my solid background in experimentation and data analysis, but also on my motivating intellectual curiosity, I hope to follow productively my interests within the scope of your company's on-going projects.

◎ Capable of integrating biological applications and computer programming skills (as evidenced by my previous work experience), I am well placed for entry into the bioinformatics field, an area to which your company has recently devoted considerable resources.

◎ Aware of the limited knowledge and capacity of Taiwan's industrial planners in tackling environmental issues, I believe that I can contribute to your company's efforts to maximize profits and continuously grow in a sustainable manner that is environmentally friendly.

◎ Despite the particularity of the expertise I learned in graduate school, I believe that employment at your company will expose me to new fields as long as I remain open and do not restrict myself to the scope of my previous academic training.

◎ If I am successful in securing employment at your company, my strong academic and practical knowledge, curricular and otherwise, will enable me to contribute positively to the corporate family.

◎ In addition to enhancing my research capabilities and professional knowledge skills, I hope to participate in your company's ground-breaking efforts to elevate IC product technology to unprecedented levels.

◎ Your company will allow me to hone my problem-solving skills, acquired during graduate school, and learn more about the challenges of the semiconductor industry. These skills will hopefully place me in line someday for a managerial position to lead one of your innovative product development projects.

◎ As a member of your corporate family, I hope to upgrade continuously my knowledge and skills so that I can remain competent within my profession. Work experiences gained so far have enticed me to understand further system-level electrical simulation for IC and electromagnetic phenomena-related research. Such an in-depth investigation would hopefully equip me with advanced professional knowledge to be in a better position to undertake IC package design.

◎ My amicable personality allows me to easily be one of a group. I generally confront the occasional disappointments of daily life with an optimistic attitude. I firmly believe that any frustrations can be alleviated with a strong, yet even-tempered will. Furthermore, in addition to constantly initiating new activities, I am responsible, and trustworthy. I am confident of my ability to achieve set goals, and exceed the expectations of my superiors. I believe that these qualities will prove beneficial to any collaborative effort in which I participate in your company.

◎ The advanced finance-related knowledge and specialized skills that graduate school gave me will allow me to contribute significantly to your company's efforts to optimize its financial structure in response to rapid changes in global financial markets.

◎ After joining your company, I will continue to upgrade my knowledge and skills by researching pertinent literature and case studies in industrial settings. Combining my work experience with state-of-the-art technologies to conduct advanced research, and with enthusiasm to grasp the latest technological concepts, I hope eventually to become an expert in IC design.

◎ After joining your company, I plan to diversify my knowledge, skills and research capabilities, especially in computer science and electronic engineering, to upgrade my design and debugging techniques. I will also devote myself to establishing my management, decision-making and critical thinking skills. I firmly believe that such skills are essential to remaining competent and competitive in this constantly evolving profession.

◎ The solid knowledge and specialized skills nurtured in graduate school will enable me to analyze effectively production data in a real environment to upgrade the quality of products to satisfy a customer's requirements. My exposure to National Science Council-sponsored projects as well as statistical and theoretical analysis will prove invaluable to any collaborative effort to which I belong in your company.

◎ Your company offers a unique environment in which I can fully grasp the latest technological trends and specialize in those areas that both satisfy my professional interests and contribute to corporate profits.

◎ I believe that employment at your company will provide me with advanced knowledge of the latest technological innovations that match my professional interests. Such knowledge will allow me to contribute not only to company profits, but also to excellence in my profession.

F In the space below, describe the field or industry to which your profession belongs.

_____

_____

_____

_____

_____

_____

_____

_____

_____

_____

_____

_____

_____

Describing the field or industry to which one's profession belongs
興趣相關產業描寫

G Look at the following examples of how to describe fields or industries to which professions belong.

Introducing a topic relevant to one's profession 介紹業界所關心的相關主題 Wafer fabrication in Taiwan is globally renowned. Technological advances have not only upgraded related machinery, but also made processes increasingly complex and precise. The contribution of individuals from diverse disciplines to the semiconductor industry is evident in wafer design, manufacturing and packaging. **Describing the importance of the topic within one's profession** 強調主題的專業 性 To ensure that a wafer has no defects, a fabricator must test it - a process commonly referred to as the Wafer Acceptance Test (WAT). Upon passing inspection, a wafer is sent to the packaging company, which makes the integrated circuit. Therefore, WAT plays (an essential or a critical) role in wafer fabrication. **Stating anticipated contribution to company in this area of expertise if employed there** 所期望對公司的專業貢獻 I am especially interested in improving control charts, an area in which I hope to gain expertise at your company.

*

Introducing a topic relevant to one's profession 介紹業界所關心的相關主題 Industrial engineering did not receive much attention among Taiwan's traditional industries as recently as two decades ago, because Taiwan's industrial sector largely comprised small to medium-scale firms that performed their activities using employees without IE backgrounds. However, as Taiwan's economy has flourished in recent decades, more large-sized and multi-national companies islandwide have realized the importance of management science as a practical discipline for the workplace. **Describing the importance of the topic within one's profession** 強調 主題的專業性 The growing tendency to adopt industrial engineering and industrial management-related practices has strengthened the local industrial sector's efficiency and competitiveness. **Complimenting the company on its commitment to excellence in this area of expertise** 讚美公司對專業的自我期許 Your company has committed itself to the highest ideals of adhering to state-of-the-art practices within the industrial engineering profession. **Stating anticipated contribution to company in this area of expertise if employed there** 所期望對公司的專業貢獻 I believe that my solid academic training and professional experiences will allow me to meet these high expectations held by your corporate family.

*

Introducing a topic relevant to one's profession 介紹業界所關心的相關主題 As China's high tech sector rapidly evolves, Taiwan continues to strengthen its global competitiveness. With its abundant natural resources, relatively inexpensive labor costs, and immense geographical area, China is aggressively developing its infrastructure and technological capabilities with foreign capital. **Describing the importance of the topic within one's profession** 強調主題的專業性 However, Taiwan still holds a competitive edge in quality control, cost control and system integration. I have decided to devote myself to industrial engineering and management, which are required on both sides of the Taiwan Strait. **Complimenting the company on its commitment to excellence in this area of expertise** 讚美公司對專業的自我期許 Your company has undertaken many successful collaborative ventures between Taiwanese and Chinese engineering firms, explaining why my interest in this area and engineering background are in line with the direction that your company is taking.

*

Introducing a topic relevant to one's profession 介紹業界所關心的相關主題 Owing to its location in the western Pacific, Taiwan finds itself in the direct path of many typhoons during the wet season. Typhoons always brings much rainfall, often resulting in severe flooding. Damaged caused by flooding poses a major threat, particularly in light of the island's dense population and industrial infrastructure. **Describing the importance of the topic within one's profession** 強調主題的專業性 Unfortunately, flood damage has caused enormous losses of lives and property in several metropolitan areas in recent years. To successfully mitigate flood hazard-related damage, the Taiwanese government is increasingly emphasizing the importance of environmental impact studies involving flood control. This trend has motivated my interest in actively participating in efforts to solve damage caused by flooding. **Complimenting the company on its commitment to excellence in this area of expertise** 讚美公司對專業的自我期許 Your consulting firm, a leader in environmental impact assessment, would provide me with a marvelous opportunity to add to my previous experience in conducting related research.

*

Introducing a topic relevant to one's profession 介紹業界所關心的相關主題 Water, the source of life, poses a major challenge for Taiwan in light of its limited supply. For example, rainfall distribution on the island is not uniform, occasionally leading to serious shortages. This potential calamity is due not only to polluted rivers in southern Taiwan, but also to the steep incline of some rivers that makes impossible the storage of a sufficient supply of water during rainy periods, such as when a typhoon approaches. The island's inhabitants thus heavily depend on the supply of groundwater for daily use. However, soil settlement and sea-water intrusion pose a threat to Taiwan's groundwater supply. An additional threat is that the subsurface water in Taiwan contains several dissolved organic liquids. **Describing the importance of the topic within one's profession** 強調主題的專業性 Therefore, studies on groundwater development in Taiwan must combine surface water flow with groundwater resources. Moreover, groundwater contamination often goes undetected by the general population. Solving the above problems heavily relies on effective ground water management and development. This fact explains why I have decided to devote myself to a career in tackling the immense water resource-related problems in Taiwan. **Stating anticipated contribution to company in this area of expertise if employed there** 所期望對公司的專業貢獻 Employment at your company would allow me to supplement my theoretical knowledge obtained at university with experience of actual cases.

*

Introducing a topic relevant to one's profession 介紹業界所關心的相關主題 Industrial engineering plays a vital role not only in traditional industries but also in high-tech ones, such as in the semiconductor sector. In a customer-oriented era, businesses heavily emphasize high product quality to meet consumers' expectations. In addition to delivering high quality, businesses must effectively address process performance and production-related costs. **Describing the importance of the topic within one's profession** 強調主題的專業性 Enhancing product quality and process performance, while minimizing production costs, is of priority concern. My graduate school education at National Chiao Tung University provided me with much theoretical knowledge about solving such problems by adopting such diverse approaches as statistics, quality control, ERP and supply chain management. **Stating anticipated contribution to company in this area of expertise if employed there** 所期望對公司的專業貢獻 Nevertheless, employment at your company would enrich my theoretical knowledge obtained from university with the practical experience that your working environment would offer.

*

Introducing a topic relevant to one's profession 介紹業界所關心的相關主題 The functions of personal computers (PC) have rapidly advanced in recent years, particularly because of advances in semiconductor technology and wafer fabrication. **Describing the importance of the topic within one's profession** 強調主題的專業性 With a wafer chip no longer limited to a single function in the PC, a chipset provides the ability to combine several single functions and thus increases the efficiency of integrated systems. **Complimenting the company on its commitment to excellence in this area of expertise** 讚美公司對專業的自我期許 SIS has played a leading role in industry for several years, not only in the field of chipsets, but also in that of advanced graphic chips on PC-based integrated systems. In so doing, SIS has positioned itself as a leader in systems-on-chips (SoCs). Unlike other IC design houses, your company has its own advanced fab, ensuring its ability to supply price-competitive, high-quality products. Your strong technical and market positions explain why I want to join your corporate family.

*

Introducing a topic relevant to one's profession 介紹業界所關心的相關主題 Taiwan's semiconductor industry has witnessed unprecedented growth for over a decade, as evidenced by the island's leading role globally in the wafer foundry sector. **Describing the importance of the topic within one's profession** 強調主題的專業性 "Self-marking" is essential to success in the intensely competitive international market. Successful entry of a local IDM company into the global market spells success for Taiwan in this rapidly growing sector. This fact explains why I have decided to devote myself to SiS, a leading chipset manufacturing company in Taiwan, with a particular interest in quality assurance.

*

Introducing a topic relevant to one's profession 介紹業界所關心的相關主題 The increasing popularity of on-line commerce has led to Taiwan's government's legislating that a digital signature has the same validity as a traditional one. Among other topics, modern cryptology concerns itself with digital signatures. My fascination with this field explains why my Master's degree is focused on cryptology. **Complimenting the company on its commitment to excellence in this area of expertise** 讚美公司對專業的自我期許 As a leader in this area of technology development, your company has distinguished itself in its commitment to in-house research projects, which match my professional interests, as evidenced by your commitment to excellence in product innovation.

*

Introducing a topic relevant to one's profession 介紹業界所關心的相關主題 Although the computer architecture market is saturated, few companies in Taiwan can design the kernel of a computer system. Most Taiwanese companies either simulate device designs on a computer or adopt designs developed abroad. **Stating anticipated contribution to company in this area of expertise if employed there** 所期望對公司的專業貢獻 Therefore, I am especially interested in studying complex issues that are more closely related to CPU design. I believe that your company would provide an environment to allow me to pursue my professional interests, regardless of the challenges they involve.

*

Introducing a topic relevant to one's profession 介紹業界所關心的相關主題 The number of computer applications has increased dramatically with the emergence of computer graphics displays. Such displays allow users to present not only numbers and text, but also pictures and graphs that illustrate the implications of related figures, and greatly add to the quality of text material. **Describing the importance of the topic within one's profession** 強調主題的專業性 Widely anticipated to become a consumer electronics product commonly found in households, the personal computer will be able to integrate graphics, audio and video features. Nevertheless, technological advances in semiconductor manufacturing technology have enabled the embedding of a graphics accelerator within the chipset (corelogic) into an integrated chip. Multimedia processes are directly sent to the integrated chip, thus reducing the overload of the processing recourse in the CPU. **Complimenting the company on its commitment to**

97

excellence in this area of expertise 讚美公司對專業的自我期許 Silicon Integrated Systems Corp. (SiS), a leading core logic and graphics chips supplier, has positioned itself to be a leading manufacturer of systems-on-chips (SoC). Your company's commitment to product excellence explains why I am eager to join your organization.

*

Introducing a topic relevant to one's profession 介紹業界所關心的相關主題 Taiwan's electronics industry did not, until as recently as a decade ago, become globally competitive. During that period, most corporations were not profitable since they focused on assembling product components; whereas overseas firms dominated the manufacturing of vital components such as the CPU and the chipset. Taiwan's government then devoted itself to developing the electronics industry and many Taiwanese corporations can now design complex chips. This ability has allowed local firms to generate considerable product revenues and capture a sizable share of the global market. **Describing the importance of the topic within one's profession** 強調主題的專業性 An increasing number of Taiwanese companies have extended their product lines to telecommunications, especially wireless communications. Such products are widely anticipated to have a high added value in the near future. These exciting trends in the telecommunications industry in Taiwan have largely determined my decision to undertake IC design research in telecommunications. **Stating anticipated contribution to company in this area of expertise if employed there** 所期望對公司的專業貢獻 I feel confident that I am heading in the right direction. Your company offers a competitive work environment and is home to highly skilled professionals: these ingredients are essential to my continually upgrading my knowledge, skills and expertise in the above area.

*

Introducing a topic relevant to one's profession 介紹業界所關心的相關主題

Designing large wafer chips of is extremely complicated, and the issue of timing has received increasing emphasis. Actually, various logic gates with distinct characteristics, including function, area and performance, are critical to the chips. Additionally, assuming that two logic gates belonging to the same critical path are far from each other implies that the required transmission time is large. **Describing the importance of the topic within one's profession** 強調主題的專業性 To solve the above problems, two methods can be adopted. The first method merges the wafer chips more closely by altering one or both of their placement coordinates. The length of their connection path is subsequently diminished. The other method, referred to as the re-structuring process, combines two gates into a single one with an equivalent logical function. More effective than the first approach, this method not only decreases the interconnection delay but also optimizes the utilization rate of the chip area. **Complimenting the company on its commitment to excellence in this area of expertise** 讚美公司對專業的自我期許 In this area of development, your company offers an excellent research environment and abundant academic resources that will enhance my research capabilities and equip me with the competence to fully realize fully my career aspirations.

*

Introducing a topic relevant to one's profession 介紹業界所關心的相關主題 Despite its renowned technological achievement, Taiwan's manufacturing sector is labor-intensive rather than intelligence-oriented. **Describing the importance of the topic within one's profession** 強調主題的專業性 Most key technologies within the island's manufacturing sector are still imported from abroad, not developed locally. Taiwan must foster its research capabilities - from constructing algorithms to developing product technologies. Doing so would allow the island to maintain its global competitiveness. **Complimenting the company on its commitment to excellence in this area of expertise** 讚美公司對專業的自我期許 Your firm has spent considerable resources in orienting local companies for the challenges of the international marketplace. **Stating anticipated contribution to company in this area of expertise if employed there** 所期望對公司的專業貢獻 I believe that my solid academic background will prove invaluable to your efforts to expand your current services.

*

Introducing a topic relevant to one's profession 介紹業界所關心的相關主題 3D models are extensively adopted in multimedia applications owing to their relatively low cost and the ease with which they construct animated 3D objects. Developing a concise and relatively easy means of constructing 3D faces has been heavily emphasized, particularly in computer animation. However, animating a human face is extremely difficult. Different models have been proposed to formulate 3D objects using expensive equipment and complex procedures. For instance, the Basin model uses a digitizer to retrieve 2D images and then transforms those images into 3D objects. Conventional 3D models are too time consuming and inaccurate when constructing digital objects since they manually retrieve 2D images. For instance, complex procedures involving the creation of digital objects require much time. **Describing the importance of the topic within one's profession** 強調主題的專業性 Such approaches not only require too many steps in constructing individual faces, but also need expensive or precise instruments such as a 3D digitizer, a laser scanner or a range finder. These obstacles create large overhead costs and are inefficient when formulating 3D faces, accounting for why many 3D facial formulation models are impractical for commercial use. A situation in which conventional models require seven steps to construct a 3D model and have an error rate of over 5% makes impossible the wide commercialization of animation software and the construction of realistic digital objects. For example, although formulating 3D objects has received increasing interest for multimedia applications, conventional models cannot meet commercial specifications. **Complimenting the company on its commitment to excellence in this area of expertise** 讚美公司對專業的自我期許 In this area, your company offers comprehensive and challenging training for those undertaking research in innovative product development of 3D displays. **Stating anticipated contribution to company in this area of expertise if employed there** 所期望對公司的專業貢獻 I am absolutely confident that my academic background, experimental and work experience in information science, desire for knowledge and love of challenges will enable me to succeed in your company's highly demanding product development projects.

H Select the correct answers to the following questions about the three stories in this unit.

1. From what will Taiwan encounter intense competition in the near future?

 A. multinational corporations

 B. global financial markets

 C. the World Trade Organization

2. What does Matt believe is essential for Taiwan ?

 A. to liberalize local markets

 B. to develop expert capabilities

 C. to implement liberal policies for mortgage securities and currency derivatives

3. Which word is most similar in meaning to "encounter"?

 A. nurture

 B. face

 C. develop

4. What has ABC Company actively implemented?

A. Financial Engineering-related practices

B. deregulation and globalization-related practices

C. innovation related-practices

5. What must Taiwan accelerate with its recent entry in the World Trade Organization?

A. interest rate derivatives and options

B. rapid changes and innovation

C. deregulation and globalization

6. When did Taiwan's electronics industry become globally competitive?

A. more than a decade ago

B. only a decade ago

C. less than a decade ago

7. What has allowed electronics firms in Taiwan to generate considerable product revenues?

A. the ability to capture a sizable share of the global market

B. the ability to design complex chips

C. the ability to make high added value products

8. What has largely determined Jack's decision to undertake IC design research?

A. the exciting trends in the telecommunications industry in Taiwan

B. the exciting trends in the electronics industry in Taiwan

C. the exciting trends in wireless communications in Taiwan

9. What area of telecommunications have Taiwanese companies extended their product lines into and is Matt interested in?

A. integrated circuits

B. wafer chips

C. wireless communications

10. What is Jack confident of?

A. that Taiwanese companies will generate high added value in wireless communications

B. that he is moving in the right direction

C. that Taiwanese electronics firms can extend their product lines to telecommunications

11. What do computer graphics displays allow users to do?

A. integrate graphics, audio and video features

B. present pictures and graphs that illustrate the implications of related figures

C. embed a graphics accelerator with the chipset (core-logic) into an integrated chip

12. Computer graphics displays add to the quality of what?

A. consumer electronics products

B. graphics, audio and video features

C. text material

13. What have enabled the embedding of a graphics accelerator within the chipset (core-logic) into an integrated chip?

A. technological advances in computer graphics displays

B. technological advances in multimedia processes

C. technological advances in semiconductor manufacturing technology

14. What reduces the overload of the processing recourse in the CPU?

A. directly sending multimedia processes to the integrated chip

B. embedding a graphics accelerator within the chipset (core-logic) into an integrated chip

C. integrating graphics, audio and video features

15. Why is Amy eager to join ABC Corporation?

A. Because of its ability to position itself to be a leading manufacturer of systems-on-chips (SoCs)

B. Because of its commitment to product excellence

C. Because of its ability to integrate graphics, audio and video features in its computer graphics displays

I Select the correct answers to the following questions about the field of industry to which one's profession belongs.

1. Which company are you interested ____ joining?

    A. to

    B. in

    C. on

2. Which industry does your profession belong ____ ?

    A. to

    B. on

    C. for

3. Which country will encounter intense competition ____ global financial markets?

    A. at

    B. from

    C. as

4. Which issues would you ____ interested in addressing if you were employed at DEF Corporation?

    A. to

    B. be

    C. are

5. Which company ____ actively implemented environmentally friendly practices?

    A. does

B. is

C. has

6. Which organization ____ Taiwan entered recently?

A. has

B. does

C. have

7. Which industry in Taiwan has rapidly expanded ____ recent years?

A. on

B. in

C. for

8. Which technologies ____ increasingly used in Taiwan's semiconductor industry?

A.does

B. is

C. are

9. Which areas ____ new development is Taiwan undergoing?

A.in

B. of

C. for

10. What are you confident ___?

A. of

B. for

C. to

11. What are some of the latest technological developments ____ your field?

A. on

B. in

C. of

12. What have an increasing number of Taiwanese companies extended their product

lines ___?

A. to

B. for

C. on

13. What are some of the exciting trends ____ the biotech industry in Taiwan?

A. with

B. by

C. in

14. What new biotechnology products are widely anticipated to be available ____ the near future?

A. with

B. in

C. on

15.What are some ____ Taiwan's globally competitive industries?

A.on

B.of

C. in

16. What decisions have you made ____ your career direction?

A. about

B. with

C. by

17. What technological capabilities ____ Taiwanese companies developed in recent years?

A. are

B. do

C. have

18. What companies have captured a sizable share ___ the global market?

A. in

B. of

C. for

19. Why are you eager ___ join ABC's corporate family?

A. with

B. for

C. to

20. Why are you so determined to succeed ___ the health care management field?

A. by

B. in

C. at

21. Why have you decided ___ enter the nursing profession?

A. to

B. for

C. on

22. Why ___ Taiwan's biotech industry increasingly competitive globally?

A. does

B. is

C. has

23. Why are an increasing number of multinational corporations investing ___ Taiwan's biotech industry?

A. on

B. in

C. to

24. Why are you confident of your ability to succeed ___ the highly competitive biotech industry?

A. in

B. on

C. for

25. Why has DEF Corporation positioned itself to _____ a leading manufacturer of semiconductor products?

A. of

B. on

C. be

26. Why does DEF Corporation's product have a wide consumer appeal _____ young people?

A. among

B. to

C. by

27. Why _____ Taiwan's biotech industry expanded rapidly in recent years?

A. is

B. has

C. does

Unit Three

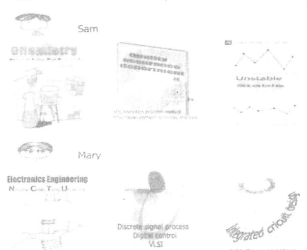

Describing participation in a project that reflects interest in a profession

描述所參與方案裡專業興趣的表現

Vocabulary and related expressions　相關字詞

working on one's degree　攻讀學位
quality control　保質控管
measurement systems analysis (MSA)
量測系統分析
concerned with　關心
reproducibility　重製性
assessment　評估
from an early age　從先前
innovative 創新的
impact on our lives　對我們生活的影響
strong research fundamentals　強力的研究根基
long been intrigued by　長久以來被吸引
renowned　有名的
simulated　模擬
practical laboratory experience
實用的實驗室經驗

develop a love for　培養喜好
statistical process control (SPC)　統計程序控制
repeatability　重現性
criteria　標準
Electrical engineering　電機工程
Electronic engineering　電子工程
solving problems logically and independently
有邏輯獨力的解決問題
pursue one's professional interests
進行某人的專業興趣
integrated circuit design　積體電路設計
culminated in　到頂點
IC design industry IC　設計產業
computer network　電腦網路
highly competitive　高度競爭的

Describing participation in a project that reflects interest in a profession
描述所參與方案裡專業興趣的表現

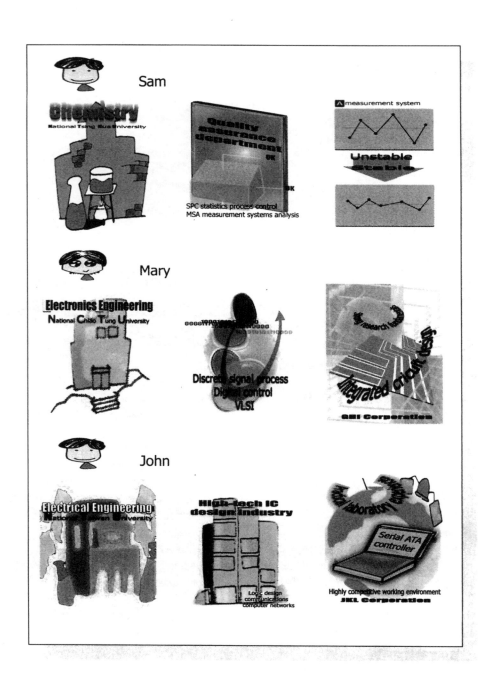

A Write down the key points of the situations on the preceding page, while the instructor reads aloud the script from the Answer Key.

Situation 1

_____

_____

_____

Situation 2

_____

_____

_____

Situation 3

_____

_____

_____

Describing participation in a project that reflects interest in a profession
描述所參與方案裡專業興趣的表現

B. Based on the three situations in this unit, write three questions beginning with **What**, and answer them. The questions do not need to come directly from these situations.

Examples

What has John long been intrigued by?

Science and technology

What does Mary believe that GHI Corporation would provide her with to further pursue her professional interests?

The ideal working environment

1. _____

_____

2. _____

_____

3. _____

_____

C Based on the three situations in this unit, write three questions beginning with **How**, and answer them. The questions do not need to come directly from these situations.

Examples

How did Sam develop a love for laboratory work and a strong interest in quality control?

By working on his Bachelor's degree in Chemistry from National Tsing Hua University

How will Mary be able to apply her strong research fundamentals to the exciting industrial field of integrated circuit design?

By becoming a member of the GHI family

1. _____

   _____

2. _____

   _____

3. _____

   _____

Describing participation in a project that reflects interest in a profession

描述所參與方案裡專業興趣的表現

D Based on the three situations in this unit, write three questions beginning with **Why**, and answer them. The questions do not need to come directly from these situations.

Examples

Why has Mary taken electrical engineering since university?

Because she has been fascinated by this topic from an early age

Why was John able successfully to complete a Master's degree in Electrical Engineering from National Taiwan University?

Because of his interest in science and technology

1. _____

   _____

2. _____

   _____

3. _____

   _____

E. Write questions that match the answers provided.

Examples

What causes errors in process control and judgment?

An unstable or inaccurate measurement system

How has graduate school taught Mary to solve problems?

Logically and independently

1. _____

   _____

   To develop an Ethernet protocol

2. _____

   _____

   The ideal working environment

3. _____

   _____

   Logic design, communications and computer networks

Unit Three

Describing participation in a project that reflects interest in a profession
描述所參與方案裡專業興趣的表現

1. Introducing the objectives of a project in which one has participated.
   介紹此方案的目標

2. Summarizing the main results of that project.
   概述該方案的成果

3. Highlighting the contribution of that project to the company or the sector to which it belongs.
   強調該方案對公司或部門的貢獻

4. Complimenting the company or organization at which one is seeking employment on its efforts in this area.
   讚美公司對業界的專業努力

Common elements in describing participation in a project that reflects interest in a profession:

1. Introducing the objectives of a project in which one has participated. 介紹此方案的目標

Consider the following examples:

◎ As evidence of my commitment to this profession, I collaborated with other statisticians in developing an efficient evaluation model capable of selecting bands of natural gas buses.

◎ Owing to my deep interest in this profession, I actively participated in a project aimed at developing an efficient response surface method capable of optimizing ordered categorical data process parameters.

◎ My strong commitment to this profession is demonstrated by my recent collaboration with colleagues in constructing an effective performance index (PCI) and developing an objective hypothesis testing procedure for PCIs, capable of assessing the operational cycle time (OCT) and delivery time (DT) for VLSI.

◎ My active participation in several projects within this field attests to my determination to pursue this career. For instance, I participated in a collaborative effort to develop a deterministic and stochastic model for simulating groundwater flow to assess monitoring network alternatives.

◎ Given my strong desire to thrive within this profession, I developed a non-aqueous phase liquid (NAPL) simulation model that includes several parameters obtained as experimental data.

2. Summarizing the main results of that project. 概述該方案的成果

Consider the following examples:

◎ The results of that project confirmed the ability of our model not only to evaluate precisely the relationship between the cost and effectiveness of all viable alternatives to bus systems, but also to generate evaluations that provide economic information on all viable alternatives to bus systems.

117

◎ The method developed in our laboratory accurately estimates the location and dispersion effects. It can be easily implemented and clearly distinguishes these effects.

◎ According to our results, the hypothesis testing procedure that we developed allows firms to assess performance indices of the operation cycle time (OCT) and delivery time (DT) of VLSI, increasing the competitiveness of suppliers.

◎ The simulation model that we developed can predict the residual level of groundwater contaminants with an accuracy of 95%.

◎ The scheme developed in our research can help IC design engineers to minimize die size, optimize design and achieve an appropriate package type, best package trace, and excellent thermal / electrical performance. The scheme can also reduce the requirement for trial-and-error to 30% lower than that of the previous stage.

3. Highlighting the contribution of that project to the company or the sector to which it belongs. 強調該方案對公司或部門的貢獻

Consider the following examples:

◎ The scheme developed in that project can shorten the design flow and dramatically reduce the time to market. The IC product's excellent characteristics can elevate a company's technical and market positions.

◎ Following that research effort, the enhanced carrier recovery on a digital receiver can exceed that of conventional models with respect to tracking, thus improving the competitiveness of communication products.

◎ Incorporating macroeconomic factors into the neural network structure developed in that research project increased its accuracy of prediction, facilitating related assessments of a mixture of investments. Investment planners can adopt the neural network structure to include bankruptcy prediction in evaluating a company's financial solvency.

◎ In addition to providing a valuable reference for government when selecting brands of bus systems, the model that we developed includes a ranking methodology that provides a more objective outcome, with weights of related decision groups, than can other methodologies.

4. Complimenting the company or organization at which one is seeking employment on its efforts in this area. 讚美公司對業界的專業努力

◎ Your company offers a competitive work environment and highly skilled professionals - ingredients which are essential to the continual upgrading of my knowledge, skills and expertise.

◎ After carefully reading the on-line promotional materials of your company, I am especially interested in your innovative product development strategy and the abundant resources that you have devoted to IC design.

◎ Your company offers comprehensive and challenging training for those undertaking research in innovative IC product development programs.

◎ Your company has distinguished itself not only by its cutting edge products and design teams, but also by its intensive training programs and comprehensive employee welfare coverage. Working in such a nurturing environment will not only foster my knowledge and management skills, but also provide me with a clearer sense of which career path I should take.

◎ Your corporation has a long tradition of providing quality information products and services as well as offering excellent technical support.

◎ ABC Corporation is recognized as the global leader in designing, producing and marketing logic design chips.

F Describe your participation in a project that reflects interest in a profession.

_____

_____

_____

_____

_____

_____

_____

_____

_____

_____

_____

_____

G Look at the following examples of how to describe your participation in a project that reflects interest in a profession.

Introducing the objectives of a project in which one has participated 介紹此方案的目標 As evidence of my commitment to this profession, I collaborated with other statisticians in developing an efficient evaluation model capable of selecting brands of natural gas buses. More specifically, the model allows decision-makers to evaluate according to an appropriate number of criteria related to cost and effectiveness. **Summarizing the main results of that project** 概述該方案的成果 The results of the project confirmed the ability of our model not only to evaluate precisely the relationship between the cost and effectiveness of all viable alternatives to bus systems, but also to generate evaluation results that provide economic information on all viable alternatives to bus systems. **Highlighting the contribution of that project to the company or the sector to which it belongs** 強調該方案對公司或部門的貢獻 In addition to providing a valuable reference for government when selecting brands of bus systems, our model has a ranking methodology that provides a more objective outcome, with weights of related decision groups, than can other methodologies. **Complimenting the company or organization at which one is seeking employment on its efforts in this area** 讚美公司對業界的專業努力 I am encouraged that your company has also devoted considerable resources to this area of research.

*

Introducing the objectives of a project in which one has participated 介紹此方案的目標 Owing to my deep interest in this profession, I actively participated in a project aimed at developing an efficient response surface method capable of optimizing ordered categorical data process parameters. **Summarizing the main**

results of that project 概述該方案的成果 In addition to accurately estimating the location and dispersion effects, the method we developed can be easily implemented and clearly distinguishes these effects. **Highlighting the contribution of that project to the company or the sector to which it belongs** 強調該方案對公司或部門的貢獻 The main contribution of the dual response surface method is that it can be used to obtain an optimal combination of process parameters and help engineers set the controlled factors, as well as alleviate the quality problem related to ordered categorical data. **Complimenting the company or organization at which one is seeking employment on its efforts in this area** 讚美公司對業界的專業努力 The fact that your organization has exerted considerable effort in this area of research largely explains why I am eager to join your corporate family.

*

Introducing the objectives of a project in which one has participated 介紹此方案的目標 Confirmation of a strong commitment to this profession can be found in my recent collaboration with colleagues in constructing an effective performance index (PCI) and developing an objective hypothesis testing procedure for PCIs, capable of assessing the operational cycle time (OCT) and delivery time (DT) for VLSI. **Summarizing the main results of that project** 概述該方案的成果 According to our results, the hypothesis testing procedure that we developed allows firms to assess the performance indices of the operation cycle time (OCT) and delivery time (DT) of VLSI, increasing the competitiveness of suppliers. **Highlighting the contribution of that project to the company or the sector to which it belongs** 強調該方案對公司或部門的貢獻 Importantly, in addition to investigating the operational cycle time (OCT) of an individual manufacturing step for VLSI, the testing procedure can be used to assess whether the delivery time meets customer requirements. **Complimenting the company or organization at which one is seeking employment on its efforts in this area** 讚美公司對業界的專

業努力 Your company's success in the area of product development explains why I would like to join the research team at your company.

*

Introducing the objectives of a project in which one has participated 介紹此方案的目標 In light of my strong desire to thrive within this profession, I developed a networked peer assessment system capable of supporting instruction and learning, to analyze students' learning outcomes in higher education. **Summarizing the main results of that project** 概述該方案的成果 The system can be used in distance learning courses, enabling students to review the homework of their peers and receive comments. At the end of a semester, educators can access the student profiles easily via this system for further analysis. Additionally, educators can identify the significant relationship between the students' attitudes and their performance, and identify appropriate reliability and validity coefficients in networked peer assessment. **Highlighting the contribution of that project to the company or the sector to which it belongs** 強調該方案對公司或部門的貢獻 In demonstrating the effectiveness of networked peer assessment, our project results confirmed its reliability and validity as an assessment strategy for distance learning. **Complimenting the company or organization at which one is seeking employment on its efforts in this area** 讚美公司對業界的專業努力 Your firm has expended considerable resources in developing distance learning systems, explaining my eagerness to join your organization.

*

Introducing the objectives of a project in which one has participated 介紹此方案的目標 A strong desire to fully devote myself to this profession is reflected in my recently completed project to develop a mathematical editor using a Java applet on the Web, capable of using a graphic user interface to edit mathematical symbols. **Summarizing the main results of that project** 概述該方案的成果 Easily implemented to edit directly mathematical symbols using a graphic user interface, the editor that we developed allows users to edit complex equations, even those containing more than 20 mathematical symbols. The easy-to-use editor can be flexibly used on the Internet in mathematical courses, helping users to edit complex mathematical symbols more easily. **Highlighting the contribution of that project to the company or the sector to which it belongs** 強調該方案對公司或部門的貢獻 While promoting the teaching of mathematics on the Web, the editor can help teachers to publish their mathematical material on-line and can be combined with other mathematical software (for example, Mathematica) to conduct mathematical examinations on the Web. **Complimenting the company or organization at which one is seeking employment on its efforts in this area** 讚美公司對業界的專業努力 In this area of development, your company offers a competitive work environment and highly skilled professionals ingredients which are essential to the continual upgrading of my knowledge, skills and expertise.

*

Introducing the objectives of a project in which one has participated 介紹此方案的目標 Actively participating in several projects within this field attests to my determination to pursue this career. For instance, I participated in a collaborative effort to develop a networked electronic portfolio system with peer assessment capabilities to provide a creative means of assessing the higher-order thinking of students. **Summarizing the main results of that project** 概述該方案的成果 The system can observe students' higher-level thinking by collecting records of their homework and interaction with peers. The system allows educators to analyze the comments that students share with peers and the content of students' reviews of peers' homework, as well as to identify the higher-order thinking component. **Highlighting the contribution of that project to the company or the sector to which it belongs** 強調該方案對公司或部門的貢獻 This component can help educators to test and verify how the proposed system affects the higher-order thinking of students. Furthermore, the networked electronic portfolio system and peer assessment can be used at all educational levels. **Complimenting the company or organization at which one is seeking employment on its efforts in this area** 讚美公司對業界的專業努力 I am encouraged that your company has also devoted considerable resources to this area of research and, therefore, would like to join your corporate family.

*

Introducing the objectives of a project in which one has participated 介紹此方案的目標 My determination to develop continuously this professional interest stems from graduate school, where I actively engaged in a National Science Council-sponsored project to develop an enhanced piecewise linearization algorithm, capable of obtaining the global optimum of a nonlinear model, for use in a web based optimization system. Our algorithm can reduce the computational time required to solve a nonlinear programming model to 50% of that required by piecewise linearization algorithms. Moreover, in addition to allowing users to make more efficient decisions, the algorithm that we developed can obtain the global optimum in general nonlinear programming models within a tolerable error and significantly increase computational efficiency by decreasing the use of 0-1 variables. **Highlighting the contribution of that project to the company or the sector to which it belongs** 強調該方案對公司或部門的貢獻 Importantly, via a web-based system also developed by our group, the algorithm can be applied in diverse fields such as medicine, biology and engineering. **Complimenting the company or organization at which one is seeking employment on its efforts in this area** 讚美公司對業界的專業努力

*

Introducing the objectives of a project in which one has participated 介紹此方

案的目標 As evidence of my commitment to this profession, I collaborated with other researchers in developing an efficient face model capable of formulating the 3D image of an individual's face from three 2D images. **Summarizing the main results of that project** 概述該方案的成果 Our results demonstrated the ability of our face model to reduce the time to construct a 3D face by 10% by optimizing the 3D model rather than manually retrieving 2D images. Additionally, the proposed model can precisely formulate an individual's face by using conventional peripheral equipment. Furthermore, steps to construct 3D digital objects in the proposed face model are simplified, reducing the related formulation costs and time to use the optimization methods. **Highlighting the contribution of that project to the company or the sector to which it belongs** 強調該方案對公司或部門的貢獻 In terms of its contribution, the model we developed can minimize the tolerable errors associated with constructing a digital face, enhancing multimedia or animation applications by reducing formulation costs and creating more realistic digital objects. The proposed model can be employed to digitize different real 3D objects. **Complimenting the company or organization at which one is seeking employment on its efforts in this area** 讚美公司對業界的專業努力 The fact that your organization has exerted considerable effort in this area of research largely explains why I am eager to join your corporate family.

*

Introducing the objectives of a project in which one has participated 介紹此方案的目標 As a testament to my commitment to acquiring pertinent knowledge and skills to rise to the challenges of this profession, I designed a GIS-based architecture that supports an automatic reporting service through handheld mobile devices. **Summarizing the main results of that project** 概述該方案的成果 This architecture can automatically page PDA users through a wireless network when desired local information becomes available. Using the global positioning system

(GPS) feature, the system will periodically send the position of the user to the server. The server will then check for any local news about disasters or roadblocks, and for advertisements. The results will be sent back to the user's machine and an event triggered to remind the user. **Highlighting the contribution of that project to the company or the sector to which it belongs** 強調該方案對公司或部門的貢獻 With its highly promising commercial applications, this GIS-based architecture can allow PDA users to access information with their geographic position functioning as a filter, thus ensuring that users are not overwhelmed with undesired information. **Complimenting the company or organization at which one is seeking employment on its efforts in this area** 讚美公司對業界的專業努力 Your firm has expended considerable resources in developing such potential commercial applications, explaining my eagerness to join your organization.

*

Introducing the objectives of a project in which one has participated 介紹此方案的目標 Owing to my deep interest in this profession, I collaboratively developed a web-based system in a PC-LAN environment, capable of detecting network problems. **Summarizing the main results of that project** 概述該方案的成果 This system can provide an efficient and inexpensive solution to enable an enterprise to maintain a stable network environment. The system we developed can detect 85% of all network problems in 5 minutes by reducing the complexity of operating a network management system. An enterprise can smoothly apply the system without complex procedures. By communicating with all remote network devices using the SNMP protocol, our system can automatically notify network administrators through e-mail, a pager or voice mail. Importantly, our system combines free software programs from the Internet to enhance the network management system. **Highlighting the contribution of that project to the company or the sector to which it belongs** 強調該方案對公司或部門的貢獻 Combining a free software program Multi Router Traffic Grapher (MRTG) and a web-based integrated interface will greatly reduce developmental costs and efforts.

*

Introducing the objectives of a project in which one has participated 介紹此方案的目標 Actively participating in several projects within this field attests to my determination to pursue this career. For instance, I developed a novel learning environment capable of assisting students in flexibly learning genetic algorithms based on computer-assisted instruction. **Summarizing the main results of that project** 概述該方案的成果 This learning environment can reduce the time required for students to complete a GA assignment to one week, increasing the number of practice exercises that can be implemented and allowing them to better learn GAs. **Highlighting the contribution of that project to the company or the sector to which it belongs** 強調該方案對公司或部門的貢獻 Importantly, this novel learning environment can eliminate the need for hand coding GA programs, simplifying the process of learning genetic algorithms. Moreover, this environment enables students to select desired system configurations, including structural settings and parametric selections, before simulation.

*

Introducing the objectives of a project in which one has participated 介紹此方案的目標 A strong desire to devote myself fully to this profession is reflected in my previous effort to develop an analytical geometric method for accurately predicting the geometric parameters of practical C4 type solder joints in flip chip technology after a reflow process. **Summarizing the main results of that project** 概述該方案的成果 In addition to calculating the effect of gravity on the buried high-lead solder bump, instead of on the semi-spherical one, this method can predict geometric parameters of a C4 type solder joint to within 5% of those obtained by a specific method found in the literature. **Highlighting the contribution of that project to the**

company or the sector to which it belongs 強調該方案對公司或部門的貢獻 Importantly the method can be used to design geometric parameters of a C4 type solder joint, enhancing the reliability of a flip chip package and reducing its stress concentration. **Complimenting the company or organization at which one is seeking employment on its efforts in this area** 讚美公司對業界的專業努力 As for this area of development, your company offers a unique environment in which I can fully grasp the latest technological trends and specialize in those areas that both satisfy my professional interests and contribute to corporate profits.

H Select the correct answers to the following questions about the three stories in this unit.

1. What does Sam occasionally perform at ABC Company?

    A. measurement systems analysis

    B. MASK inspection

    C. statistical process control

2. What is the name of the department in which Sam works at ABC Company?

    A. Statistical Process Control

    B. Measurement Systems Analysis

    C. Quality Assurance

3. What kind of measurement system causes errors in process control and judgment?

    A. an imprecise or unreliable one

    B. an inexpensive or time consuming one

    C. an unstable or inaccurate one

4. What has Sam developed a strong interest in while working at ABC Company?

    A. quality control

    B. laboratory work

129

C. process control and judgment

5. Sam is concerned with criteria for assessing what?

A. MASK inspection

B. process control and judgment

C. a measurement system

6. What has fascinated Mary from an early age?

A. electronic engineering

B. electrical engineering

C. electronics

7. Mary is interested in how what impacts our lives?

A. discrete signal processing technologies

B. digital control technologies

C. integrated circuit technologies

8. What does Mary believe that GHI Corporation would provide the ideal working environment for her to do?

A. solve problems logically and independently

B. further pursue her professional interests

C. research integrated circuit technologies

9. Besides signal processes and VLSI, what does Mary's graduate school research focus on?

A. digital control

B. integrated circuit technologies

C. electronics-related topics

10. What does Mary believe that she will be able to apply as a member of the GHI family?

A. her ability to solve problems logically and independently

B. her strong research fundamentals

C. her professional interests

11. What industrial field does Mary's research belong to?

    A. VLSI

    B. digital control

    C. integrated circuit design

12. What has John's intrigue with science and technology culminated in?

    A. entry into the hi-tech IC design industry

    B. successful completion of a Master's degree in Electrical Engineering

    C. Involvement in a project in which he simulated an Ethernet protocol

13. Which is the most similar in meaning to "culminated in"?

    A. led to

    B. developed

    C. cultivated

14. What was John's first project at JKL Corporation?

    A. to research logic design, communications and computer networks

    B. to develop an Ethernet MAC controller

    C. to develop a Serial ATA controller

15. What is John doing now at JKL Corporation?

    A. developing a Serial ATA controller

    B. researching logic design, communications and computer networks

    C. developing an Ethernet MAC controller

16. Which word is most similar in meaning to "renowned"?

    A. arrogant

    B. amicable

    C. distinguished

> **I** Select the correct answers to the following questions about one's participation in a project that reflects interest in a profession.

1. What did you develop a love for ____ at National Tsing Hua University?

   A. during

   B. while

   C. with

2. What major projects have you participated in ____ an engineer?

   A. by

   B. to

   C. as

3. What specific tasks ___ you performed while conducting laboratory experiments?

   A. have

   B. did

   C. does

4. What do you feel that your personal strengths are ____ participating in a project?

   A. during

   B. when

   C. with

5. What research skills would you like to develop further ___ you gain employment at DEF Corporation?

   A. by

   B. if

   C. with

6. What experience do you have in participating ___ biotechnology projects?

   A. in

B. from

C. which

7. What are you especially concerned ____ when participating in biotechnology projects?

A. from

B. by

C. with

8. What have you developed a strong interest ____ while participating in biotechnology projects?

A. in

B. for

C. on

9. How will you be able to apply the strong research fundamentals taught ____ National Chiao Tung University?

A. for

B. at

C. to

10. How did you ____ involved in this project?

A. become

B. be

C. is

11. How ____ you develop your interest in electrical engineering?

A. was

B. did

C. were

12. How did you become fascinated ____ biotechnology-related topics?

A. by

B. on

C. to

13. How did you learn innovative ways ____ solving problems logically and independently?

A. to

B. of

C. in

14. How ____ computer technology impacted our daily lives?

A. are

B. is

C. has

15. How can GHI Corporation provide the ideal working environment ____ you can further pursue your professional interests?

A. in which

B. to which

C. for which

16. How much longer do you have ____ completing a Master's degree in Health Care Management?

A. before

B. after

C. for

17. How long has it ____ since you received your Bachelor's degree in Nursing?

A. does

B. have

C. been

18. Why have you long been intrigued ____ science and technology?

A. by

B. for

C. on

19. Why has your interest in electronic products culminated ____ successful completion of a Master's degree in Electrical Engineering from National Taiwan University?

A. on

B. to

C. in

20. Why did you enter the hi-tech IC design industry ____ pursue a career as an engineer?

A. for

B. to

C. on

21. Why are you able to apply the practical laboratory experiences ____ graduate school to your current working environment?

A. from

B. on

C. with

22. Why ____ your company offer such a highly competitive work environment?

A. are

B. do

C. does

23. Why did you develop a love ____ nursing while at university?

A. at

B. for

C. on

24. Why is your personality conducive ____ stressful work situations?

Describing participation in a project that reflects interest in a profession
描述所參與方案裡專業興趣的表現

A. to

B. by

C. on

25. Why ____ you become involved in this project?

A. before

B. was

C. did

27. Why did you first ____ interested in participating in health care management?

A. be

B. become

C. are

Unit Four

Describing academic background and achievements relevant to employment

描述學歷背景及已獲成就

Vocabulary and related expressions   相關字詞

desiring   意欲
theoretical and professional knowledge
理論及專業知識
consulting firm   顧問公司
wide array   大量
certification   認證
formation   形成
a specialization in   專攻
architectural   建築學的
proceeds to   繼續
implementing   執行
balance   平衡
premier   主要的
departmental curricula   科系課程
fundamental   根基的
Local Area Network (LAN)   區域網路
analytical   分析的
view   觀點
setbacks   挫折

competitive edge   競爭優勢
strengthen   強化
exposed   使暴露於
pollution control   污染控管
training course   訓練課程
valuable member   有價值成員
hardware   硬體
simulate   模擬
time to market   入市場時間
optimizing   最佳化
product quality   產品品質
solid background   強有力背景
absorb   吸收
wireless   無線的
communication skills   溝通技巧
experimentation   實驗法
bottlenecks in research   研究瓶頸
perseverance   堅持

A Write down the key points of the situations on the preceding page, while the instructor reads aloud the script from the Answer Key.

Situation 1

_____

_____

_____

Situation 2

_____

_____

_____

Situation 3

_____

_____

_____

Describing academic background and achievements relevant
to employment
描述學歷背景及已獲成就

B Based on the three situations in this unit, write three
questions beginning with **What**, and answer them.
The questions do not need to come directly from
these situations.

Examples

What did Jerry acquire a degree in from National Chiao Tung University?

Environmental Engineering

What does Joy believe is necessary to balance time to market with product quality?

Simulation and analysis

1. _____

_____

2. _____

_____

3. _____

_____

C Based on the three situations in this unit, write three questions beginning with **Where**, and answer them. The questions do not need to come directly from these situations.

Examples

Where did Jerry receive certification as an "Air Pollution Control Equipment Technician"?

At the R.O.C. Environmental Protection Administration

Where did Max receive a Master's degree in Electronics Engineering?

National Taiwan University

1. _____

   _____

2. _____

   _____

3. _____

   _____

D Based on the three situations in this unit, write three questions beginning with *Which*, and answer them. The questions do not need to come directly from these situations.

Which topics did Jerry's intensive training course cover?

The formation and prevention of air pollutants

Which tasks does Joy prefer to undertake in computer architecture?

Creating organizational and architectural designs and then writing programs to simulate their effectiveness

1. _____

_____

2. _____

_____

3. _____

_____

E Write questions that match the answers provided.

Examples

1. _____

_____

Developing a wireless Local Area Network

2. _____

_____

As challenges rather than setbacks

3. _____

_____

A wide array of pollution control technologies and equipment

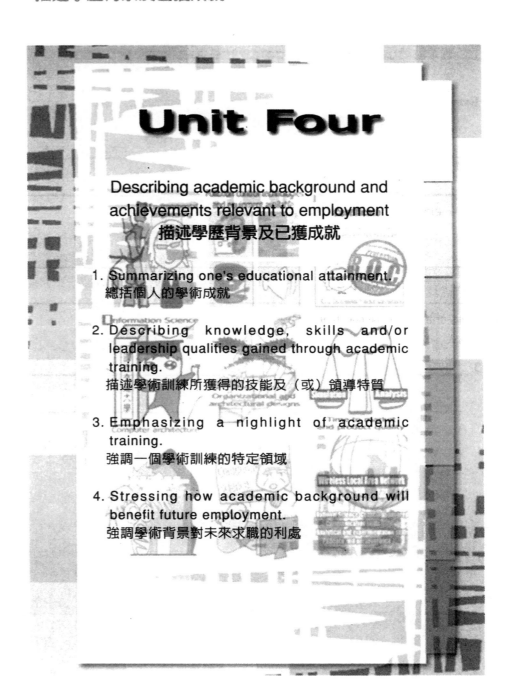

Unit Four

Describing academic background and
achievements relevant to employment
描述學歷背景及已獲成就

1. Summarizing one's educational attainment.
   總括個人的學術成就

2. Describing knowledge, skills and/or
   leadership qualities gained through academic
   training.
   描述學術訓練所獲得的技能及（或）領導特質

3. Emphasizing a nighlight of academic
   training.
   強調一個學術訓練的特定領域

4. Stressing how academic background will
   benefit future employment.
   強調學術背景對未來求職的利處

Common elements in describing academic background and achievements include:

1. Summarizing one's educational attainment　總括個人的學術成就

◎ Undergraduate studies exposed me to diverse disciplines, thus allowing me to choose a career path more objectively than if I had a bias for a particular area.

◎ While my Master's degree in Biochemistry prepared me for the rigorous demands of conducting original research in this field and publication of those findings in international journals, doctoral level studies in the same field equipped me with the required knowledge, skills and professional expertise to excel in the biotechnology profession.

◎ Widely recognized as one of Taiwan's leading institutes of learning, the Experimental High School in Hsinchu Science-based Industrial Park from which I graduated, is renowned for its mathematics and physics departments, providing special science education programs that include visits by well-known academics who conduct workshops and seminars for students.

◎ As a diligent student at Jones University, I was on the Dean's List several times and graduated with honors in the class of 1998.

◎ I received my undergraduate and graduate training in Industrial Engineering at National Chiao Tung University and National Tsing Hua University, respectively, higher institutions of learning at which many staff of the Hsinchu Science-based Industrial Park developed their professional skills.

◎ Immediately following four years of highly theoretical study and intellectual rigor at National Taiwan University in successful pursuit of a Bachelor's degree in Chemistry, I gained entry to the highly prestigious doctoral program in the same field at National Tsing Hua University.

◎ I majored in Computer Science during university and later received a Master's degree in the same field, specifically with the intention of acquiring sufficient to contribute more effectively to society in the future.

◎ The enclosed academic transcripts reveal that I excelled in a diverse range of electrical engineering courses during university, allowing me to bring a solid

Unit Describing academic background and achievements relevant
Four to employment
描述學歷背景及已獲成就

academic foundation and sufficient knowledge and skills in this area to your
company

◎ Instead of reflecting a lack of academic ability, my comparatively low grade point
average largely follows from the fact that I graduated with nearly thirty credits more
than graduation required. With an average semester course load of over twenty
credits, I concentrated on exposing myself to seemingly polar disciplines, ranging
from Electronics to Religion. I believe that exposing myself to diverse
undergraduate curricula has given me a more objective view of which career path to
pursue.

◎ My unflattering grade point average of 3.39 during undergraduate studies should be
seen in light of the fact that I attended a high school and university that are regarded
as among the most prestigious and academically challenging in Taiwan.
Nevertheless, a GPA of 3.75 during my final two years of university reflects my
determination not only to improve my academic standing, but also to acquire the
knowledge and skills necessary for the workplace.

◎ I have always striven for a well-balanced personality to remain strong in a
competitive environment by aspiring to academic excellence and by participating in
activities. While serving as class president, my grade point average dipped during
my sophomore year of university. Instead of relinquishing my extracurricular
activities, I had to reestablish my priority of balancing social and academic activities.
My grade point average stabilized, as evidenced by my accompanying academic
transcripts.

◎ Following participation in a highly competitive selective scheme for talented
students in math and science, run by the Ministry of Education, I gained entry to the
Hsinchu First Girl's Senior High School in 1999.

◎ My rather late decision to switch my major to Psychology during my senior year
explains why I remained in university for another year. However, I do not regret this
decision, as the additional time allowed me to focus more clearly on my career
direction.

2. Describing knowledge, skills and/or leadership qualities gained through academic training 描述學術訓練所獲得的技能及（或）領導特質

◎ Although I did not perform well academically during my freshman year in university, I buckled down and concentrated on my studies, resulting in a gradual improvement in my grades until graduation. This gradual improvement in my academic performance reflects my determination in setting realistic goals, regardless of how formidable they appear at the moment.

◎ My diverse academic interests reflect my ability to view beyond the conventional limits of a discipline and fully comprehend how it relates to other ones. Solid training at this prestigious institute of higher learning equipped me with strong analytical skills and research fundamentals.

◎ Undergraduate and graduate level courses in mechanical engineering often involved term projects that allowed me to apply theoretical concepts in a practical context and to develop my problem-solving skills.

◎ In the accompanying academic transcripts, high marks on those courses that equipped me with a solid theoretical background in electrical engineering reflect my commitment to acquiring knowledge and skills that will not only make me competent, but also allow me to thrive in the workplace.

◎ Through my academic training, I acquired specialized knowledge of finance-related issues and developed my ability to work independently.

◎ By equipping me with the fundamentals of computer science, undergraduate courses underpinned the professional training that I received in graduate school.

◎ Critical thinking skills developed during undergraduate and graduate studies have enabled me not only to explore finance-related issues beyond their initial appearances and delve into the underlying issues, but also to conceptualize problems in different ways.

◎ Equipped with strong analytical and experimental skills acquired during graduate school, I am able to find a practical context for applying the theoretical concepts taught in the classroom and understand how they relate to the hi tech sector.

◎ Doctoral studies increased the breadth and depth of my understanding of electrical engineering, as evidenced by my doctoral dissertation, and some of those findings were published in several international journals.

◎ Besides developing my academic abilities, the strong departmental curricula strengthened my resolve to apply my newly acquired knowledge and skills in an interdisciplinary manner.

◎ Actively participating in several National Science Council-sponsored projects not only bolstered my commitment to laboratory work but also broadened my outlook on research by collaborating with experimenters of various backgrounds.

◎ Management training courses in which I enrolled following university graduation not only made me acutely aware of global trends in management practices, but also motivated me to upgrade continuously my knowledge and skills to remain competitive in a hi tech sector that continues to evolve at a dizzying pace.

◎ Successfully completing a senior year term project on biotechnology strengthened my resolve to pursue this field professionally and acquire the necessary skills to thrive in this exciting profession.

◎ Despite majoring in chemistry during university, I retained an open mind towards other disciplines in order not to limit myself, as attested by my decision to minor in English literature and computer science.

◎ Graduate study in Construction Engineering made me aware of the importance of financial planning and evaluating a project's success. The balance of academic training and practical knowledge acquired through exposure to actual construction projects during graduate school will prove to be an invaluable asset to any company to which I belong - I hope that company is yours.

◎ My outstanding academic performance during university and graduate school attests to my diligence and creativity. The challenges encountered during doing my Master's thesis, a seminal work that dated groundwater using carbon 14, developed my ability to solve problems logically and efficiently.

◎ I was diligent in my studies during university. During the first three years of university, my grade point average was lower than 80 because I participated in many extracurricular activities. In my junior year, I was determined to raise my grade point average. I took rigorous courses such as Mathematical Analysis and Advanced Engineering Mathematics and received grades above 80.

◎ Studying at National Tsing Hua University, one of Taiwan's premier institutes of higher learning, strongly motivated me to acquire the latest knowledge, skills and technical information. More specifically, I learned how to analyze problems, find solutions, and implement them according to the concepts taught in class. I also participated in a research project during my senior year, learning how to be a contributing team member and developing a thorough understanding of teamwork. I also attended several international conferences that addressed biotechnological issues to broaden my perspective on potential applications of biology and computers- these areas are now my main areas of interest.

◎ My high marks in language courses reflect my strong command of English composition and conversation.

3. Emphasizing a highlight of academic training 強調一個學術訓練的特定領域

◎ My teachers often commended me on my ability to approach problems with which I was previously unfamiliar, logically and methodically. This trait not only allowed me to grasp new concepts quickly, but also to understand the depth and implications of complex problems.

◎ A rich blend of theoretical knowledge and practical concepts taught in undergraduate biology courses facilitated my understanding of how this field can be integrated in the hi tech sector.

◎ Serving as a teaching assistant nurtured my ability to clarify and present complex questions and concepts orally and in written form.

◎ While heavily emphasizing self-directed learning and development aimed at contributing to collaborative research efforts, graduate school ignited within me a strong desire to diversify my knowledge and skills to adopt multi-disciplinary approaches in an industrial setting.

◎ My curiosity and determination to adopt unconventional or multi-disciplinary approaches to solve networking problems not only distinguished me from other graduate research students, but also led to my developing a software program that has already been commercialized.

◎ Graduate school instilled in me the need for harmony among research collaborators to achieve the desired outcome. As group leader, I often organized discussion groups on how to implement operating systems developed in our laboratory. In addition to exchanging relevant theoretical knowledge and individual expertise, our group formed a bond that greatly facilitated accumulation and analysis of data and, eventually, the publishing of our research findings in several renowned international journals.

◎ This course motivated me to identify how information science concepts can applied in other disciplines to create potential industrial applications that would have been otherwise impossible without such an integration of seemingly polar fields. Bioinformatics is a notable example.

◎ My graduate school research often involved deriving complex mathematical models and then presenting the results clearly in written form and orally. This continual activity of explaining concepts to those outside my field of expertise was invaluable training for what I often encounter in the workplace - the need to provide sufficient details for non-technical professionals to make management decisions.

◎ Writing my Master's thesis proved to be a valuable exercise in adopting a multi-disciplinary approach to integrating knowledge and skills from different fields.

◎ Besides providing a practical context for the academic fundamentals of information management, a senior seminar on database applications in industry required me to collaborate closely with classmates by simulating an industrial project to fulfill course requirements.

◎ A graduate seminar on Internet-based technologies made me aware of their rapid growth and incorporation into areas in which they had not been previously applied, such as education, language learning and medicine.

◎ During university, I constantly read commentaries and papers on the latest developments in biology to broaden my perspective on potential technological and industrial applications.

◎ A cumulative grade point average of 4.0 during graduate school speaks for my professional grasp of the latest technological trends in information management.

4. Stressing how academic background will benefit future employment　強調學術背景對未來求職的利處

◎ Graduate school has equipped me with much knowledge and logical skills to address problems effectively in the workplace, even though I may lack experience of a particular topic. After clarifying the problem at hand and identifying its component parts, I divide it into individual questions, clarify all the variables, their effects and the possible consequences. After careful consideration, I then make a logical conclusion based on available information and propose available options for further research. I believe that you will find these qualities a valuable asset at your company.

◎ I am absolutely confident that my academic background, experimental and work experience in materials science, desire for knowledge and love of challenges will enable me to succeed in your company's highly demanding product development projects.

◎ Extensive laboratory training extended my ability to define specific situations, think logically, collect related information, and analyze problems independently. These qualities will prove to be a valuable asset to any collaborative effort in which I am involved in your company.

F　In the space below, describe your academic background and achievements.

_____

_____

_____

_____

Describing academic background and achievements relevant to employment

描述學歷背景及已獲成就

_____

_____

_____

_____

_____

_____

_____

_____

G Look at the following examples of describing academic background and achievements.

Summarizing one's educational attainment 總括個人的學術成就 I received a Master's degree in Electronics Engineering from one of Taiwan's premier universities, National Taiwan University, in 1994. **Describing knowledge, skills and/or leadership qualities gained through academic training** 描述學術訓練所獲得的技能及（或）領導特質 By providing me with a solid background in computer science, the departmental curricula allowed me to absorb fundamental knowledge and obtain practical laboratory experience simultaneously. **Emphasizing a highlight of academic training** 強調一個學術訓練的特定領域 During graduate school, I participated in a National Science Council-sponsored research project aimed at developing a wireless Local Area Network. My collaboration in a team enhanced my communication skills and the research effort fostered my analytical and experimentation skills. **Stressing how academic background will benefit future employment** 強調學術背景對未來求職的利處 This solid academic training challenged me to view bottlenecks in research as challenges rather than setbacks, thus increasing my patience and perseverance in future investigations. These qualities will benefit any collaborative effort that I belong to within your company.

*

Summarizing one's educational attainment 總括個人的學術成就 The strong academic fundamentals in Electrical Engineering acquired during my undergraduate studies at National Tsing Hua University prepared me for the rigorous demands of pursuing a Master's degree at the same institution. **Describing knowledge, skills and/or leadership qualities gained through academic training** 描述學術訓練所獲得的技能及（或）領導特質 Building upon those fundamentals during graduate school, I was able to broaden my professional knowledge in communications and signal processing-related courses such as Communication Principles, Communication System Experimentation, Error Control Coding, Digital Signal Processing, Video Signal Processing, Speech & Audio Signal Processing and Pattern Recognition. I also served as a teaching assistant in departmental courses on Electronic Experimentation (I) and Logic Design. These courses provided a detailed theoretical understanding that has further enriched my academic background.

*

Solid undergraduate and graduate academic training in science at National Taiwan University of Science and Technology, a widely respected university in Taiwan, has allowed me to develop my solid logical and professional skills.

153

*

Summarizing one's educational attainment 總括個人的學術成就 I received a Master's degree in Chemistry from Fu Jen University in 1994, where I concentrated on the theoretical analysis of chemical reaction mechanisms, thermal relations and material synthesis.

*

Summarizing one's educational attainment 總括個人的學術成就 I will meet the requirements of my Master's degree in Industrial Engineering from National Chiao Tung University in the spring of 2002. **Emphasizing a highlight of academic training** 強調一個學術訓練的特定領域 In addition to researching topics related to quality control, data analysis and system integration, I have participated in research projects involving customer relations, 6 sigma and financial evaluation. **Stressing how academic background will benefit future employment** 強調學術背景對未來求職的利處These experiences have enhanced my ability to plan, execute, and orally present research findings. I also served as a research assistant in a university-sponsored project on health promotion. Such solid graduate training has equipped me for the rigorous demands of the highly competitive workplace of your company.

*

Summarizing one's educational attainment 總括個人的學術成就 Graduate school research has allowed me to understand thoroughly the characteristics of flooding in Taiwan. My research focus has thus centered on the feasibility of effectively forecasting flood discharge. **Emphasizing a highlight of academic training** 強調一個學術訓練的特定領域 More specifically, in my Master's thesis "Applying an Artificial Neural Network Algorithm to Forecast the Catchment Outflow", I developed a method for estimating the flood discharge more easily than by conventional methods, which depend on several given hydraulic parameters of flooding. Portions of this thesis have already been published in the Journal of

Hydroscience and Hydraulic Engineering. Additionally, participation in several domestic and international conferences has enhanced my ability to present orally my research findings on flood control. **Stressing how academic background will benefit future employment** 強調學術背景對未來求職的利處 I believe that the above experiences will prove invaluable to any research team to which I belong within your organization.

*

Summarizing one's educational attainment 總括個人的學術成就 I received a Bachelor's degree from the Department of Soil and Water Conservation at National Chung Hsing University in 1994. **Describing knowledge, skills and/or leadership qualities gained through academic training** 描述學術訓練所獲得的技能及（或）領導特質 The departmental curricula provided me with a solid theoretical understanding of mechanical engineering, solid mechanics and fluid mechanics. Upon graduation, I successfully gained entry into the Institute of Civil Engineering at National Chiao Tung University in pursuit of a Master's degree from 1994 to 1996. **Emphasizing a highlight of academic training** 強調一個學術訓練的特定領域 My research focused on developing groundwater numerical models and I simulated the groundwater flow of the Cho-Shui River fan using deterministic and stochastic models. More recently, in 1999, I passed a rigorous nationwide examination in which I received accreditation as a water conservancy engineer.

*

Summarizing one's educational attainment 總括個人的學術成就 While pursuing a Master's degree in Electrical Engineering, I took a diverse range of courses within the department, such as Semiconductor Physics, Semiconductor Devices, Memory Design and Integrated Circuit Design. These professionally designed and delivered courses made me aware of the seemingly unlimited theoretical and practical applications of electrical engineering. Equipped with strong academic fundamentals necessary for graduate level research, as well as a burning desire for advanced knowledge in the field, I scored highly on an intensely competitive nationwide graduate school entrance examination and subsequently entered the prestigious Institute of Electrical Engineering at National Cheng Kung University to engage in semiconductor research. **Describing knowledge, skills and/or leadership qualities gained through academic training** 描述學術訓練所獲得的技能及（或）領導特質 The Institute's widely praised curricula instilled in me advanced knowledge and skills in theoretical and practical contexts, allowing me to refine my research capabilities, as evidenced by the considerable time I spent conducting independent research in the laboratory. Once having acquired a sound theoretical and practical understanding of sensors and actuators, I actively engaged in collaborative research to improve the structures and their performance of recently developed sensors. The findings of this research were published in Electrical Device Letters and received considerable praise.

*

I majored in Computer Science at National Cheng Kung University, where I later received a Master's in the same field.

*

Summarizing one's educational attainment 總括個人的學術成就 A solid academic background in Computer Science and Information Engineering at one of Taiwan's premier universities, National Tsing Hua University, provided me with the fundamental skills required for IC design. **Describing knowledge, skills and/or leadership qualities gained through academic training** 描述學術訓練所獲得的技能及（或）領導特質 Graduate research in the microprocessor and ASIC design for multimedia applications equipped me with advanced knowledge and skills necessary to remain competitive in the workplace - hopefully at your company.

*

Summarizing one's educational attainment 總括個人的學術成就 A solid academic background in Information Engineering gained at National Tsing Hua University provided me with the fundamental skills required for advanced research in IC design. **Emphasizing a highlight of academic training** 強調一個學術訓練的 特定領域 I have spent considerable time in multimedia related hardware design, mostly developing image processing and computer graphics hardware. Those experiences have provided me with an in-depth knowledge of ASIC design for multimedia applications.

*

Summarizing one's educational attainment 總括個人的學術成就 The Institute of Computer Information Science at National Chiao Tung University provided me with solid background knowledge of mathematics and programming during my undergraduate studies. While working on my Master's degree, I participated in many projects and performed many experiments to enhance my research and problem-solving skills. **Describing knowledge, skills and/or leadership qualities gained through academic training** 描述學術訓練所獲得的技能及（或）領導特 質 These experiences reinforced my belief that success is only fully realized through a diligent and persevering attitude towards life's challenges.

*

Summarizing one's educational attainment 總括個人的學術成就 As a graduate student, I was fascinated by telecommunications. I decided to pursue a communications-related career, with a particular focus on digital signal processes, digital communications and coding theory. **Describing knowledge, skills and/or leadership qualities gained through academic training** 描述學術訓練所獲得的 技能及（或）領導特質 Relevant knowledge and skills have allowed me to design a filter used in sample rate conversion. Using this filter, a sample rate source can be easily converted into another one. Additionally, this filter can be used as an audio processor. For example, a listener wants to enjoy music stored on a hard disc. However, the wave files have many different sample rate formats, preventing the listener from accessing them directly. Therefore, the data must be processed by a filter and, then, sent to the speaker or headphone. Designing a good filter is a difficult challenge because, in addition to providing high quality music, the computational power must be minimized. To do so, many series of coefficients used in the FIR filter must be obtained and filters must be compared in terms of their characteristics. Our intensive study has revealed that a filter with a series of coefficients can attain high quality, according to a general measurement criterion and the requirement of minimal computational power.

*

Summarizing one's educational attainment 總括個人的學術成就 My studies at the Institute of Electronics Engineering at National Chiao Tung University provided me with a solid background knowledge of telecommunications and signal processing, as well as the desire to become a designer in this exciting field. My graduate level research included signal processing. **Describing knowledge, skills and/or leadership qualities gained through academic training** 描述學術訓練所獲得的技能及（或）領導特質 Collaborative teamwork has encouraged close cooperation among research collaborators and the minimization of design complexity, ultimately lowering product cost. I have also been able to excel in logic design-related skills, such as Modelsim, Debussy, Mat lab and HDL. Moreover, these experiences have sharpened my ability to analyze the merits and limitations of these methods, think logically, collect related information, and meet customer specifications while using minimal resources. **Stressing how academic background will benefit future employment** 強調學術背景對未來求職的利處 Accordingly, I am determined to devote myself to a career in telecommunications-related research so that I can continuously refine my professional skills that are necessary to thrive in this highly competitive environment.

*

Summarizing one's educational attainment 總括個人的學術成就 After studying Chemical Engineering at a technological institute, I received a Bachelor's degree in Environmental Engineering from National Taipei University of Technology. Desiring to strengthen my theoretical and professional knowledge, I acquired a Master's degree in Environmental Engineering from National Chiao Tung University two years later. Graduate level research also allowed me to actively participate in several projects that exposed me to a wide array of pollution control technologies and available equipment. **Emphasizing a highlight of academic training** 強調一個學術訓練的特定領域 As evidence of my desire continuously to upgrade my research capabilities, I received certification as an "Air Pollution Control Equipment Technician" from the R.O.C. Environmental Protection Administration following an intensive training course. The course shed further light on the formation and prevention of air pollutants.

*

Summarizing one's educational attainment 總括個人的學術成就 I received a Master's degree in Electronic Engineering at National Chiao Tung University in 1994. The departmental curricula provided me with a theoretical and practical understanding of electrical engineering. Moreover, courses such as Circuit Design and Design Automation were particularly effective in enhancing my ability to analyze EDA field-related problems. **Emphasizing a highlight of academic training** 強調一個學術訓練的特定領域 In my Master's thesis, I proposed a novel automation algorithm that significantly enhances the results of cell placement. Portions of the thesis have been submitted for publication in the Journal of Design Automation.

Describing academic background and achievements relevant to employment
描述學歷背景及已獲成就

*

Summarizing one's educational attainment 總括個人的學術成就 Following undergraduate studies, I pursued a Master's degree in Industrial Engineering at National Chiao Tung University. **Emphasizing a highlight of academic training** 強調一個學術訓練的特定領域 Concentrating on quality control research, I participated in several projects related to Six-Sigma quality control, customer satisfaction at Applied Materials Taiwan, and an analysis of the salary structure at the Biomedical Engineering Center, Industrial Technology Research Institute. These projects allowed me not only to apply my academic skills to practical situations, but also to foster my ability to solve problems logically.

*

Summarizing one's educational attainment 總括個人的學術成就 In addition to providing me with a solid background knowledge of electronics, my studies at the Institute of Electrical and Electronic Engineering at National Taiwan University allowed me to acquire advanced research skills and numerous laboratory experiences. **Emphasizing a highlight of academic training** 強調一個學術訓練的特定領域 My Master's thesis focused on filter design and compression algorithms to reduce the cost of implementing a filter. New algorithms were also developed to compress audio data. Our filters can operate more efficiently and economically than conventional ones under the same conditions. Characterized by their simplicity, our new compression algorithms offer an alternative means of processing audio data.

*

Summarizing one's educational attainment 總括個人的學術成就 Solid undergraduate and graduate academic training in science at National Taiwan University of Science and Technology, a widely respected university in Taiwan, has allowed me to develop my solid logic and professional capabilities. To acquire finance-related knowledge, I returned to National Taiwan University of Science and

Technology, following considerable work experience, to acquire another Master's degree, this time in Finance, from the Institute of Finance. Owing to my strong analytical skills, I have focused my graduate research on financial topics related to engineering, such as pricing derivatives, fitting yield curves, and designing innovative financial products.

*

Summarizing one's educational attainment 總括個人的學術成就 Solid undergraduate and graduate academic training in science at National Taiwan University, the premier university in Taiwan, has allowed me to develop strong analytical skills and professional capabilities. Ranking first academically in my graduating class attests to my academic excellence. Following graduation, I worked as an engineer for six years. After that work experience, I switched the focus of my career to the financial sector and returned to National Taiwan University to pursue another Master's degree, this time in Finance from the Institute of Finance. Owing to my strong analytical skills, I focused my graduate research on financial engineering, such as pricing derivatives, fitting yield curves, and designing innovative financial products. **Emphasizing a highlight of academic training** 強調一個學術訓練的特定領域 Several academic awards, an overall academic ranking of first out of a class of 28 and a cumulative GPA of 3.9 reflect my diligence and advanced professional knowledge. **Stressing how academic background will benefit future employment** 強調學術背景對未來求職的利處 I believe my solid academic training will give me a competitive edge in the workplace, hopefully at your company.

*

Summarizing one's educational attainment 總括個人的學術成就 During graduate school, I served as a teaching assistant for courses in Quality control and Statistical analysis methods. **Describing knowledge, skills and/or leadership qualities gained through academic training** 描述學術訓練所獲得的技能及（或）

領導特質 These courses allowed me not only to instruct others on SAS and STATISTICA software, but also to become skilled in using the software and performing data analysis. In addition, I participated in several National Science Council-sponsored projects in which I realized how my theoretical knowledge could be implemented in a workplace. **Emphasizing a highlight of academic training** 強調一個學術訓練的特定領域 For instance, I was able to facilitate wafer quality inspection through the more effective use of a control chart. In a project at the Biomedical Engineering Center, I adopted the regression method to assess the salary structure of staff and accurately determine employees' salary over a certain period. **Stressing how academic background will benefit future employment** 強調學術背景對未來求職的利處 Full participation in these projects not only enhanced my research skills, but also fostered my interest in Industrial Engineering. These attributes, I believe, are sought by your company.

*

Summarizing one's educational attainment 總括個人的學術成就 After passing a rigorous nationwide university entrance examination in 1990, I was admitted to the Department of Power Mechanical Engineering at National Tsing Hua University, one of Taiwan's premier institutes of higher learning. This four year academic training introduced me to the dynamic nature of mechanical engineering-related research. Upon graduation, I successfully passed the graduate school examination to take a Master's degree in the same field. **Describing knowledge, skills and/or leadership qualities gained through academic training** 描述學術訓練所獲得的技能及（或）領導特質 My particular emphasis on combustion turbo engine-related research provided me with a theoretical and practical understanding of fields related to aerodynamic and fluid mechanics. **Stressing how academic background will benefit future employment** 強調學術背景對未來求職的利處 The training and skills I acquired in experimental design and data analysis will make me a valuable member of any research team to which I belong in your company.

*

Summarizing one's educational attainment 總括個人的學術成就 At graduate school, I audited courses in the training of civil engineers, which covered technologies involved in construction engineering as well as tunnel construction in Taiwan. I also attended many international conferences and won recognition for my contributions. **Describing knowledge, skills and/or leadership qualities gained through academic training** 描述學術訓練所獲得的技能及（或）領導特質 These experiences reinforced my dedication to pursuing a career in civil engineering. Although occasionally frustrated by a bottleneck in a project I'm working on, I view such obstacles as stimuli for striving harder. **Stressing how academic background will benefit future employment** 強調學術背景對未來求職的利處 I believe that your company adopts the same attitude in developing construction technologies, as I have often heard through other companies in the field. After careful consideration, I feel that I would adjust well to the competitive working environment that your company offers.

*

Summarizing one's educational attainment 總括個人的學術成就 As an undergraduate student at National Tsing Hua University, I actively engaged in turbo air-jet engine research sponsored by the National Science Council. Our group attempted to identify air flow phenomena inside the turbo engine. This investigative work provided me with solid background knowledge of experimentation and data analysis, as well as enthusiasm to pursue a career in engineering. To enhance my research abilities, I attended several international conferences and audited related courses on campus.

*

Summarizing one's educational attainment 總括個人的學術成就 I received a

Bachelor's degree in Civil Engineering from Chung Hsing University in May 2001. **Describing knowledge, skills and/or leadership qualities gained through academic training** 描述學術訓練所獲得的技能及（或）領導特質 The departmental curricula provided me a sound theoretical knowledge of fluid motion, including fluid properties, regimes of flow and fluid kinematics. Of particular interest were engineering courses such as structural rheology and soil mechanics. Part-time work as a laboratory assistant exposed me to fundamental laboratory practices, including taking measurements and analyzing samples. **Stressing how academic background will benefit future employment** 強調學術背景對未來求職的利處 In sum, my undergraduate experiences have provided a solid academic foundation on which employment at your company would allow me to further develop my laboratory and professional skills.

*

Summarizing one's educational attainment 總括個人的學術成就 At graduate school, the departmental curricula provided me with a theoretical and practical understanding of materials science and engineering, especially in the extraction, melting and casting, welding and the heat treatment of various metallic materials. At the same time, I participated in a National Science Council research project aimed at improving the process method of magnesium alloys. **Describing knowledge, skills and/or leadership qualities gained through academic training** 描述學術訓練所獲得的技能及（或）領導特質 Fully engaging in each stage of the projects, from forming the original concepts and designing the experimental process, to implementing the experiments , not only improved my research skills but also deepened my knowledge of related fields. In addition, my research results have received considerable praise, as evidenced by my participation in several conferences and publications in related journals. **Stressing how academic background will benefit future employment** 強調學術背景對未來求職的利處 I

164

believe that my solid graduate training has equipped me for the rigorous demands of your company.

H Select the correct answers to the following questions about the three stories in this unit.

1. Where did Jerry work following graduation?

    A. National Chiao Tung University

    B. a consulting firm

    C. the R.O.C. Environmental Protection Administration

2. When did Jerry receive certification as an "Air Pollution Control Equipment Technician?

    A. following graduation

    B. following completion of a Master's degree in Environmental Engineering

    C. following an intensive training course

3. What did Jerry's work experience following graduation expose him to?

    A. training skills that will make him a valuable member of any research team

    B. a wide array of pollution control technologies and equipment

    C. ways to continually improve his research skills

4. Which word is most similar in meaning to "intensive"?

    A. concentrated

    B. diffused

    C. satisfactory

5. Which word is most similar in meaning to "exposed"?

    A. covered

    B. closed

    C. unprotected

6. What was Joy's specialization while acquiring her Master's degree in Information Science?

    A. hardware design

    B. time to market for products

    C. computer architecture

7. What kind of programs does Joy prefer to write?

    A. those for IC design houses to ensure market for products

    B. those to simulate the effectiveness of organizational and architectural designs

    C. those for simulating and analyzing product quality

8. What do IC design houses increasingly emphasize?

    A. time to market for products

    B. implementing and optimizing hardware

    C. modifying software design to improve product performance

9. Which word is most similar in meaning to "simulate"?

    A. simplify

    B. model

    C. tempt

10. What do IC design houses find extremely difficult?

    A. analyzing simulation results and modifying software design

    B. increasing profits by emphasizing time to market

    C. implementing and optimizing the hardware

11. What did Max aim to develop while participating in a National Science Council-sponsored research project?

    A. an analytical system for Electronic Engineering

    B. a wireless Local Area Network

    C. fundamental laboratory practices

12. What was Max able to foster while participating in the research effort during

graduate school?

    A. his patience and perseverance

    B. his practical laboratory experience

    C. his analytical and experimentation skills

13. How was Max able to enhance his communication skills?

    A. by collaborating in a research team

    B. by increasing his patience and perseverance with other collaborators

    C. by absorbing fundamental knowledge and obtaining practical laboratory experiences

14. What does Max believe will give him a competitive edge in the workplace?

    A. his patience and perseverance

    B. his solid academic training

    C. his fundamental research skills

15. Which word is the most similar in meaning to "perseverance"?

    A. optimism

    B. creativity

    C. insistence

Select the correct answers to the following questions about one's academic background and achievements.

1. At what university _____ you acquire a Master's degree in Environmental Engineering?

    A. did

    B. do

    C. are

2. What motivated your desire to strengthen your theoretical and professional

knowledge ___ Food Science?

A. on

B. in

C. of

3. What capacity did you work ___ at the consulting firm following the completion of your graduate studies?

A. for

B. in

C. on

4. What practical work experiences did you acquire _____ university?

A. for

B. during

C. while

5. What training do you hope to receive ____ the company at which you are seeking employment?

A. from

B. on

C. to

6. What have you ____ to enhance your research skills?

A. did

B. done

C. are

7. What projects did you actively engage ____ following the completion of your graduate studies?

A. for

B. on

C. in

8. What did your graduate school research focus on ____ you pursued a Ph.D. in Computer Science??

    A. in

    B. while

    C. during

9. What did you receive certification ____ while working in the semiconductor company?

    A. to

    B. of

    C. for

10. Where ____ you receive a Master's degree in Information Science?

    A. were

    B. do

    C. did

11. Where did you acquire specialized training ____ Radiology?

    A. while

    B. in

    C. during

12. Where would you prefer to work in the electronics industry ____ completion of your graduate studies?

    A. following

    B. while

    C. as

13. Where did you first work after acquiring a Bachelor's degree in Nursing ____ Yuan Pei University of Science and Technology?

    A. from

    B. on

Unit Describing academic background and achievements relevant
Four to employment
描述學歷背景及已獲成就

C. towards

14. Where ____ you receive a solid academic background in Nursing?

A. was

B. did

C. were

15. Where would you like to pursue a Master's degree ___ the opportunity arises?

A. for

B. if

C. in

16. Where ___ you gain a radiology certification?

A. did

B. does

C. were

17. Where ___ you receive your nursing training?

A. are

B. were

C. did

18. Where did you become familiar ___ the latest trends in biotechnology?

A. by

B. with

C. to

19. Which National Science Council-sponsored research projects ___ you participate in while pursuing a Master's degree in Food Science?

A. did

B. do

C. was

20. Which courses did you audit ____ in university?

A. in

B. while

C. during

21. Which topic did you research _____ your post-doctorate work?

A. during

B. on

C. while

22. Which challenges _____ you encounter during your graduate school research?

A. are

B. did

C. were

23. Which skills were you able to enhance _____ collaborating with others in a research group?

A. at

B. for

C. by

24. Which of your personal strengths enabled you _____ get along with others in the research group?

A. by

B. to

C. in

25. Which qualities do you think are essential _____ a nursing professional to advance in a highly competitive environment?

A. on

B. to

C. for

26. Which of your achievements during university are you the most proud _____?

A. of

B. in

C. on

27. Which setbacks did you encounter _____ your research, but were able to overcome eventually?

A. while

B. during

C. on

Unit Five

Bill

Benson

Introducing research and professional experiences relevant to employment

介紹研究及工作經驗

Vocabulary and related expressions 相關字詞

solid background knowledge　強有力背景知識
compulsory military service　當兵義務
collaborative teamwork　小組合作
colleagues　同事
design complexity　設計的複雜性
excelled　優於
merits　優點
logically　合邏輯地
minimal resources　最小的資源
refine　精煉
highly competitive　高度競爭
public engineering projects　公共工程計畫
Taipei Rapid Transit System　台北捷運系統
governmental deficit　政府赤字
construction projects 建設工程計畫
innovative　創新的
Industrial Technology Research Institute (ITRI)
工研院
acquired　獲得
data analysis　資料分析
collaborating　合作
audited　審核
Reliability Engineering　可靠度工程

technological setting　科技環境
telecommunications　電信
undertake　著手
stressed　著重
minimization　縮至最小
ultimately　最終地
sharpened his ability to　敏捷他的能力
limitations　限制
customer specifications　客戶需求
continually　繼續地
thrive　繁榮
actively engaged in　主動地從事
Taiwan High Speed Rail project　台灣高速鐵路計畫
National Highway projects　國家高速公路計畫
trend　流行
strong analytical skills　強有力的分析技巧
statistician　統計員
hands-on knowledge　親自經手的知識
knowledge management 知識管理
customer relations　客戶關係
Financial Investment　財務投資
Human Relations　人際關係

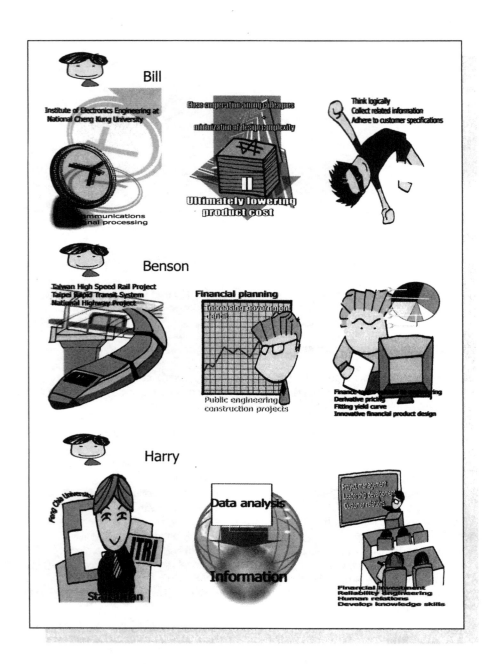

A Write down the key points of the situations on the preceding page, while the instructor reads aloud the script from the Answer Key.

Situation 1

_____

_____

_____

Situation 2

_____

_____

_____

Situation 3

_____

_____

_____

B Based on the three situations in this unit, write three questions beginning with **Why**, and answer them. The questions do not need to come directly from these situations.

Examples

Why did Bill join ABC Corporation?

To undertake signal processing-related research

Why would Harry be an invaluable engineer at ABC Company?

Because of his ability to develop knowledge-related skills and then apply them to management in a technological setting

1. _____

_____

2. _____

_____

3. _____

_____

C Based on the three situations in this unit, write three questions beginning with **How**, and answer them. The questions do not need to come directly from these situations.

Examples

How did Harry learn much about project management, leadership development and customer relations?

By collaborating with several companies on numerous projects

How has collaborative team work at ABC Corporation benefited the company?

It has ultimately lowered product costs through close cooperation among colleagues and the minimization of design complexity.

1. _____

   _____

2. _____

   _____

3. _____

   _____

D Based on the three situations in this unit, write three questions beginning with *What*, and answer them. The questions do not need to come directly from these situations.

Examples

What did Benson actively engage in during his six years as an engineer?

Several large public engineering projects, such as the Taiwan High Speed Railway, the Taipei Rapid Transit System and National Highway Projects.

What were some of the relevant areas in which Harry audited courses?

Financial Investment, Reliability Engineering and Human Relations

1. _____

   _____

2. _____

   _____

3. _____

   _____

E　Write questions that match the answers provided.

Examples

How long has Benson been an engineer?

Six years

How did Bill's work experience at ABC Corporation help him?

It sharpened his ability to analyze the merits and limitations of methods, think logically, collect related information, and meet customer specifications, while using minimal resources.

1. _____

   _____

   Pricing derivatives, fitting yield curves, and designing innovative financial products

2. _____

   _____

   Modelsim, Debussy, Mat lab, and HDL

3. _____

   _____

   Because of the increasing governmental deficit and the trend to finance large public engineering construction projects

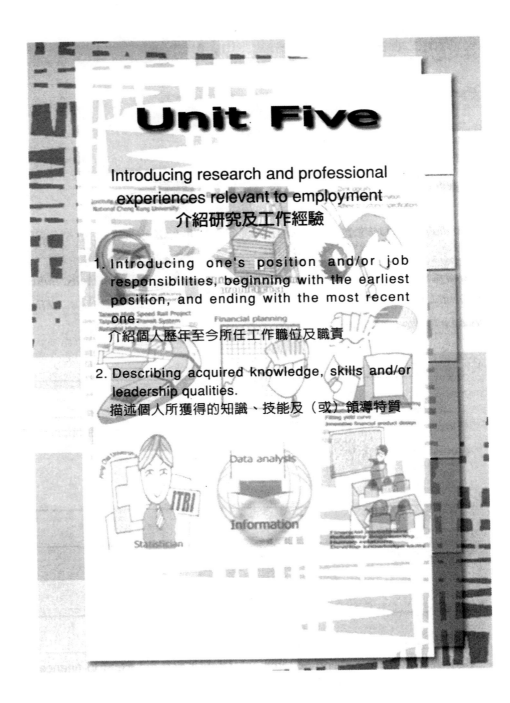

Unit Five

Introducing research and professional experiences relevant to employment
介紹研究及工作經驗

1. Introducing one's position and/or job responsibilities, beginning with the earliest position, and ending with the most recent one.
介紹個人歷年至今所任工作職位及職責

2. Describing acquired knowledge, skills and/or leadership qualities.
描述個人所獲得的知識、技能及（或）領導特質

Common elements in introducing one's professional and/or research experiences include:

1. Introducing one's position and/or job responsibilities, beginning with the earliest position and ending with the most recent one. 介紹個人歷年至今所任工作職位及職責

◎ As a commissioned officer in our country's compulsory military service, I arranged the daily schedule of all the cadres in the platoon, served as a communication link between those cadres and higher-level officers, and coordinated missions within the unit, often assigned on short notice by those ranking officers.

◎ While effectively coordinating the manpower and other resources in the department, I was also responsible for identifying market trends across the entire semiconductor industry and assessing our company's most effective responses.

◎ A large portion of my most recent work focused on increasing the company's revenue from the supply end - including the fab wafer start plan, IC assembly, testing, R&D design status - to the demand end - including customers' design-in status and demand forecasting.

◎ As an administrative manager, besides fostering a closer relationship with our customers, I spent much time in understanding IC market trends.

◎ As an administrative coordinator in an environmental protection agency, I actively engaged in planning policy-making projects on various scales and with different aims.

◎ Of all the projects in which I was involved, I enjoyed those that aimed to foster public awareness of environmental issues. Not only do such projects provide coordinators with unique opportunities to participate constructively in developing the public awareness of the need to protect the environment, but they also challenge Taiwan's governmental officials to tackle pertinent issues of economic development.

◎ While conducting a recent audit of a company's financial records, I became aware of my limited knowledge of how global economic activities affect small- to medium-sized firms. I believe that employment at your company would compensate for my lack of expertise in this area.

◎ I began working as a financial planner in a well-known investment group that specializes in the semiconductor industry.

◎ My enclosed curriculum vitae reflects abundant management experience in the semiconductor industry spanning more than a decade, as made possible by graduate training at one of Taiwan's finest institutes of higher learning as well as collaboration with many globally renowned industrial partners.

◎ After serving for five years as an administrative assistant to the general manager, in which role I mediated between management goals and departmental progress, I was promoted to assistant manager of the procurement department, becoming adept in information gathering, data evaluation, price negotiations, and budgetary review.

◎ My previous work experiences attest to my ability to comprehend fully the administrative activities of a hi-tech company and how to coordinate such activities efficiently to maximize inter-departmental harmony and, ultimately, corporate profits.

◎ While working at an engineering consultancy firm, I was responsible for coordinating several public engineering projects simultaneously. Successfully implementing a project requires carefully arranging a schedule, closely monitoring the schedule until completion, and collaborating with colleagues in (various OR different) departments. Executing tasks on schedule is essential in an engineering consultancy firm; any delay will cause serious losses. I will take the same responsible attitude towards future tasks, hopefully at your company.

◎ After receiving a Master's degree in Power Mechanical Engineering from National Tsing Hua University and completing our country's compulsory military service immediately thereafter, I began working at ABC Corporation, a leading manufacturer of chipsets and designer of graphic ICs. Despite my solid academic foundation, I still felt somewhat unprepared for the rapid pace of emerging technologies in the work place, particularly in electromagnetics, which fact explains why I returned to university for doctoral studies. As I will meet my doctoral degree requirements shortly, I look forward to applying my newly acquired knowledge and skills to employment at a globally renowned corporation such as yours.

◎ Serving as a research assistant in several National Science Council-sponsored projects on biotechnology familiarized me with the operations of a research laboratory, including weekly progress reports and regular seminars. I find the work highly stimulating and rewarding and, based on my past academic performance and recent laboratory experiences, am confident of my ability to contribute to your company's R&D efforts.

◎ Intensive laboratory and theoretical training in a summer internship before my senior year of university marked a turning point as I decided to pursue a career in biotechnology research to remain abreast of the latest developments in this rapidly evolving field.

2. Describing acquired knowledge, skills and/or leadership qualities. 描述個人所獲得的知識、技能及（或）領導特質

◎ Collaborating with others in several National Science Council-sponsored projects has made me more self-confident when encountering obstacles to the progress of research. I now view such obstacles as opportunities to adopt different approaches to the problem at hand.

◎ Within our research group, I assumed a leadership role by drawing others into discussion and exchanging opinions with our project leader.

◎ Regardless of the complexity of a problem, I am always determined to solve it. If unable to solve it by myself, I often consult my colleagues and assign different aspects of a problem according to a particular member's intellectual strengths, to solve the problem collaboratively and efficiently.

◎ The unique perspective I have acquired from conducting research in different countries and under varying circumstances has proven invaluable to my later professional endeavors.

◎ My most recent employment involved coordinating the activities of different departments, and exposed me to a wide spectrum of temperaments and working stylesof various colleagues from administrative assistants to senior researchers. Working in different environments, even within the same company, made me more adaptable to unforeseeable circumstances.

◎ My previous employment instilled in me the importance of working efficiently. As project leader of an IC design venture with an American company, I submitted

183

weekly reports. During video conferences with our overseas counterparts, I strove to cover all of the pertinent issues as thoroughly as possible within a given time constraint. Working under tight time constraints proved to be invaluable training in in meeting targets more efficiently.

◎ My clinical work with terminally ill patients has taught me that attending to their physical needs is only one aspect of the profession. Helping patients understand the nature of their disease and attempting to view things from their perspective are also equally important tasks of a health care professional.

◎ Occasional frustrations with slow progress in research strengthened my resolve to excel in the laboratory, making me more tenacious. Extensive laboratory work also exposed me to advanced experimental techniques and significantly improved my analytical skills and data collection capabilities.

◎ Considerable laboratory experience has given me a comprehensive view of the intricate aspects of research and factors that spell success as an experimenter.

◎ While I find the research process extremely satisfying, I also realize that continuous progress hinges on a persistent and tenacious attitude towards laboratory work.

◎ Driven by the sense of achievement that follows a successful project, I have a personality that is conducive to thorough yet efficient laboratory work as part of a collaborative effort.

◎ Numerous work experiences have made my thinking more deliberate and opened my mind toward emerging opportunities.

◎ My superiors have often commented on my adaptability, receptivity, responsibility and diligence when venturing into new projects.

◎ The sense of accomplishment from developing programs that will potentially benefit millions of Internet users is immense.

◎ Working in the pharmaceutical sector for more than a decade has clarified my current educational needs and the career path that I should take to remain abreast of the latest trends in this increasingly hi tech market.

◎ By assuming such responsibilities, I acquired a breadth of experiences in dealing with complex environmental issues. In addition to refining my ability to coordinate related activities, these experiences enabled me to examine an array of issues in economic, social, political and public financial contexts.

◎ This project gave me an in-depth understanding of the workings of Taiwan's semiconductor industry.

◎ During graduate school, I analyzed the most pertinent information within my field of interest and then identified research questions and hypotheses. This methodological approach to solving problems will make me competent in the workplace, hopefully at your company.

◎ My success in research stems from my avid interest in continuously reading pertinent literature and investigating the source of the problem, whenever I encounter a bottleneck in my work.

◎ Working there, I increasingly realized the importance of establishing feasible short-term and long-term goals as foundations to a manufacturer's continued survival. Interacting with other financial planners from other hi tech sectors broadened my views on the most effective investment strategies in the volatile technology market.

◎ As an investment planner, I focused on acquiring strong analytical skills and quickly absorbed as much knowledge of the hi tech sector as possible to supply my clients with valuable advice on the latest trends and major breakthroughs.

◎ Responsible for coordinating inter-departmental activities to utilize effectively the company's manpower and resources, I learned how to incorporate the seemingly polar approaches of different departments to solve a particular problem in a cohesive framework that drew upon the strengths of the departments involved. Doing so involved not only absorbing other colleagues' perspectives, but also learning how to carefully negotiate with others so that the dignity of each collaborator was maintained.

◎ My colleagues and superiors can attest to my enthusiasm and perseverance in taking strenuous on-the-job training courses. These courses provided fundamental knowledge of the telecommunications field. Despite their difficulty, these courses further solidified my academic background to realize fully the theoretical implications of this discipline in an industrial setting and to conduct advanced research. When assigned a project, I quickly generate a schedule, draft the details and implement the project sequentially. By applying this same responsible attitude, I firmly believe that I can contribute positively to any research group to which I belong, as evidenced by my enthusiasm for solving problems efficiently and accepting difficult challenges confidently.

◎ As a quality engineer, I have continuously striven to upgrade my knowledge and skills and then apply them to researching and developing a variety of technologies. Remaining confident in the feasibility of applying new processes, I am especially drawn to technological innovations, new product technologies, and advanced skills that are necessary in the constantly evolving hi tech sector.

◎ I am conscientious, responsible and diligent. When undertaking a project, I always strive for excellence and efficiency. Nevertheless, I am aware of overhead costs and approach tasks carefully and methodologically. My superior often reminded me to follow the uniform procedure especially on construction sites. Now, when I am involved in a project, I quickly draft the project schedule and determine how to achieve the tasks in (order OR sequential steps).   Consequently, I have become more deliberate and confident in my work style.

◎ I am friendly, communicative and adventurous. When exposed to a new working environment, I can quickly become a member of the group I am with by trying to understand their perspectives and needs. Based on this understanding, I try to retain good relations with my colleagues. Moreover, I am determined when taking on new adventures and accepting challenges. I strongly believe that an impossibility can often be transformed into an opportunity if I remain diligent. Temporary setbacks or even failures provide a valuable reference for the future. I believe that my strong personality will prove invaluable in my career.

◎ Having served as a research assistant in several National Science Council-sponsored research projects, I firmly believe that acquiring knowledge and skills from diverse research experiences is more productive and fulfilling than passively receiving information in a classroom. Without a practical context, knowledge appears to lack value.

◎ From these experiences, I became highly motivated to succeed in whatever endeavor I undertook, as evidenced by my ability to identify quickly goals associated with a particular task and then map out realistic steps to attain them.

◎ The hands-on experience in a laboratory setting provided me with numerous opportunities to corroborate what I had learned from textbooks and then extend that knowledge to an independent search for innovative solutions. While also aware of my lack of skills in experimental design, I believe that laboratory research has nurtured skills in data evaluation and collaboration within a research group, , which will prove beneficial to future research projects to which I belong, hopefully at your company.

◎ Working in the chemical engineering profession for nearly two decades has made me highly adaptive to change, responsive to sudden fluctuations in technological trends, and flexible in acquiring diverse skills demanded by a competitive corporate climate.

◎ My most recent managerial position allowed me to interact with clients from all over the world, expanding my understanding of global affairs and making me more confident in succeeding in the face of time and budgetary constraints as well as cultural differences. I have been able to succeed by setting realistic goals and pursuing them relentlessly.

◎ Working in a family-owned machinery business exposed me to the multi-faceted operations of small- to medium-sized enterprises, the prevalence of which represents a unique feature of Taiwanese entrepreneurs. It also extended my academic knowledge across a diversity of business disciplines such as finance, marketing and personnel management. My efforts to develop and implement new business strategies to overcome increasing competition provided an invaluable experience, on which I will be able to draw in the future.

◎ Several years in management positions have taught me the importance of sound accounting practices to a firm's long-term success. A firm's accounting practices not only make managers responsible for the welfare of its employees, but also allow strategic and financial planners to aggressively pursue available contracts.

Introducing research and professional experiences relevant to employment

介紹研究及工作經驗

F In the space below, introduce your professional and/or research experiences.

_____

_____

_____

_____

_____

_____

_____

_____

_____

_____

_____

_____

_____

G Look at the following examples of introducing one's professional and/or research experiences.

Introducing one's position and/or job responsibilities, beginning with the earliest position, and ending with the most recent one 介紹個人歷年至今所任工作職位及職責 My extensive work experience in civil engineering has enabled me to share hands-on tunnel construction experiences with classmates in training courses as well as in collaborative instruction on the latest technological approaches adopted in Taiwan. Following graduate studies, I continued to work in a consulting company that coordinates many construction projects involving bridges and super-highways. **Describing acquired knowledge, skills and/or leadership qualities** 描述個人所獲得的知識、技能及（或）領導特質 I adjust well to intensely competitive working environments and totally immerse myself in new challenges within the construction field. I believe my intellect and determination will prove invaluable in your company's challenging work environment.

*

Introducing one's position and/or job responsibilities, beginning with the earliest position, and ending with the most recent one 介紹個人歷年至今所任工作職位及職責 Beyond my solid academic background, I participated in a research project coordinated by Chunghwa Telecommunication Labs that strengthened my practical laboratory experience. Related to Mandarin speech recognition, this project was a collaborative effort with leading universities in Taiwan, including National Taiwan University, National Tsing Hua University, National Chiao Tung University, and National Central University. **Describing acquired knowledge, skills and/or leadership qualities** 描述個人所獲得的知識、技能及（或）領導特質 Such large-scale teamwork enhanced my ability to coordinate and communicate with others. Within the framework of a National Science Council-sponsored project, I also assisted my advisor in collecting Mandarin speech samples locally and then compiling them in a Mandarin database. This project allows researchers and companies interested in Mandarin speech recognition to develop their own models and verify their algorithms using the speech database.

*

Introducing one's position and/or job responsibilities, beginning with the earliest position, and ending with the most recent one 介紹個人歷年至今所任工作職位及職責 Upon graduation, I switched my career focus to the financial sector and worked in the fixed income department of a securities house to learn about the design, pricing, placement, and promotion of fixed income products. Then, I worked at the Financial Department of GHI Company to implement overseas financing projects, such as GDR, and ECB issuance. **Describing acquired knowledge, skills and/or leadership qualities** 描述個人所獲得的知識、技能及（或）領導特質 I believe my solid academic training and valuable work experience will give me a competitive edge in the workplace, hopefully at your company.

*

Introducing one's position and/or job responsibilities, beginning with the earliest position, and ending with the most recent one 介紹個人歷年至今所任工作職位及職責 Following a stint of nearly two years in our country's compulsory military service, I worked at two companies as an engineer, developing a vacuum system for use in the electronics sector and constructing a five-inch wafer fab for the semiconductor industry. Having worked at SiS for over a year, I am responsible for coordinating the R&D activities of the DCVD process team. Our close team collaboration has allowed us to successfully complete many projects, such as improving the HDP-CVD gap-fill, the dual Damascene and low K ARC setting and in-situ ILD-SRO setting. In the future, I hope to acquire more knowledge of semiconductor processes to contribute more significantly to SIS.

*

Introducing one's position and/or job responsibilities, beginning with the earliest position, and ending with the most recent one 介紹個人歷年至今所任工作職位及職責 After performing military service, as is compulsory in our country, I first worked as an application engineer at a vacuum systems company, performing a wide spectrum of engineering tasks and acquiring a diverse array of industrial knowledge and skills. I then switched to working at a five-inch foundry fab, where I received basic semiconductor process training. I joined SiS in 2000, and am responsible for developing DCVD-related processes. **Describing acquired knowledge, skills and/or leadership qualities** 描述個人所獲得的知識、技能及（或）領導特質 A strong team collaborative spirit has allowed our research group to successfully complete many projects, especially those in HDP-CVD gap-fill improvement, dual Damascene and low K ARC setting, as well as in-situ ILD-SRO setting. I hope to acquire more process experience and more significantly contribute to my company in the future.

*

Introducing one's position and/or job responsibilities, beginning with the earliest position, and ending with the most recent one 介紹個人歷年至今所任工作職位及職責 After receiving a Master's degree from National Tsing Hua university, I became a process engineer in the semiconductor industry. I diagnosed wafer defects and devised strategies for their prevention. My subsequent transfer to the quality assurance department was a logical step. I now focus on guaranteeing product quality. **Describing acquired knowledge, skills and/or leadership qualities** 描述個人所獲得的知識、技能及（或）領導特質 With a solid background in process engineering, I am able to identify quickly the root cause of a product's inferiority and prescribe preventative measures. My responsible attitude towards my job will prove an invaluable asset to your company.

*

Introducing one's position and/or job responsibilities, beginning with the earliest position, and ending with the most recent one 介紹個人歷年至今所任工作職位及職責 After graduating from the Computer Information Science Department at National Chiao Tung University in 1996, I devoted myself to robotics-related research. **Describing acquired knowledge, skills and/or leadership qualities** 描述個人所獲得的知識、技能及（或）領導特質 Fully engaging in each project and experimental processes not only enhanced my research skills, but also deepened my knowledge of related fields. This solid training allowed me to solve problems logically, which ability proved to be helpful in writing my Master's thesis.

*

Introducing one's position and/or job responsibilities, beginning with the earliest position, and ending with the most recent one 介紹個人歷年至今所任工作職位及職責 As a quality assurance engineer, I must ensure that our company's products adhere to customers' and industrial specifications. Accordingly, I must not only closely examine the wafer testing procedure to evaluate parameters, but also learn the computer languages used to run the testing equipment. Reviewing different kinds of product specifications occupies most of my working time. This tight schedule requires that I manage my time efficiently.

*

Introducing one's position and/or job responsibilities, beginning with the earliest position, and ending with the most recent one 介紹個人歷年至今所任工作職位及職責 As an industrial engineer at SIS, I am responsible for the capacity planning of our wafer fab. Accordingly, I must study the standard throughput of the equipment. Capacity planning includes static and dynamic. At SIS, we use MS Excel and the AP Simulation system to run our capacity models for long term planning and short term planning, respectively. This information provides a valuable reference for the Marketing Department when ordering materials and also helps them understand the actual productivity.

*

Introducing one's position and/or job responsibilities, beginning with the earliest position, and ending with the most recent one 介紹個人歷年至今所任工作職位及職責 As a quality service engineer in the semiconductor industry, I review test programs for the mass production of wafer products. Although not trained as an electrical engineer, I am learning the theory and principles underlying design for test (DFT), and recognizing the key parameters that account for most of the decrease in the fault coverage. **Describing acquired knowledge, skills and/or leadership qualities** 描述個人所獲得的知識、技能及（或）領導特質 Closely examining pertinent technical publications has also allowed me to address problems in current test programs more effectively, thereby upgrading the company's approaches to testing increases the quality of our products

*

Introducing one's position and/or job responsibilities, beginning with the earliest position, and ending with the most recent one 介紹個人歷年至今所任工作職位及職責 Several years of work experience have provided me with the fundamental skills and practical knowledge to be a highly competent quality service engineer. Internal training courses on Quality Assurance (QA), Automatic Test Equipment (ATE), and Very High Speed Integrated Circuit Hardware Description Language (VHDL) have been particularly helpful in fostering my professional capabilities. **Describing acquired knowledge, skills and/or leadership qualities** 描述個人所獲得的知識、技能及（或）領導特質 Moreover, fully engaging in each stage of testing for mass production, from ATE testing to module testing, has thoroughly familiarized me with all aspects of the wafer testing process.

*

As a quality service engineer, I find my work quite challenging. By consulting with designers, reading pertinent literature, and performing experiments, I have been able to detect numerous test modes and effective paths that were previously overlooked. These discoveries have significantly contributed towards achieving minimum fault coverage. Moreover, these experiences have reinforced my dedication to the quality assurance field.

*

Introducing one's position and/or job responsibilities, beginning with the earliest position, and ending with the most recent one 介紹個人歷年至今所任工作職位及職責 Following graduation, I joined a leading engineering consultancy firm in Taiwan, DEF Engineering Consultants, as an hydrogeology engineer. During my six years as an engineer, I have actively engaged in several large public engineering projects, such as the Taiwan High Speed Rail Project, the Taipei Rapid Transit System, and the National Highway Project. Owing to the increasing governmental deficit and its financing of large public engineering construction, I have had to learn how to evaluate a project in terms of its financial planning. After returning to university to acquire a Master's degree in Finance, I switched my career focus to the financial sector and worked in the fixed income department of a securities house to learn of the design, pricing, placement, and promotion of fixed income products. Then, I worked at the Financial Department of GHI Company to implement overseas financing projects, such as GDR and ECB issuance. **Describing acquired knowledge, skills and/or leadership qualities** 描述個人所獲得的知識、技能及（或）領導特質 I believe my solid academic training and valuable work experience will give me a competitive edge in the workplace, hopefully at your company.

*

Introducing one's position and/or job responsibilities, beginning with the earliest position, and ending with the most recent one 介紹個人歷年至今所任工作職位及職責 As an engineer at Taiwan's most prestigious engineering consultancy firm for six years, I actively engaged in several large-scale public construction projects, such as the Taiwan High Speed Rail Project, the Taipei Rapid Transit System, and the National Highway Project. These valuable work experiences not only reinforced my professional knowledge and skills, but also enhanced my ability to solve problems logically. With an increasing governmental deficit, many large, publicly financed construction projects are financed by BOT. Engineers thus heavily prioritize the importance of evaluating a public engineering project in terms of its financial planning. To strengthen my finance-related knowledge, I returned to National Taiwan University to acquire another Master's degree, this time in Finance with a particular emphasis on financial engineering. **Describing acquired knowledge, skills and/or leadership qualities** 描述個人所獲得的知識、技能及（或）領導特質 Graduate study provided me with a theoretical and practical understanding of financial issues. Upon graduation, I switched my career focus to the financial sector and worked in the fixed income department of a securities house to learn of the design, pricing, placement, and promotion of fixed income products. Following employment in a security house for a relatively short period, I worked in the Financial Department of ABC Corporation, implementing overseas financing projects, such as GDR and ECB issuance. I believe my solid academic training and valuable work experiences will give me a competitive edge in the workplace, hopefully at your company.

*

Introducing one's position and/or job responsibilities, beginning with the earliest position, and ending with the most recent one 介紹個人歷年至今所任工

作職位及職責 A solid background of work experience in SiS provided me with the fundamental skills and practical knowledge to be a highly competent quality service engineer. Internal training courses on Quality Assurance (QA), Automatic Test Equipment (ATE) and Very High Speed Integrated Circuit Hardware Description Language (VHDL) have been particularly helpful in fostering my professional capabilities. Moreover, fully engaging in each stage of testing for mass production, from ATE testing to module testing, has thoroughly familiarized me with all aspects of the wafer testing process.

*

Introducing one's position and/or job responsibilities, beginning with the earliest position, and ending with the most recent one 介紹個人歷年至今所任工作職位及職責 I have actively engaged in semiconductor research with a particular emphasis on sensors and actuators. This growth sector of electrical engineering has extensive applications in medicine and telecommunications. After I thoroughly reviewed pertinent literature and closely collaborated with my thesis research advisor, my graduate research focused on developing a novel structure for infra-red light sensors of an improved cantilever type, made of new, light-absorbing material. This research uses this new light-absorbing material in infra-red sensors for the first time.

*

As a testing engineer, I find my work physically and mentally challenging, yet personally fulfilling, since I can contribute to the development of wafer chip technology and gain advanced professional knowledge simultaneously.

*

As an engineer in the highly competitive IC design sector, I have been involved in most **Introducing one's position and/or job responsibilities, beginning with the earliest position, and ending with the most recent one** 介紹個人歷年至今所任工

196

作職位及職責 phases of IC design. In particular, I participated in designing chipsets for Pentium series CPUs from 1996 to 1997. I am now responsible for hardware emulation, that is, constructing a realistic environment in which to verify logic designs, enhancing my analytical and research skills. Moreover, the tedious and complex process of debugging and verification has made me more persevering and focused. In sum, SiS has provided an environment that has nurtured my knowledge and skills in this constantly fluctuating field.

*

Introducing one's position and/or job responsibilities, beginning with the earliest position, and ending with the most recent one 介紹個人歷年至今所任工作職位及職責 After I completed our country's compulsory military service, I worked in the environmental engineering department of a consultancy firm. During my work, I coordinated and executed many soil and groundwater projects and monitored electronics factories. These projects focused mainly on monitoring wells to detect contaminants from leaking pipes or tanks. These projects provided me with advanced professional knowledge on groundwater contamination and available technologies to abate it.

*

Introducing one's position and/or job responsibilities, beginning with the earliest position, and ending with the most recent one 介紹個人歷年至今所任工作職位及職責 As a research assistant at the Sanitary and Health Care Center in National Chiao Tung University for two years and in Industrial Technology Research Institute (ITRI) for six months, I have acquired much professional, hands-on knowledge of data analysis that would prepare me for a career in health-related research and knowledge management at an international level. Collaborating with Applied Materials of Taiwan, Chailease Finance and ITRI on numerous projects, I have learned much about project management, leadership and customer relations. I would also like to audit courses in relevant areas, such as Financial Investment, Reliability Engineering, Data Envelopment Analysis, Neural networks, and Human Relations. **Describing acquired knowledge, skills and/or leadership qualities** 描述個人所獲得的知識、技能及（或）領導特質 The ability to develop knowledge and skills continuously and then apply them to management in a technological setting will prove invaluable as an engineer at your company.

*

Introducing one's position and/or job responsibilities, beginning with the earliest position, and ending with the most recent one 介紹個人歷年至今所任工作職位及職責 Before entering graduate school, I worked at the Mechanical Industrial Research Laboratories of the Industrial Technology Research Institute in a team effort to develop GIS software. Although working there for only two months, I learned about the merits of solving problems logically and the importance of team collaboration. During graduate study, in addition to participating in several National Science Council sponsored projects, I undertook process capability index research related to Quality Control. These experiences have fostered the professional skills needed to thrive in the work place, hopefully at your company.

*

Holding a hydraulic engineering conference in Taiwan requires close collaboration with organizational committee members to ensure success. As one of the organizers, I had to delegate tasks, such as issuing a call for papers to encourage participation, preparing the conference proceedings, and making stage decorations, to various staff members. Doing so ensured that the paper presentations went smoothly. **Describing acquired knowledge, skills and/or leadership qualities** 描述個人所獲得的知識、技能及（或）領導特質 This unique leadership opportunity not only enhanced my ability to integrate different activities into a single concerted effort, but also provided a more thorough understanding of hydraulic engineering developments in Taiwan.

*

Introducing one's position and/or job responsibilities, beginning with the earliest position, and ending with the most recent one 介紹個人歷年至今所任工作職位及職責 Undergraduate Industrial and Management courses at National Chiao Tung University provided me with a solid academic background in the field. Graduate study in the same field later provided me with advanced professional knowledge in quality control. In addition to contributing to related theories, I participated in many National Science Council-sponsored projects to balance my academic skills with practical work experiences. **Describing acquired knowledge, skills and/or leadership qualities** 描述個人所獲得的知識、技能及（或）領導特質 These experiences have led to my current research project of designing an on-line control process for wafer fabrication. I believe this research will offer me a glimpse into the exciting field of industrial research aimed at continuously upgrading wafer quality. I believe that you will find this mixture of solid academic training and advanced professional knowledge gained through graduate school to be an asset to your company.

*

Introducing one's position and/or job responsibilities, beginning with the earliest position, and ending with the most recent one 介紹個人歷年至今所任工作職位及職責 My graduate studies focused on the processing of magnesium alloys, with a particular emphasis on how the their mechanical properties and thermal-mechanical processing are related. To enhance my research abilities, I participated in a National Science Council research project aimed at improving the method of processing magnesium alloys. During that period, I attended several domestic and international conferences. My findings culminated in the publication of several journal papers. I believe that my solid graduate training has equipped me for the demands of your company.

*

Introducing one's position and/or job responsibilities, beginning with the earliest position, and ending with the most recent one 介紹個人歷年至今所任工作職位及職責 In addition to having a strong academic background, as a graduate, I actively participated in a National Science Council-sponsored project related to flood forecasting in the Wu-Shi Basin. I also attended an international symposium on flood control in Beijing and visited the Yangtse Gorges. My advanced research capabilities will become more refined with professional work experience at your company.

H Select the correct answers to the following questions about the three stories in this unit.

1. The Institute of Electronic Engineering at National Cheng Kung University provided Bill with solid background knowledge of what?

    A. telecommunications and logic design-related systems

    B. telecommunications and signal processing

    C. Debussy, Mat lab and HDL

2. What did Bill do after receiving his Master's degree in Electronic Engineering?

    A. joined ABC Corporation

    B. began a career in telecommunications-related research

    C. completed Taiwan's compulsory military service

3. Why is Bill determined to devote himself to a career in telecommunications-related research?

    A. to continually refine his professional skills to thrive in this highly competitive environment

B. to excel in logic design-related systems

C. to minimize design complexity and reduce product costs for his company

4. Which word is similar in meaning to "thrive"?

A. decline

B. succeed

C. organize

5. At which university did Bill receive a Master's degree in Electronic Engineering?

A. National Taiwan University

B. National Chiao Tung University

C. National Cheng Kung University

6. For how many years has Benson been an engineer?

A. three

B. five

C. six

7. Why has Benson had to learn how to evaluate a project's financial plan?

A. owing to the increasing governmental deficit

B. owing to the trend to finance large public engineering construction projects

C. both A and B

8. Which word is the most similar in meaning to "innovative"?

A. creative

B. hostile

C. innocent

9. Which word is the most similar in meaning to "analytical"?

A. determined

B. innovative

C. logical

10. Which word is the most similar in meaning to "deficit"?

A. surplus

B. shortage

C. abundance

11. Where did Harry serve as a statistician for two years?

A. Industrial Technology Research Institute (ITRI)

B. Feng Chia University

C. ABC Company

12. What kind of hands-on knowledge has prepared Harry for a career in health-related research and knowledge management?

A. knowledge of financial investment

B. knowledge of project management

C. knowledge of data analysis

13. Where would Harry like to work as an engineer?

A. ABC Company

B. Industrial Technology Research Institute (ITRI)

C. Feng Chia University

14. Which word is the most similar in meaning to "hands-on"?

A. theoretical

B. practical

C. fundamental

15. Which word is the most similar in meaning to "relevant"?

A. rare

B. suspicious

C. pertinent

Ⅰ Select the correct answers to the following questions about one's professional and/or research experiences.

1. Why are you determined to devote yourself to a career ____ telecommunications-related research?

   A. on

   B. of

   C. in

2. Why did you decide to work in the medical profession ____ a radiology technician?

   A. as

   B. with

   C. through

3. How did the Institute of Communications Engineering at National Chiao Tung University provide you with a solid background knowledge ____ telecommunications and signal processing?

   A. to

   B. of

   C. in

4. Why did you join ABC Corporation after completing Taiwan's compulsory military service ____ nearly two years?

   A. by

   B. to

   C. of

5. Why did the company that you worked for stress close cooperation ____ colleagues?

   A. through

   B. among

C. across

6. Why do you believe that you can thrive ____ the highly competitive environment

of the semiconductor industry?

A. in

B. of

C. for

7. Why are you able to analyze the merits and limitations of conventional methods

____selecting the most appropriate one?

A. to

B. before

C. through

8. Why are you able to still think logically____ stressful work situations?

A. on

B. in

C. for

9. How did the company that you work for require that you collect marketing

information and try your best ____ meet customer specifications?

A. to

B. by

C. for

10. How were you able to cope ____ the stress of working in the intensively

competitive environment of your previous employment?

A. by

B. with

C. through

11. How did you learn ____ your previous work to evaluate a project's financial plan?

A. of

B. by

C. in

12. How did you actively engage in the projects in which you participated ____ working for an electronics company?

A. through

B. during

C. while

13. How were you able to strengthen your analytical skills ____ the company that you worked for?

A. to

B. in

C. by

14. How did you develop your interest in designing semiconductor products while working ____DEF Corporation?

A. across/although

B. to/by

C. for/at

15. How did you become so determined to devote yourself ____ a career in nursing?

A. from

B. to

C. by

16.How were you able to secure a good position within the company ____ such a relatively short time?

A. in

B. with

C. for

17. How did you first learn ____ the company at which you are seeking employment?

    A. to

    B. about

    C. from

18. How were you able continually to refine your professional skills ____ the company at which you worked previously?

    A. that

    B. which

    C. at

19. What important lessons have you learned while collaborating ____ several companies on numerous projects?

    A. to

    B. on

    C. with

20. What university courses did you audit ____ work?

    A. after

    B. between

    C. to

21. What position did you hold ____ the Sanitary and Health Care Center of Feng Chia University?

    A. through

    B. at

    C. while

22. What company have you been working at ____ the past six months?

    A. with

    B. through

C. for

23. What career has your professional, hands-on knowledge of nursing prepared you
____?

A. for

B. on

C. to

24. What have you learned about good customer relations ____ the healthcare
management industry?

A. on

B. for

C. in

25. What period ____ time have you been working for DEF Corporation?

A. of

B. on

C. with

26. What expertise do you have ____ managing biotechnology projects?

A. to

B. of

C. in

Unit Six

Alex

I fostered my collaborative, coordinating, organization and communicative skills.

Carey

Environmental protection
Nature Science

Describing extracurricular activities relevant to employment

Confidence

描述與求職相關的課外活動

Vocabulary and related expressions 相關字詞

counselor 顧問
grasp the basic concepts of 掌握基本觀念
roundtable discussions 合桌開會
collaborative 合作的
organizational 組織的
environmental protection 環保
an extension of 延伸
balance 平衡
practical contexts 實用背景
framework 骨架
systematically applying 有系統地應用
rewarding experiences 有益經驗
actively introduce 主動引介
rigorous 嚴格的

curricular materials 課程資料
enabled 使有能力
sharpen his presentation skills 敏捷他的簡報技能
unique opportunity 獨特的機會

sponsored by 贊助
curriculum 課程
address 發表描述
coordinating 協調的
communicative 溝通的
adversely impacts 不利地衝擊
theoretical foundation 理論基礎
grasp 掌握
broadening his horizons 擴展他的視野
collaborating 合作
knowledge and skills 知識及技能
realizing 瞭解
recruit 招收新成員
nationwide university entrance examination
全國大學聯招
monitored 監控
implement 實行
broaden his knowledge base 擴展他的知識
根基

A Write down the key points of the situations on the preceding page, while the instructor reads aloud the script from the Answer Key.

Situation 1

_____

_____

_____

Situation 2

_____

_____

_____

Situation 3

_____

_____

_____

B Based on the three situations in this unit, write three questions beginning with *What*, and answer them. The questions do not need to come directly from these situations.

Examples

What was one of the most rewarding experiences of his undergraduate years?

Developing his communication skills in an environmental protection organization

What was the purpose of the Electrical Engineering camp that Jason worked with other classmates toorganize?

To inform students of the programs that they can pursue at the Department at National Cheng Kung University

1. _____

_____

2. _____

_____

3. _____

   _____

C Based on the three situations in this unit, write three questions beginning with **Why**, and answer them. The questions do not need to come directly from these situations.

Examples

Why were the roundtable discussions held nightly during camp helpful to Alex?

They addressed difficulties in instruction and reviewed the following day's schedule.

1. _____

   _____

2. _____

   _____

3. _____

   _____

D Based on the three situations in this unit, write three questions beginning with **Where**, and answer them. The questions do not need to come directly from these situations.

Examples

Where was the Electrical Engineeering camp, that Jason worked with other classmates to organize, to be held?

On the campus of National Cheng Kung University

Where did Alex serve twice as a counselor?

In the Electrical Engineering Camp held at National Taiwan Science and Technology University

1. _____

   _____

2. _____

   _____

3. _____

   _____

E　Write questions that match the answers provided.

Examples

1. _____

   _____

   It helped him implement the knowledge that he had learned in the classroom and sharpen his presentation skills

2. _____

   _____

   Trying to grasp scientific knowledge in practical contexts

3. _____

   _____

   His work performance

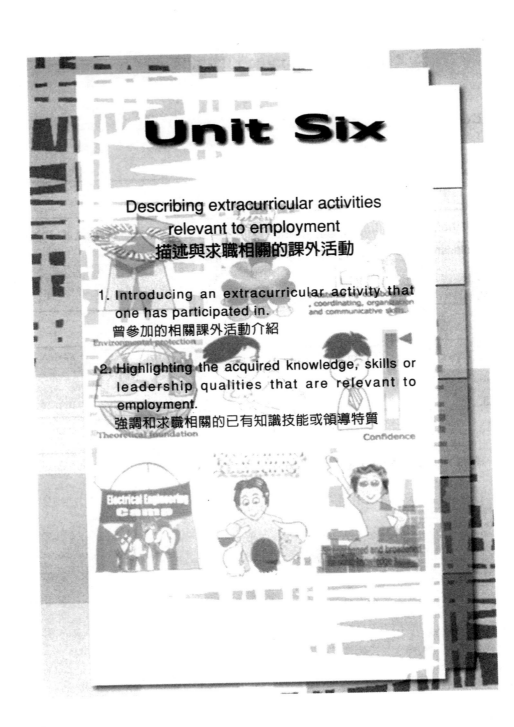

Common elements in describing extracurricular activities that are relevant to employment include the following:

1. Introducing an extracurricular activity that one has participated in 曾參加的相關課外活動介紹

◎ In addition to striving relentlessly for academic excellence at undergraduate school, I matured as an individual by actively participating in various extra-curricular activities.

◎ For nearly a decade, I have devoted myself to developing the skills to support physically and mentally challenged individuals. While experiencing the joy of assisting less fortunate people and fulfilling my social responsibilities, I have frequently coordinated volunteers with various fields of expertise but with the same conviction, in organizing a wide spectrum of events to bring value to others' lives.

◎ I enjoy browsing the Internet for knowledge . I can easily communicate with classmates, exchange information, gain access to databases and even publish papers on-line.

◎ On campus, I spent time developing my own interests and focusing on personal growth, not just academia.

◎ In addition to acquiring professional knowledge through graduate school and work, I cultivated my social skills and collaborative spirit through mountain-climbing with a campus organization. When climbing, I release the pressure of work by testing my own physical limits and making myself healthier.

◎ was member of the high school track team, for which I ran the 100 m dash and received a silver medal in a regional contest. I also participated in our department's student association, increasing knowledge of organizational operations and cultivating my communication skills. I also volunteered for the Mental Retardation Foundation. These rewarding experiences have strengthened my coordinating and leadership capabilities.

◎ An outstanding manager must balance academic and social skills. Therefore, to apply my knowledge skills systematically and broaden my horizons, I actively participated in our university's Student Union, the most reputable student organization on campus. After several years of involvement, I served as a vice-president of the association in which role I was responsible for various tasks, such as coordinating student welfare and communicating those needs to pertinent school authorities; holding campus events, and contacting student unions of other universities to set up collaborative events.

◎ I must confess to spending too much time on extracurricular activities during my first two years at university, causing my grade point average to slip early on. Nevertheless, during my junior and senior years, I refocused on strengthening my academic skills and dramatically improved my cumulative GPA.

◎ As a class representative for three years during undergraduate school, I earned the respect of classmates and faculty, largely owing to my ability to communicate effectively and motivate others.

◎ My participation in summer youth camps for underprivileged children aroused my commitment to charitable causes and equipped me with the communication skills necessary for coordinating large groups of volunteers.

◎ At undergraduate school, I organized a private consultancy group of university students who tutored junior high school students in an array of subjects. Despite the initial difficulty in establishing this group, I was able to recruit a large number of tutors, rent a location, purchase teaching materials, and design a daily study schedule to help the students keep up with the curriculum. The community response was overwhelming, as evidenced by the large number of students who enrolled in our tutorial courses.

◎ During university, I organized and led a campus orchestral group to perform at public events. The numerous tasks included matching the musical talents of individual members with the group's needs; finding sponsors to hold performances, and arranging demanding practice schedules that did not interfere too much with the members' academic studies.

◎ As a volunteer for the Society for Chemical Engineers at graduate school, I was responsible for organizing academic workshops, managing departmental publications, performing various administrative tasks, and organizing book exhibitions. This experience instilled in me the importance of synergy and efficiency when collaborating with others.

2. Highlighting the acquired knowledge, skills or leadership qualities that are relevant to employment 強調和求職相關的已有知識技能或領導特質

◎ Volunteer social work allowed me to view others' circumstances objectively, often difficult for someone who has been engrossed with academia since childhood.

◎ Coordinating club activities and closely collaborating with other volunteers provided a valuable point of reference when I later organized my Master's thesis.

◎ My congenial personality, nurtured by these extracurricular activities, allows me to mix well with others from diverse backgrounds.

◎ Showing a strong academic performance, I acquired solid communication and coordination skills while leading our department's student association for two years. The collaborative skills demanded by the position speak of another trait of my personality and won me the respect of my peers, faculty members and staff.

◎ Extensive global travel for business or recreation has made me more receptive to the sometimes opposing values of different countries. Closely observing and comparing different societies, rather than making sweeping generalizations about a particular country or group of people, have allowed me to understand various management practices in different cultures.

◎ The numerous extracurricular activities in which I participated in during university taught me how to organize activities efficiently; express my opinions clearly; communicate with others effectively; transform conflicts into constructive situations that promote collaboration, and cope with failure by analyzing the underlying problems that prevent success.

◎ The way in which I depend on and support my fellow mountain-climbers has instilled in me the need for team spirit. As well as viewing majestic scenery from above, I can also observe the topography of the land. I have also learned about the aquatic environment, geology and geomorphology.

◎ As the leader of the harmonica club at university, I was able fully to express not only my enthusiasm for music but also for working with others who share my passion. In addition to broadening my horizons and nurturing communication skills with members with diverse interests and backgrounds, I was able to quickly adjust to new surroundings and make new friends as well.

◎ Participating in the university Heart club, a social service organization, helped me nurture leadership and collaborative skills in a leadership role in which I organized and coordinated many activities. ALE, an acronym for Actual Living English, not only strengthened my listening, speaking, reading and writing skills, but also allowed me to make new friends from different cultures and to express my feelings in another language, which is challenging for me. Experiences gained through my participation in extracurricular activities have greatly enriched my life have greatly enriched my life by enabling me to achieve the necessary balance of academic and social skills.

◎ These experiences strengthened my communicative, organizational, leadership, and management skills. Additionally, this challenging work made me confident in my ability to achieve goals by systematically applying knowledge skills.

◎ These activities instilled in me the importance of developing an outgoing personality, excellent communicative skills, and an assiduous working attitude to implement club activities successfully. For instance, I often spent much time preparing presentations before our group meetings and articulated my opinions at the appropriate time.

◎ As this was my first entrepreneurial experience, albeit not an overly successful one, I learned much about pricing, marketing and budgeting. While contributing to the community and allowing me to earn a meager income at the same time, this activity exposed me to the wide range of management decisions that must be made to be successful.

◎ While leading the campus orchestral group, I learned how to motivate group members to hone their individual talents for a common goal. Dealing with the occasional frustrations of fiercely individualistic orchestral members when trying to reach a consensus has made me a strong leader. I was able to listen patiently to individual concerns and tried to incorporate them in a group consensus. I believe that that role was good training for the workplace.

◎ Extensive travel to more than twenty countries has not only broadened my perspective on living a fulfilling life, but also emboldened me to incorporate the practices of seemingly polar lifestyles into my own.

◎ Working part-time as a network manager at an Internet service provider not only taught me a great deal about Internet communication, but also instilled in me the necessity of systematically and methodically making concerted efforts with others , something which is vital in a research career.

F In the space below, describe your extracurricular activities that are relevant to employment.

_____

_____

_____

_____

_____

_____

_____

_____

_____

_____

_____

G Look at the following examples of how to describe extracurricular activities that are relevant to employment.

Introducing an extracurricular activity that one has participated in 曾參加的相
關課外活動介紹 During graduate school at National Tsing Hua University, I twice
served as a counselor in the Electrical Engineering Camp sponsored by our
department. This camp helps high school students to grasp the basic concepts of
Electrical Engineering and Electronics. All counselors thoroughly discuss the
curriculum several times beforehand to arrange all the details. Roundtable
discussions held nightly during the camp examined difficulties in instruction and
reviewed the following day's schedule. **Highlighting the acquired knowledge,
skills or leadership qualities that are relevant to employment** 強調和求職相關
的已有知識技能或領導特質 These two activities fostered my collaborative,
coordinating, organizational and communicative skills. I believe that such
experiences greatly facilitate my work performance.

*

Introducing an extracurricular activity that one has participated in 曾參加的相
關課外活動介紹 I enjoy reflecting on the past and thinking about the future, which
fact explains why I participated in the campus debating club at university. During
this period, I took many opportunities to identify and defend a particular position.
**Highlighting the acquired knowledge, skills or leadership qualities that are
relevant to employment** 強調和求職相關的已有知識技能或領導特質 I also
participated in many debating matches, which trained my mental alertness and
ability to respond quickly. Similarly, in my job, I face daily challenges that enable
me to adopt the skills gained in the university debating club to assess situations
rationally and make right decisions.

*

Introducing an extracurricular activity that one has participated in 曾參加的相關課外活動介紹 Realizing that the faculty and students of the Electrical Engineering department should actively introduce its programs to recruit senior high school students, I worked with other classmates in organizing an Electrical Engineering camp on the university campus. This camp attempted to inform students of the programs they can pursue after successfully passing a rigorous nationwide entrance examination to enter this department at National Tsing Hua University. In this camp, I was responsible for preparing curricular materials, teaching in the classroom and assisting students to complete experiments. I also closely monitored the students to assist them in finishing activities. **Highlighting the acquired knowledge, skills or leadership qualities that are relevant to employment** 強調和求職相關的已有知識技能或領導特質 These responsibilities allowed me to implement the knowledge that I had learned in the classroom. They also sharpened my presentation skills. Moreover, this diverse experience strengthened and broadened my solid knowledge base, and further enhanced my ability to collaborate closely with my peers. This unique opportunity proved to be one of the most rewarding experiences of my undergraduate years.

*

Introducing an extracurricular activity that one has participated in 曾參加的相關課外活動介紹 Among the many extracurricular activities in which I participated at university were the campus social service organization and the photography club, and the "peer group". The campus social service organization held sports, entertainment and health-related activities in remote areas. As a leader of this organization, I realized that executing these activities required coordination among team members and related social entities, and the work strengthened my negotiation skills and broadened my horizons. **Highlighting the acquired knowledge, skills or**

leadership qualities that are relevant to employment 強調和求職相關的已有知識技能或領導特質 Learning photography sharpened my observational skills and enhanced my aesthetic appreciation of nature and humans. I even won the grand prize in the campus photography contest. The "peer group", which aims to enhance students' well being, trained students to help other classmates through psychological courses, psychological testing, counseling and even dramatic theater. The peer group heightened my sensitivity to those around me and greatly improved my communication skills.

*

Introducing an extracurricular activity that one has participated in 曾參加的相關課外活動介紹 Owing to the occasionally monotonous and tedious nature of electrical engineering research, working in the semiconductor industry requires both a top-notch physical condition and strong analytical capabilities. This fact explains why I strive for a balance between work and leisure. I enjoy recreational sports such as swimming, volleyball, jogging and hiking. An overseas vacation once or twice annually is a welcome break from my hectic work schedule. Traveling overseas provides an objective perspective on our daily lives and can broaden one's horizons. Extracurricular activities can offer a diverse education, and enhance our sensitivity towards other cultures. For instance, the fog's rising above the San Francisco Bay area has inspired me and adventures at Disney Land have left treasured memories. **Highlighting the acquired knowledge, skills or leadership qualities that are relevant to employment** 強調和求職相關的已有知識技能或領導特質 Global travel allows people to apply their knowledge in unconventional ways...from practicing language skills to distinguishing between a country's history and its current situation. Without venturing to a castle, an individual would have great difficulty in appreciating the greatness of a previous empire. In addition to reenergizing individuals to return to work, balanced extracurricular activities can help produce well-rounded people.

*

Introducing an extracurricular activity that one has participated in 曾參加的相關課外活動介紹 In addition to undergoing rigorous training through coursework, I participated in our university department's student association. I actively coordinated a diverse spectrum of academic activities, which enhanced my communication and collaborative skills and revealed the inner workings of an organization.

H Select the correct answers to the following questions about one's extracurricular activities that are relevant to employment.

1. At what camp did Alex serve twice as a counselor?

   A. his department's Electronic Engineering camp

   B. his department's Electrical Engineering camp

   C. his department's Industrial Engineering camp

2. Who attends this camp?

   A. vocational students

   B. junior high school students

   C. high school students

3. Why do counselors thoroughly discuss the curriculum before the camp?

   A. to arrange the details

   B. to review the following day's schedule

   C. to address difficulties in instruction

4. How often were roundtable discussions held at the camp?

   A. weekly

B. once every two days

C. nightly

5. What does Alex believe that such experiences have greatly improved?

A. his coordinating skills

B. his work performance

C. his organizational skills

6. What does Carey consider to be an extension of science?

A. nature

B. industry

C. knowledge and skills

7. What kind of knowledge does Carey believe should be grasped in practical contexts?

A. theoretical

B. systematic

C. scientific

8. What was one of the most rewarding experiences of Carey's undergraduate years?

A. increasing his confidence in achieving goals by systematically applying knowledge and skills

B. developing communication skills

C. developing a theoretical foundation to balance nature and science

9. Which word is most similar in meaning to "framework"?

A. background

B. hypothesis

C. outline

10. Which word is the most similar in meaning to "adversely"?

A. negatively

B. optimistically

C. realistically

11. Whom did Jason work with in organizing an Electrical Engineering camp on the university campus?

    A. faculty members

    B. other classmates

    C. senior high school students

12. Which word is the most similar in meaning to "rigorous"?

    A. stringent

    B. flexible

    C. compromising

13. Which word is the most similar in meaning to "recruit"?

    A. exploit

    B. solicit

    C. manage

14. Which word is the most similar in meaning to "collaborate"?

    A. compete

    B. struggle

    C. cooperate

15. What was Jason responsible for in this camp?

    A. preparing curricular materials

    B. teaching in the classroom

    C. both A and B

I Select the correct answers to the following questions about one's professional and/or research experiences.

1. What did you serve ____ in the Electrical Engineering Camp sponsored by your university department?

   A. for

   B. as

   C. at

2. What extracurricular activities did you participate ____ during university?

   A. with

   B. on

   C. in

3. What did the volunteer activities ____ you participated in during university help others to do?

   A. that

   B. which

   C. how

4. What skills did you develop ____ participating in extracurricular activities at university?

   A. by/while

   B. on/at

   C. with/across

5. What were some of your responsibilities in the extracurricular activities ____ which you participated during university?

   A. across

   B. to

   C. in

6. What did you learn from your extracurricular activities at university that will be helpful ____ the future?

A. on

B. for

C. in

7. What personal traits did you realize that you have by participating ____ extracurricular activities at university?

A. to

B. in

C. as

8. What kind of relationships did you form in the extracurricular activities ____ which you participated at university?

A. in

B. on

C. from

9. Why did you become involved in an environmental protection organization ____ the university campus?

A. at

B. in

C. on

10. Why did you start participating in the student volunteer organization ____ your university?

A. at/in

B. on/by

C. from/towards

11. Why did the extracurricular activities in which you participated at university heavily influence your decision ____ pursue a career in health care management

A. by

B. from

C. to

12. Why did your extracurricular activities at university strongly influence your interest ____ the nursing profession?

A. in

B. from

C. at

13. Why did you ____ involved in helping youth?

A. are

B. become

C. be

14. Why do you feel ____ participating in extracurricular activities is important?

A. that

B. which

C. how

15. Why did extracurricular activities make you aware ____ your social responsibilities?

A. of

B. in

C. for

16. Why do you feel that effective communications skills are essential ____ successful collaboration within a group?

A. by

B. for

C. on

17. Where did you volunteer your time ____ helping troubled youth?

A. of

B. for

C. in

18. Where _____ you become involved in helping youth?

A. were

B. did

C. does

19. Where did you acquire the unique leadership opportunity _____ help youth?

A. for

B. of

C. to

20. Where did you learn how to execute a comprehensive camp schedule _____ closely collaborating with others?

A. by

B. with

C. to

21. Where did you learn how to collaborate closely _____ others?

A. to

B. with

C. from

22. Where did you learn _____ to foster your communication skills?

A. for

B. by

C. how

23. Where did you come into contact _____ other youth volunteers?

A. with

B. from

C. while

24. Where _____ you learn how to develop your leadership skills?

A. were

B. did

C. does

Appendix A

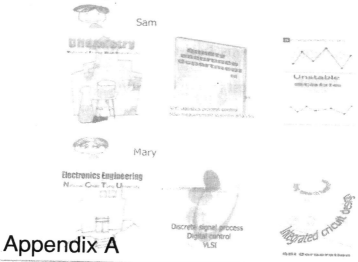

Appendix A

Asking academic questions that are relevant to the workplace

問學術方面的問題，為了工作需求

Exercise 1

Asking academic questions, beginning with "Which", on one's

interest in a field of study

學術方面問題／表達學習領域興趣

1. At which university _____ you hope to pursue a Ph.D. in Computer Science?

   A. are B. does C. do

2. Which field of research _____ you study at graduate school?

   A. am B. did C. are

3. Which topic _____ you research at graduate school?

   A. is B. are C. did

4. Which topic _____ you fascinated with?

   A. are B. have C. is

5. Which topic _____ you interested in researching during your graduate studies?

   A. have B. is C. are

6. At which department at Yuan Pei University of Science and Technology _____
   you acquire a Bachelor's degree?

   A. have B. are C. did

7. Which university _____ one of Taiwan's premier institutes of higher learning?
   A. is B. were C. are

8. Which degree _____ you near completing?
   A. is B. have C. are

9. At which university _____ you receive a Master's degree?
   A. have B. did C. is

10. At which university _____ you obtain a Bachelor's degree?
    A. are B. was C. did

Exercise 2

Asking academic questions, beginning with "What", on one's

interest in a field of study

學術方面問題／表達學習領域興趣

1. What university did you graduate _____ ?

    A. of B. from C. at

2. What university did you receive a Bachelor's degree _____ ?

    A. in B. by C. from

3. What did you major _____ at National Cheng Chi University?

    A. from B. in C. by

4. What do you plan to do _____ graduate school?

    A. while B. by C. after

5. What have you dreamed _____ since childhood?

    A. of B. for C. at

6. What have you aspired to become _____ childhood?

    A. before B. at C. since

7. What do you hope that your graduate school research will center _____?

A. for B. on   C. by

8. What has prepared you _____ advanced study in graduate school?

A. in B. at C. for

9. What kind of person have you become because of your dreams _____ a world free of pollution?

A. by B. in C. of

10. What university do you intend to apply _____ for graduate school?

A. to B. for C. in

Exercise 3

Asking academic questions, beginning with "Why", on one's

interest in a field of study

學術方面問題／表達學習領域興趣

1. Why do you want _____ attend graduate school?

   A. in B. by C. to

2. Why do you feel _____ studying interactive marketing research is important?

   A. by B. that C. which

3. Why do you wish to further your knowledge _____ interactive marketing research?

   A. of B. in C. at

4. Why did you select Yuan Pei University of Science and Technology to acquire a

   Bachelor's degree _____ Medical Technology?

   A. of B. for C. in

5. Why do you want your graduate studies to focus _____ interactive marketing

   research?

   A. at B. on C. in

6. Why did you select this university as the place _____ pursue a Bachelor's degree?

   A. in B. at C. to

7. Why have you studied Marketing _____ high school?

   A. during B. since C. on

8. Why are you interested _____ the increasing number of customer-oriented

   administrative database systems and customer/supplier relations?

   A. in B. for C. with

9. Why _____ Marketing interest you?

   A. is B. does C. do

10. Why did you immerse yourself _____ customer service-related issues early on?

   A. in B. with C. on

Exercise 4

Asking academic questions, beginning with "Which", on one's

interest in a field of study

學術方面問題／表達學習領域興趣

1. Where do you hope to be admitted _____ graduate school?

    A. for B. to C. in

2. Where _____ you receive your Bachelor's degree?

    A. do B. does C. did

3. Where did you major _____ Business Administration?

    A. in B. on C. at

4. Where would you _____ interested in attending graduate school?

    A. are B.with C. be

5. Where did you become interested _____ total systems intervention?

    A. on B. in C. for

6. Where would you like _____ attend graduate school?

    A. for B. be C. to

7. Where _____ you want to pursue an MBA?

    A. do B. were C. does

8. Where is your first choice _____ doctoral studies?

   A. in B. with C. for

9. Where would you like to study _____ a doctoral degree?

   A. at B. for C. with

10. Where _____ MIT located?

   A. are B. be C.is

Exercise 5

Asking academic questions, beginning with "What", on one's

current knowledge of a field of study

學術方面問題／展現已有的學習領域知識

1. What motivates you _____ attend graduate school?

   A. for B. to C. in

2. What would you like to focus on _____ studying for a Ph.D. in Management?

   A. while B. during C. for

3. What have you decided _____ study?

   A. for B. to C. in

4. What career path do you intend to take _____ completing your Ph.D.?

   A. during B.after C.on

5. What is the reason for your decision to study _____ a Ph.D. in Management?

   A. on B. in C. for

6. What can you tell us _____ Taiwan's economic situation?

   A. on B. about C. with

7. What _____ you know about Taiwan's economic situation?

   A. do B. are C. am

8. What is your motivation to study _____ a Ph.D. in Management?

   A. in B. with C. for

9. What is the current situation _____ Taiwan's economy?

   A. on B. for C. of

Exercise 6

Asking academic questions, beginning with "Which", on one's

current knowledge of a field of study

學術方面問題／展現已有的學習領域知識

1. Which factor most motivates you to pursue a graduate degree _____ International

   Finance?

   A. of B. at C. in

2. Which career are you interested in pursuing _____ you complete a degree in

   International Finance?

   A. after B. during C. on

3. Which topic are you interested in researching _____ graduate school?

   A. of B. by C. during

4. Which field are you interested _____ acquiring a graduate degree in?

   A. in B.for C. on

5. Which country is undergoing rapid changes _____ regulation and innovation?

   A. of B. in C. for

6. Which field have you decided to concentrate _____ while pursuing a graduate

   degree in International Finance?

A. for B. with C. on

7. Which topic in international trade are you the most familiar _____?

A. for B. with C. to

8. Which career direction do you want to take _____ completing a graduate degree in International Finance?

A. after B. for C. to

9. At which university do you want to pursue a graduate degree _____ International Finance?

A. of B. with C. in

Exercise 7

Asking academic questions, beginning with "Why", on one's

current knowledge of a field of study

學術方面問題／展現已有的學習領域知識

1. Why do you want to pursue an advanced degree _____ the Institute of Public Health of Harvard University?

   A. at B. for C. with

2. Why have you decided to devote yourself _____ effectively addressing public health issues in Taiwan following graduate school?

   A. in B. for C. to

3. Why are you interested in researching public health issues _____ Harvard University?

   A. for B. at C. with

4. Why did you choose a career _____ public health after completing your advanced degree at Harvard University?

   A. at B. for C. in

5. Why are you motivated _____ research public health issues at Harvard University?

   A. to B. for C. with

6. Why did you select Harvard University as the place _____ research public health issues?

   A. for B. with C. to

7. Why _____ Taiwan's public health system interest you?

   A. do B. does C. is

8. Why does Taiwan have an unequal distribution of public health resources _____ urban and rural areas?

   A. with B. for C. in

9. Why _____ equitable health care essential for Taiwan?

   A. does B. is C. are

Exercise 8

Asking academic questions, beginning with "How", on one's

current knowledge of a field of study

學術方面問題／展現已有的學習領域知識

1. How did you select _____ degree to pursue in graduate school?

   A. which   B. at   C. with

2. How _____ you develop your knowledge of International Finance?

   A. was   B. were   C. did

3. How did you develop your interest _____ Taiwan's economy?

   A. of   B. in   C. to

4. How _____ you remain abreast of the latest topics in International Finance?

   A. does   B. do   C. are

5. How _____ you become interested in Taiwan's economy?

   A. was   B. were   C. did

6. How do you plan to research the way _____ which domestic companies can

   compete with multinational corporations?

   A. in   B. of   C. for

7. How _____ you select at which university to pursue a graduate degree?

   A. have B. did C. do

8. How _____ Taiwan's economy flourished in recent decades?

   A. have B. did C. has

9. How can Taiwan enhance _____ local competitiveness?

   A. their B. its C. his

Exercise 9

Asking academic questions, beginning with "Why", on one's

academic background and achievements

學術方面問題／描述學歷背景及已獲成就

1. Why did you major in Finance _____ National Cheng Kung University?

   A. in B. on C. at

2. Why did you choose National Cheng University as the place to pursue a

   Bachelor's degree _____ Finance?

   A. of B. in C. with

3. Why _____ you decided to pursue advanced study in this field?

   A. has B. have C. did

4. Why are you equipped to meet the rigorous demands _____ advanced study in

   Finance?

   A. of B. in C. for

5. Why did you perform so well _____ your undergraduate studies?

   A. about B. to C. in

6. Why did you concentrate _____ developing your analytical skills and research

   fundamentals during undergraduate school?

   A. in B. at C. on

7. Why did you refuse several employment offers in the financial sector _____ completing your undergraduate studies?

　A. on　B. after　C. in

8. Why _____ you take the highly competitive nationwide university entrance examination?

　A. were　B. was　C. did

9. Why are you confident _____ your ability to meet the rigorous demands of graduate study?

　A. to　B. with　C. for

10. Why do you feel that you can meet the rigorous demands _____ graduate study?

　A. for　B. about　C. of

Exercise 10

Asking academic questions, beginning with "What", on one's

academic background and achievements

學術方面問題／描述學歷背景及已獲成就

1. At what university _____ you receive your Bachelor's degree?

   A. do B. did C. does

2. What courses interested you most _____ National Chiao Tung University?

   A. at B. for C. on

3. What courses in the Department _____ Industrial Engineering did you enjoy the most?

   A. in B. of C. on

4. What university did you graduate _____?

   A. in B. by C. from

5. What courses _____ you audit at National Chiao Tung University?

   A. were B. did C. was

6. What fundamental skills did you acquire _____ National Chiao Tung University?

   A. about B. for C. at

7. What opportunities did you have to come into contact _____ actual enterprises?

   A. by　B. with　C. for

8. What department _____ you receive your bachelor's degree from?

   A. were　B. was　C. did

9. What did the coursework _____ your junior and senior years emphasize?

   A. on　B. during　C. about

10. What did a solid academic background in Food and Beverage Management at

    Yuan Pei Medical Institute of Technology provide you _____ ?

   A. on　B. for　C. with

Exercise 11

Asking academic questions, beginning with "Where", on one's

academic background and achievements

學術方面問題／描述學歷背景及已獲成就

1. Where did you foster your interest _____ this field of study?

   A. with B.in C. to

2. Where did you gain a further glimpse _____ food science-related research?

   A. on B.with C. into

3. Where did you foster your ability _____ solve problems logically?

   A.how B. to C. with

4. Where did you graduate _____ in 2001?

   A. by B. for C. from

5. Where _____ you develop your analytical skills?

   A. does B. did C. were

6. Where _____ you gain practical laboratory experiences?

   A. was B. were C. did

7. Where did you acquire theoretical knowledge _____ factory automation in Taiwan?

A. for B. of C. by

8. Where did you learn _____ to conduct research independently?

A. which B. by C. how

9. Where did you serve _____ a teaching assistant?

A. as   B. in C. at

Exercise 12

Asking academic questions, beginning with "Which", on one's

academic background and achievements

學術方面問題／描述學歷背景及已獲成就

1. Which domestic and international conferences _____ you attended?

   A. has B. have C. did

2. Which National Science Council research projects did you participate _____
   during graduate school?

   A. in B. on C. for

3. Which of your works have received praise from peers _____ your field?

   A. of B. to C. in

4. Which topics did you study in the research projects _____ you participated in?

   A. that B. in C. for

5. Which stage _____ the National Science Council research projects did you
   participate in?

   A. for B. of C. on

6. At which university _____ you participate in several National Science Council
   research projects?

   A. were B. was C. did

7. Which research group did you belong to _____ participating in National Science Council research projects?

   A. while   B. for   C. in

8. Which professor supervised the research group _____ which you belonged?

   A. through   B. by   C. to

9. Which professor supervised you while you wrote _____ master's thesis?

   A. its   B. your   C. his

10. Which master's degree program _____ you decided to enroll in?

   A. have   B. did   C. were

Exercise 13

Asking academic questions, beginning with "Where", on one's

research and professional experiences

學術方面問題／介紹研究及工作經驗

1. Where were the several international conferences _____ you attended held?

   A. to B. that C. for

2. Where did you learn _____ to publish a research paper?

   A. by B. for C. how

3. Where _____ you audit management courses?

   A. were B. did C. was

4. Where _____ you enhance your research abilities?

   A. do B. does C. did

5. Where did you learn _____ modern management practices are related?

   A. how B. on C. from

6. Where did you learn how _____ conduct research?

   A. by B. through C. to

7. Where _____ you complete your undergraduate studies?

A. do B. were C. did

8. Where did you learn _____ to write a research paper?

A. by B. how C. to

9. Where did you come _____ contact with researchers in your field of study?

A. with B. on C. into

Exercise 14

Asking academic questions, beginning with "What", on one's

research and professional experiences

學術方面問題／介紹研究及工作經驗

1. At what institute at National Taiwan University _____ you research food science-related topics?

   A. were B. was C. did

2. What part time work did you take while working _____ your bachelor's degree?

   A. on B. in C. from

3. What skills _____ your studies at the Institute of Food Research at National Taiwan Normal University provide you with?

   A. were B. was C. did

4. What else did you _____ while working on your bachelor's degree?

   A. does B. do C. did

5. What were you responsible _____ while working at the Food Safety Laboratory?

   A. in B. at C. for

6. What work experiences did you acquire _____ working on your bachelor's degree?

   A. in B. at C. for _____ working on your bachelor's degree?

A. on　B. while　C. for

7. What did you learn from your work _____ the Food Safety Laboratory?

A. at　B. by　C. on

8. What practical skills _____ you develop while working at the Food Safety Laboratory?

A. were　B. was　C. did

9. What _____ the relationship between your undergraduate studies and your work at the Food Safety Laboratory?

A. were　B. was　C. did

Exercise 15

Asking academic questions, beginning with "Why", on one's

research and professional experiences

學術方面問題／介紹研究及工作經驗

1. Why do you feel _____ conducting educational research offers many valuable experiences?

   A. for B. on C. that

2. Why are you confident that you _____ become a distinguished researcher someday

   A. have B. can C. has

3. Why are you ready to immerse yourself _____ academia?

   A. in B. on C. by

4. Why do you believe that you can meet the challenges _____ graduate school?

   A. for B. of C. to

5. Why _____ you enjoy performing educational research?

   A. does B. do C. are

6. Why are you preparing _____ the exciting challenges of a research career?

   A. for B. with C. to

7. Why do you feel _____ undertaking educational research is important for graduate study?

　A. what　B. by　C. that

8. Why _____ you aspire to become a distinguished research in the educational field?

　A. do　B. does　C. are

9. Why must you work diligently to become a distinguished researcher _____ the educational field?

　A. with　B. in　C. to

10. Why did you become interested _____ performing educational research?

　A. of　B. to　C. in

Exercise 16

Asking academic questions, beginning with "Which", on one's

research and professional experiences

學術方面問題／介紹研究及工作經驗

1. Which occupation have you worked _____ at Chang Gung Memorial Hospital for
   the past five years?
   A. for B. in C. on

2. Which hospital have you worked _____ during the past five years?
   A. while B. to C. at

3. Which profession _____ you worked in for the past five years?
   A. have B. has C. are

4. Which aspect _____ your work do you enjoy the most?
   A. for B. of C. to

5. Which aspect _____ your work do you find the most challenging?
   A. from B. to C. of

6. Which tasks in your job _____ you enjoy the most?
   A. does B. are C. do

7. Which skills have you developed _____ working at the hospital?

   A. for B. to C. while

8. Which work opportunities did you have while working _____ your bachelor's degree?

   A. for B. on C. at

9. Which awards or recognition _____ you received for your work as a physical therapist?

   A. have B. has C. are

Exercise 17

Asking academic questions, beginning with "Where", on one's

extracurricular activities relevant to study

學術方面問題／描述與學習有關的課外活動

1. Where did you participate _____ a social service organization that held summer youth camps?

   A. of B. for C. in

2. Where _____ you become involved in helping youth?

   A. were B. did C. does

3. Where did you acquire the unique leadership opportunity _____ help youth?

   A. for B. of C. to

4. Where did you learn how to execute a comprehensive camp schedule _____ closely collaborating with others?

   A. by B. with C. to

5. Where did you learn how to collaborate closely _____ others?

   A. to B. with C. from

6. Where did you learn _____ to foster your communication skills?

   A. for B. by C. how

7. Where did you come into contact _____ other youth volunteers?

   A. with　B. from　C. while

8. Where _____ you learn how to develop your leadership skills?

   A. were　B. did　C. does

9. Where did you realize the importance _____ doing volunteer work?

   A. of　B. to　C. for

10. Where did you become aware _____ your social responsibilities?

   A. to　B. with　C. of

Exercise 18

Asking academic questions, beginning with "What", on one's

extracurricular activities relevant to study

學術方面問題／描述與學習有關的課外活動

1. What extracurricular activities _____ you participate in during university?

   A. were B. did C. does

2. What is a valuable lesson that you learned _____ participating in extracurricular activities during university?

   A. because B. as C. while

3. What personal traits did you realize that you _____ by participating in extracurricular activities during university?

   A. have B. did C. was

4. What skills _____ you develop while participating in extracurricular activities during university?

   A. was B. did C. were

5. What did you learn _____ your extracurricular activities during university that will be helpful in the future?

   A. as B. with C. from

6. What _____ some of your responsibilities in the extracurricular activities that you participated in during university?

   A. does B. were C. did

7. What skills do you believe that a good manager should _____?

   A. did B. had C. have

8. What allows you _____ adjust easily to different cultures?

   A. by B. to C. with

9. What kind of relationships did you form _____ the extracurricular activities in which you participated during university?

   A. as B. because C. through

Exercise 19

Asking academic questions, beginning with "Which", on one's

extracurricular activities relevant to study

學術方面問題／描述與學習有關的課外活動

1. Which extracurricular activity _____ you participate in that heavily influenced your decision to pursue a career in marketing?

   A. were B. was C. did

2. Which personal interests did you develop _____ participating in extracurricular activities during university?

   A. as B. while C. for

3. Which profession did you become interested _____ while participating in extracurricular activities during university?

   A. in B. to C. for

4. Which skills did you develop while participating _____ extracurricular activities during university?

   A. on B. of C. in

5. Which responsibilities did you have in the extracurricular activities that you participated in _____ university?

   A. at B. for C. because

6. Which valuable lessons _____ you learn while participating in extracurricular activities during university?

A. were B. did C. does

7. Which volunteer experience strengthened you _____ an individual the most?

A. at B. by C. as

8. Which volunteer experience left a deep impression _____ you?

A. in B. on C. for

9. Which personal qualities did you develop _____ participating in extracurricular activities during university?

A. on B. to C. while

Exercise 20

Asking academic questions, beginning with "What", on one's

personal qualities relevant to study

學術方面問題／描述與學習有關的個人特質

1. What do you feel that your personal strengths_____?

   A. is　B. are　C. do

2. What is an example _____ your diligence?

   A. of　B. for　C. to

3. What activities have you participated _____ that reflect your personal strengths?

   A. on　B. in　C. to

4. What makes you determined _____ pursue a Master's degree in Food Science?

   A. of　B.for　C.to

5. What factor _____ inspired you to be a high achiever?

   A. had　B. has　C. was

6. What challenges in life have _____ you a strong individual?

   A. made　B. makes　C. make

7. What obstacles have you had to overcome _____ your studies that have made you

a better individual?

A. for B.of C. during

8. What courses during university challenged you the _____?

A. most B. better C. best

9. What personal qualities _____ you develop at undergraduate school?

A. were B. did C. was

Exercise 21

Asking academic questions, answered with "Yes" or "No", on

one's personal qualities relevant to study

學術方面問題／描述與學習有關的個人特質

1. Can you often pinpoint the untapped market demand _____ a certain group?

   A. of B. on C. at

2. _____ you a reliable individual?

   A. Do B. Is C. Are

3. Do you feel that creativity can _____ nurtured through training?

   A. of B. be C. for

4. Do you remain abreast _____ the latest technological trends in your field?

   A. for B. with C. of

5. Are you in tune _____ popular trends in your field?

   A. for B. with C. by

6. Are you motivated properly _____ study in graduate school?

   A. to B. as C. with

7. _____ you determined to meet the challenges of graduate school?

   A. Is B.Are C. Have

8. Do you believe that you can contribute to the efforts _____ your research group in graduate school?

A. with B. for C. of

9. Can you rise _____ the rigorous challenges of graduate study?

A. to B. for C. on

Exercise 22

Asking academic questions, beginning with "Which", on one's

personal qualities relevant to study

學術方面問題 / 描述與學習有關的個人特質

1. Which factor _____ you believe is essential to success in academic studies?

    A. does B. are C. do

2. Which personal quality do you think is the most important _____ graduate study?

    A. for B. on C. by

3. Which of your personal strengths _____ helped you in academic studies the most?

    A. has B. have C. are

4. Do you remain abreast _____ the latest technological trends in your field?

    A. for B. with C. of

5. Which factors influenced your decision _____ pursue a graduate degree in Medical Technology?

    A. for B. to C. by

6. Which person _____ inspired you the most to be a high achiever?

    A. has B. have C. did

7. Which obstacles have you overcome to succeed _____ academia?

    A. for　B.　with　C. in

8. Which teacher challenged you the most to strive _____ academic excellence?

    A. with　B.　for　C. of

9. Which activities have you undertaken _____ which you contributed to a group effort?

    A. in　B. from　C. by

Exercise 23

Asking academic questions, beginning with "Why", on one's

personal qualities relevant to study

學術方面問題 / 描述與學習有關的個人特質

1. Why is your personality suitable _____ graduate study?

    A. on   B. for   C. with

2. Why are you able to interact _____ individuals from diverse backgrounds?

    A. with   B. to   C. on

3. Why can you easily adapt yourself _____ new circumstances?

    A. for   B. to   C. are

4. Why do you feel highly competent _____ collaborating with others in a group?

    A. on   B. in   C. to

5. Why are you able _____ assess different situations rationally?

    A. when   B. for   C. to

6. Why do you believe that you can rise _____ the challenges of graduate school?

    A. for   B. to   C. in

7. Why do you believe that you possess the skills necessary to thrive _____ graduate

school?

A. to B. by C. in

8. Why did you have many opportunities to collaborate _____ others during undergraduate school?

A. with B. on C. to

9. Why were you able occasionally to meet _____ entrepreneurs during university?

A. with B. from C. by

Exercise 24

Asking academic questions, beginning with "Why", on one's

career objectives

學術方面問題 / 概述未來工作目標

1. Why do you want to complete a Master's degree _____ Medical Technology?

   A. of B. in C. for

2. Why have you decided _____ enter the health care profession?

   A. for B. of C. to

3. Why do you feel that you can contribute more significantly in the workplace

   _____ further academic training?

   A. as B. with C. to

4. Why are you receptive _____ novel concepts in the workplace?

   A. to B. in C. by

5. Why are you able to respond effectively to the latest technological advances _____

   the workplace?

   A. on B. in C. as

6. Why do you believe that you will be in line _____ a managerial position in just a

   few years?

A. from B. with C. for

7. Why do you plan to work _____ a multinational corporation or research institute
   after completing your graduate degree?
   A. in B. after C. from

8. Why _____ you chosen a career in Nursing?
   A. were B. have C. did

9. Why do you believe that the skills nurtured _____ graduate school will help you in
   the workplace?
   A. in B. as C. to

Exercise 25

Asking academic questions, beginning with "What", on one's

career objectives

學術方面問題 / 概述未來工作目標

1. What career path _____ you chosen?
   A. has B. did C. have

2. What line _____ work do you plan to take after graduation?
   A. on B. of C. with

3. What plans do you have _____ teaching in a university after you complete your graduate studies?
   A. at B. as C. for

4. What skills did you focus _____ nurturing during your graduate studies?
   A. by B. on C. with

5. What is the importance _____ establishing an extensive personal network in your profession?
   A. as B. within C. of

6. What work experience _____ you hope to acquire following graduation?
   A. does B. were C. do

7. What do you hope to contribute _____ the medical profession?

    A. to B. from C. for

8. What can you offer _____ the medical technology profession?

    A. on B. by C. to

9. What opportunities _____ you believe are available in the nursing profession?

    A. are B. do C. is

Exercise 26

Asking academic questions, beginning with "Where", on one's

career objectives

學術方面問題 / 概述未來工作目標

1. Where do you plan to continue _____ your graduate studies after you complete your Bachelor's degree?
   A. to B. with C. on

2. Where would like your career focus to _____ in the future?
   A. at B. be C. as

3. Where do you see yourself _____ ten years from now?
   A. of B. in C. at

4. Where would you like to nurture your research and management skills _____ future employment?
   A. to B. for C. at

5. Where are the most job opportunities _____ the nursing profession available?
   A. of B. to C. in

6. Where do you hope to teach _____ graduate school?
   A. after B. as C. by

7. Where do you hope to gain further experience _____ the medical technology profession?

A. of B. in C. by

8. Where would you be _____ a better position to understand the latest technological trends in medicine?

A. in B. to C. as

Exercise 27

Asking academic questions, beginning with "Where", on one's

career objectives

學術方面問題／概述未來工作目標

1. Where would you like to begin your career _____ the medical technology profession?

   A. of B. on C. in

2. Where would you like to work _____ graduation?

   A. following B. for C. in

3. Where _____ your career direction leading you?

   A. are B. is C. were

4. Where would you like your career path _____ begin?

   A. by B. for C. to

5. Where do you think that you would be able to nurture the skills necessary _____ the workplace?

   A. as B. for C. of

6. Where are you most interested in working _____ your graduate studies?

   A. after B. although C. as

7. Where _____ you consider working after undergraduate school?

   A. are　B. does　C. would

8. Where do you think that you would be able _____ realize your career goals the most?

   A. to　B. in　C. on

Exercise 28

Asking academic questions, beginning with "Which", on one's

career objectives

學術方面問題／概述未來工作目標

1. Which company would you like to work _____ after graduating from university?

   A. as B. by C. for

2. Which university do you think would prepare you best for a career _____ Nursing?

   A. in B. on C. with

3. Which profession have you chosen to work _____?

   A. by B. for C. in

4. Which career direction _____ you taking?

   A. are B. do C. will

5. Which profession are you interested _____ joining after you complete your studies?

   A. on B. in C. to

6. Which university do you believe will provide you _____ valuable experiences that will benefit your career?

   A. to B. on C. with

7. Which university do you believe would allow you _____ acquire advanced knowledge and specialized skills?

A. to B. on C. as

8. Which university do you believe would make you better equipped _____ the workplace?

A. to B. for C. on

9. Which company would place you _____ a better position to realize fully your career goals?

A. with B. in C. to

Exercise 29

Asking academic questions, beginning with "Where", on why an

institution was selected for advanced study

學術方面問題／解釋選擇該校原由

1. Where do you intend to enhance your education _____ a graduate degree program in Medical Technology?

   A. as B. through C. for

2. Where do you want to apply to _____ graduate school?

   A. at B. on C. for

3. Where do you feel that you will be able to receive the necessary training and skills _____ a leader in your organization?

   A. with B. for C. on

4. Where will you be able to foster the skills needed _____ become a successful information specialist?

   A. as B. for C. to

5. Where will you be able to build upon and refine the fundamental skills that you gained _____ undergraduate study?

   A. during B. on C. as

6. Where did you learn _____ the most appropriate graduate program for you?

    A. with B. for C. about

7. Where have you decided to apply to _____ graduate school?

    A. for   B. when C. of

8. Where did you first become interested in the field in which you want _____ pursue graduate study?

    A. from B. as C. to

9. Where do you want to study _____ a Master's degree?

    A. on B. for C. in

Exercise 30

Asking academic questions, beginning with "What", on why an

institution was selected for advanced study

學術方面問題／解釋選擇該校原由

1. What was your reason _____ applying to this university?

   A. to   B. for   C. of

2. What motivated you to apply ____ this university for graduate school?

   A. to   B. for   C. by

3. What factor influenced you the most ____ applying to this university?

   A. for   B. to   C. when

4. What features _____ this university are most attractive to you?

   A. by   B. of   C. for

5. What ____ this institution attracts you the most for graduate study?

   A. in   B. on   C. to

6. What about the university is pleasing _____ you?

   A. of   B. to   C. for

7. What university's graduate program _____ consistently ranked high nationally?

A. has B.did C. have

8. What university has a highly qualified and experienced faculty with frequent publications _____ prestigious journals?

A. on B. in C. with

9. What university _____ seemingly unlimited academic resources?

A. have B. is C. has

Exercise 31

Asking academic questions, beginning with "Why", on why an

institution was selected for advanced study

學術方面問題／解釋選擇該校原由

1. Why do you want to apply to the Department of Information Science _____ MIT?

   A. of B. at C. in

2. Why did your professor recommend Indiana University _____ doctorate studies?

   A. in B. of C. for

3. Why is applying _____ this university a logical choice for you?

   A. in B. with C. to

4. Why are you drawn _____ the university's graduate program in Food Science?

   A. to B. on C. with

5. Why do you believe that you can contribute to the rich pool _____ talented

   individuals at this university?

   A. of B. with C. for

6. Why are you convinced that this university is the one that you are looking _____ ?

   A. at B. for C. from

7. Why _____ the university's graduate program consistently rank high nationally?

   A. does　B.　is　C. has

8. Why do you feel that you can easily adjust _____ undergraduate life at this university?

   A. of　B. for　C. to

9. Why does this university draw a diverse student body _____ many countries?

   A. at　B. from　C. in

Exercise 32

Asking academic questions, beginning with "Which", on why an

institution was selected for advanced study

學術方面問題／解釋選擇該校原由

1. Which university has significantly contributed _____ the development of
computer science?

   A. for B. in C. to

2. Which university program prepares _____ graduates to rise to the challenges of a
career in Biotechnology?

   A. their B. its C. his

3. Which factor influenced you the _____ in your decision to attend this university?

   A. best B. good C. most

4. Which department _____ National Tsing Hua University do you want to pursue a
bachelor's degree in Food Science?

   A. for B. at C. in

5. Which university do you intend _____ apply to so that you can pursue a Bachelor's
degree in computer science?

   A. for B. in C. to

6. Which field of research are you interested in _____ your graduate studies?

A. at B. for C. with

7. Which university offers what you are looking _____ in a Bachelor's degree program in Food Science?

A. for B. at C. to

8. Which graduate program in Nursing _____ you most interested in?

A. have B. are C. has

9. Which country plays a dominant role _____ developing finance-related theories and applications?

A. in B. of C. in

Exercise 33

Asking academic questions that are answered with a "Yes" or

"No" reply, when recommending a student for study (Part A):

Introduction and qualification to make recommendation

學術方面問題／撰寫推薦信函（A部分）

推薦信函開始及推薦人的資格

1. Is Professor Chang the chairperson _____ the Ecology Department at National Tsing Hua University?

    A. for B. in C. of

2. Is Professor Smith qualified to recommend you _____ graduate study in Nursing?

    A. on B. to C. for

3. Has Professor Chang _____ the opportunity to observe you closely during your undergraduate studies in Medical Technology?

    A. have B. had C. did

4. Has Professor Chang _____ able to monitor your academic progress during university?

    A. be B. to C. been

5. Have you enrolled in several of Professor Chang's courses _____ the past four years?

A. over B. with C. by

6. Is Professor Chang impressed _____ your overall academic performance during university?

A. at B. for C. with

7. Is Professor Chang aware _____ the numerous departmental activities that you participated in during your undergraduate studies?

A. for B. of C. to

8. Is Professor Su aware of how you contributed to a group effort _____ completing an assigned project?

A. on B. during C. while

9. Is Professor Su aware of _____ you played an instrumental role in a group effort?

A. to B. what C. how

Exercise 34

Asking academic questions, beginning with "What", when recommending a student for study (Part A): Introduction and qualification to make recommendation

學術方面問題／撰寫推薦信函（A部分）推薦信函開始及推薦人

的資格

1. What progress did the team that you participated _____ make during Professor Chang's course of Biotechnology?

   A. from B. in C. by

2. What _____ you contribute to Professor Lin's Accounting Course?

   A. did B. was C. does

3. What insight did your team provide _____ Total Quality Management during Professor Su's class?

   A. from B. by C. into

4. What role did you play in the group effort that you participated _____ during Professor Su's class?

   A. over B. in C. to

5. What points did you stress _____ orally presenting your group's findings during

Professor Su's class?

A. for B. when   C. to

6. What role _____ you play in inspiring other students to participate more actively in Professor Su's Biotechnology course?

A. was B. were C. did

7. What work did you assign to other members _____ the group in which participated during Professor Su's course?

A. of B. with C. for

8. In what student organizations within your department _____ you serve as an officer?

A. was B. did C. were

9. What confidence does Professor Su _____ in your ability contribute to a group effort?

A. have B. had C. has

Exercise 35

Asking academic questions, beginning with "Where", when recommending a student for study (Part A): Introduction and qualification to make recommendation

學術方面問題／撰寫推薦信函（A部分）推薦信函開始及推薦人

的資格

1. Where did you first become acquainted _____ Professor Yu?

    A. by B. to C. with

2. Where _____ you enroll in Professor Chang's course in Global Economics?

    A. was B. did C. were

3. Where did you first learn _____ Global Economics?

    A. about B. in C. to

4. Where is Professor Su the chairperson _____ the Finance Department?

    A. in B. on C. of

5. Where _____ Professor Su chair the Technical Management program?

    A. do B. does C. is

6. Where does Professor Yu believe that you can meet the academic requirements

_____ its Master's degree program in Strategic Management?

A. of B. to C. by

7. Where was Professor Chang able _____ monitor your academic progress at university?

A. in B. for C. to

8. Where did Professor Su become aware of how your ability to contribute to a group effort _____ completing an assigned project?

A. on B. during C. while

9. Where _____ Professor Su become aware of your ability to play an instrumental role in a group effort while completing an assigned project?

A. how B. was C. did

Exercise 36

Asking academic questions, beginning with "How", when recommending a student for study (Part A): Introduction and qualification to make recommendation

學術方面問題／撰寫推薦信函（A部分）推薦信函開始及推薦人

的資格

1. How _____ Professor Smith qualified to recommend you for graduate study in
   Nursing?
   A. are B. is C. does

2. How did Professor Chang _____ the opportunity to observe you closely during
   your undergraduate studies in Medical Technology?
   A. do B. has C. have

3. How did Professor Chang _____ impressed with your overall academic
   performance during university?
   A. be B. become C. has

4. How _____ you contribute to Professor Wei's courses, Introduction to Art and
   Art Theory?
   A. was B. were C. did

5. How did you inspire other students to participate more actively _____ Professor

Wei's courses of Art and Art Theory?

A. to B. in C. on

6. How _____ you assign work to other team members in the group effort in which you participated during Professor Su's course?

A. did B. were C. was

7. How did Professor Chang become aware of the numerous departmental activities that you participated _____ during your undergraduate studies?

A. to B. in C. of

8. How did Professor Su become aware of your contribution _____ a group effort when completing an assigned project?

A. to B. of C. for

9. How did Professor Su become confident in your ability _____ contribute to a group effort??

A. on B. to C. for

Exercise 37

Asking academic questions, beginning with "What", when recommending a student for study (Part B): Personal qualities of the candidate that are relevant to Graduate Study, and Closing

學術方面問題 /撰寫推薦信函 (B 部分) 被推薦人與進階學習有關的個人特質及信函結尾

1. What did you often serve _____ in Professor Li's research group?
   A. by B. at C. as

2. What role did you play _____ the weekly group meetings held in Professor Lin's laboratory?
   A. to B. in C. with

3. What does Professor Li largely attribute the team's excellent performance _____?
   A. by B. to C. in

4. What about you never ceased _____ amaze Professor Li?
   A. to B. for C. in

5. What impression does Professor Li have _____ the way in which you interacted with other group members?
   A. as B. to C. of

6. What does Professor Li believe that you appear to _____ learned?

　A. did　B. has　C. have

7. What about you does Professor Li believe will be a great asset to any future research effort to _____ you belong?

　A. which　B. that　C. in

8. What impression did you make _____ Professor Li with respect to your ability to successfully complete your graduate studies?

　A. for　B. in　C. on

Exercise 38

Asking academic questions, beginning with "Why", when recommending a student for study (Part B): Personal qualities of the candidate that are relevant to Graduate Study, and Closing

學術方面問題／撰寫推薦信函（B 部分）被推薦人與進階學習有關的個人特質及信函結尾

1. Why does Professor Lin believe that the opportunity to pursue advanced study _____ MIT's graduate program will benefit you?

   A. at   B. in   C. for

2. Why does Professor Lin believe you have selected nursing as your career _____ choice?

   A. with   B. for   C. of

3. Why is Professor Lin confident _____ your ability to conduct independent research?

   A. for   B. of   C. in

4. Why does Professor not hesitate to recommend you _____ admission into MIT's graduate program?

   A. for   B. at   C. with

5. Why does Professor Lin believe _____ your analytical skills are exemplary?

   A. for   B. which   C. that

6. Why _____ Professor Li encourage the admissions committee to contact her?

   A. does   B. is   C. has

7. Why _____ you never ceased to amaze Professor Li?

   A. do   B. have   C. had

8. Why have you left such a deep impression _____ Professor Li?

   A. on   B. for   C. in

9. Why _____ Professor Lin believe that you are a highly promising candidate for graduate study?

   A. is   B. does   C. do

Exercise 39

Asking academic questions, beginning with "How", when

recommending a student for study (Part B): Personal qualities of

the candidate that are relevant to Graduate Study, and Closing

學術方面問題 /撰寫推薦信函 (B 部分) 被推薦人與進階學習有

關的個人特質及信函結尾

1. How _____ you proven that you are an optimistic individual?
   A. do   B. have   C. has

2. How did you actively participate in weekly group meetings _____ involve journal
   discussions and oral reports?
   A. that   B. which   C. did

3. How do you react _____ a bottleneck in your research?
   A. to   B. for   C. when

4. How _____ you displayed your determination to pursue a career in Finance?
   A. have   B. do   C. was

5. How _____ you contribute to Professor Smith's research group?
   A. are   B. were   C. did

6. How did you encourage other research collaborators to participate fully _____ related projects?

A. at   B. in   C. for

7. How did you actively participate in weekly group meetings _____ involved journal discussions and oral reports?

A. that   B. which   C. did

8. How _____ you leave such a deep impression on Professor Li with respect to your research capabilities?

A. were   B. did   C. was

9. How do you intend _____ convince the admissions committee at MIT to accept you into the graduate school program in Nursing?

A. to   B. with   C. for

Exercise 40

Asking academic questions, beginning with "Which", when recommending a student for study (Part B): Personal qualities of the candidate that are relevant to Graduate Study and Closing

學術方面問題 /撰寫推薦信函 (B 部分) 被推薦人與進階學習有

關的個人特質及信函結尾

1. Which renowned program at Harvard University are you applying _____?
   A. in B. to C. at

2. Which trait do you think is important _____ conducting graduate level research?
   A. for B. to C. as

3. Which topic did you seek Professor Li's advice _____ in your research project?
   A. by B. to C. on

4. Which of your strengths _____ Professor Lin respect the most?
   A. do B. does C. is

5. Which graduate school program _____ Professor Li encouraged you to apply to?
   A. has B. did C. does

6. Which topics did you discuss in the weekly group meetings _____ Professor Li's

research group?

A. by　B. at　C. of

7. Which department have you worked _____ for the past five years?

A. in　B. to　C. at

8. Which of your skills _____ you think are the most exemplary?

A. are　B. does　C. do

9. Which tasks are you responsible _____ performing when conducting experiments?

A. on　B. to　C. for

Appendix B

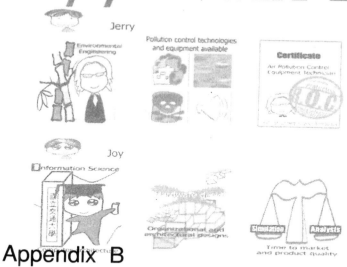

Appendix B

Useful phrases in an effective employment application statement

工作自傳的參考例句

· My fascination with computers explains why I completed my undergraduate studies in Information Science at National Tsing Hua University, one of Taiwan's premier institutes of higher learning.

· Offering a unique workplace in which I can put my academic skills into practice, your company can provide me an excellent opportunity to foster my professional skills.

· I believe that my solid academic foundation and advanced research expertise will prove invaluable to any project team to which I belong at your company.

· As an engineer in this intensely competitive hi-tech sector, I believe that I can contribute to your company's efforts to manufacture high quality telecommunication products.

· Despite my lack of professional experience, I believe that my solid academic background and knowledge base can contribute positively to your company.

· I knew that to prepare for employment in this highly competitive field, I should hone my research skills, which explains why I went on to complete a Master's degree in Biotechnology before entering the workforce.

· University sparked my fascination with multimedia applications, my desire to enter this exciting field and my eventual success in securing employment.

· The unique environment that your company offers would allow me to meet my own personal goals as well as contribute to society.

· I am interested in investigating topics related to this very important problem in the IC design field.

· I hope to contribute to advancing computer design and creating more flexible and advanced devices.

· Becoming a member of your corporate family would also allow me to apply my strong research fundamentals to this exciting industrial field of integrated circuit design.

· This advanced professional knowledge, in combination with my already strong research fundamentals, has equipped me to accept rigorous challenges in the workplace.

· Language training courses within the company allow me to communicate easily with others. I feel that I am heading in the right direction.

· Equipped with solid academic fundamentals and determined to enhance my professional knowledge of telecommunications, I later received a Master's degree in Electronic Engineering from National Chiao Tung University.

· Many research opportunities within this constantly evolving field have equipped me with advanced professional skills in telecommunications that have enabled me to rise to the challenges of a career within this industry.

· I firmly believe that my creativity and industrious attitude will prove invaluable to any collaborative effort to which I belong within your company.

· Employment at your company would enrich my theoretical knowledge obtained from university with the practical experience that your working environment would offer.

· Acquiring invaluable work experience at your company would be the most effective way for me to realize what this vibrant industry can offer.

· With my fascination with how integrated circuit technologies have dramatically impacted our lives, I believe that your company would provide the ideal working environment in which I can further pursue my professional interests.

· Graduate studies in this field, with a particular emphasis on computer-aided design, further strengthened my solid academic background.

· With its excellent design facilities and seemingly unlimited resources, your company provides a conducive working environment that would allow me to put my solid academic training into practice.

· I am confident of my ability to apply my practical laboratory experience from graduate school to the highly competitive working environment that your company offers.

· I believe that your company provides a unique working environment in which I can fully develop my professional interests.

· I believe that my solid background in knowledge management will prove to be a valuable asset to your company.

· Your company thrives among tough competition in the constantly changing computer technology field. This seemingly unlimited change would provide an exciting environment in which I can strive to advance my professional skills.

· My strong background in Electrical Engineering, with a particular focus on IC design, will not only be a valuable asset to your company's research and development team, but also allow me to develop professional skills in a leading multinational company.

· I believe that my solid academic background will compensate for my lack of professional experience, allowing me to contribute to your corporate family.

· As a proud member of this distinguished profession, I hope to contribute significantly to advancing computer design and creating more reliable devices.

· Upon completing my Master's degree, I hope to bring my solid academic skills in these areas to your company.

· I hope that employment at your company will allow me to realize more fully the practical applications of these important disciplines in the workplace.

· Eager to contribute to the strengthening of your company's organizational culture, I have been preparing for several years to enter the challenging semiconductor industry.

· I believe that employment at your renowned company will provide not only a dynamic environment in which I can apply my academic skills but also invaluable training to become an effective manager.

· Having developed an interest in this dynamic field, I look forward to joining your company so that I can more fully understand related industrial applications and become an accomplished engineer.

· I believe that your company would provide a unique environment in which I could build on a solid academic background to hone my professional skills.

· My evidenced commitment and solid academic foundation in this area would prove to be an invaluable asset for projects within your company.

· I firmly believe that the research fundamentals acquired during graduate school will give me a competitive edge in the workplace, hopefully at your company.

· I am especially interested in improving control charts, an area in which I hope to gain expertise at your company.

· Your company has committed itself to the highest ideals of adhering to state-of-the-art practices within the industrial engineering profession. I believe that my solid academic training and professional experiences will allow me to meet these high expectations held by your corporate family.

· Your company has undertaken many successful collaborative ventures between Taiwanese and Chinese engineering firms, explaining why my interest in this area and engineering background are in line with the direction that your company is taking.

· Your consulting firm, a leader in this emerging technology field, would provide me with a marvelous opportunity to add to my previous experience in conducting related research.

· Employment at your company would allow me to supplement my theoretical knowledge obtained at university with experience of actual cases.

· This fact explains why I have decided to devote myself to a career in tackling the immense water resource-related problems in Taiwan.

· Your strong technical and market positions explain why I want to join your corporate family.

· As a leader in this area of technology development, your company has distinguished itself in its commitment to in-house research projects, which match my professional interests, as evidenced by your commitment to excellence in product innovation.

· I believe that your company would provide an environment to allow me to pursue my professional interests, regardless of the challenges they involve.

· Your company's commitment to product excellence explains why I am eager to join your organization.

· Your company offers a competitive work environment and is home to highly skilled professionals: these ingredients are essential to my continually upgrading my knowledge, skills and expertise in the above area.

· In this area of development, your company offers an excellent research environment and abundant academic resources that will enhance my research capabilities and equip me with the competence to fully realize fully my career aspirations.

· Your firm has spent considerable resources in orienting local companies for the challenges of the international marketplace.

· I believe that my solid academic background will prove invaluable to your efforts to expand your current services.

· I am absolutely confident that my academic background, experimental and work experience in information science, desire for knowledge and love of challenges will enable me to succeed in your company's highly demanding product development projects.

· I am encouraged that your company has also devoted considerable resources to this area of research.

· The fact that your organization has exerted considerable effort in this area of research largely explains why I am eager to join your corporate family.

· Your company's success in the area of product development explains why I would like to join the research team at your company.

· My collaboration in a team enhanced my communication skills and the research effort fostered my analytical and experimentation skills.

· This solid academic training challenged me to view bottlenecks in research as challenges rather than setbacks, thus increasing my patience and perseverance in future investigations.

· These courses provided a detailed theoretical understanding that has further enriched my academic background.

· Participation in several domestic and international conferences has enhanced my ability to present orally my research findings.

· I believe that the above experiences will prove invaluable to any research team to which I belong within your organization.

· These experiences reinforced my belief that success is only fully realized through a diligent and persevering attitude towards life's challenges.

· The training and skills I acquired in experimental design and data analysis will make me a valuable member of any research team to which I belong in your company.

· Although occasionally frustrated by a bottleneck in a project I'm working on, I view such obstacles as stimuli for striving harder. I believe that your company adopts the same attitude in developing construction technologies, as I have often heard through other companies in the field.

· After careful consideration, I feel that I would adjust well to the competitive working environment that your company offers.

- My undergraduate experiences have provided a solid academic foundation on which employment at your company would allow me to further develop my laboratory and professional skills.

- My research results have received considerable praise, as evidenced by my participation in several conferences and publications in related journals.

- I adjust well to intensely competitive working environments and totally immerse myself in new challenges within the construction field. I believe my intellect and determination will prove invaluable in your company's challenging work environment.

- My responsible attitude towards my job will prove an invaluable asset to your company.

- This unique leadership opportunity not only enhanced my ability to integrate different activities into a single concerted effort, but also provided a more thorough understanding of hydraulic engineering developments in Taiwan.

- I believe that you will find this mixture of solid academic training and advanced professional knowledge gained through graduate school to be an asset to your company.

- My advanced research capabilities will become more refined with professional work experience at your company.

- These activities fostered my collaborative, coordinating, organizational and communicative skills. I believe that such experiences will greatly facilitate my work performance, hopefully at your company.

· Similarly, in my job, I face daily challenges that enable me to adopt the skills gained in the university debating club to assess situations rationally and make right decisions.

· The peer group heightened my sensitivity to those around me and greatly improved my communication skills.

· I actively coordinated a diverse spectrum of academic activities, which enhanced my communication and collaborative skills and revealed the inner workings of an organization.

Answer Key

解　答

Answer Key
Expressing interest in a profession
表達工作相關興趣

A.

Situation 1

A solid background in quality control, financial analysis, and industrial management at National Chiao Tung University explains Bob's determination to become a successful manager. During graduate school, he participated in many collaborative projects that involved industrial organizations such as ITRI, AMAT and Chailease Finance. This invaluable exposure made ABC Corporation a logical choice for his first employment upon graduation, owing to its active role among global enterprises. Eager to contribute to the strengthening of ABC's organizational culture, Bob has been preparing for several years to enter the challenging semiconductor industry. As is well known, the intensely competitive global market is driven by customers who demand the highest quality products. With this in mind, Bob believes that ABC company will provide him not only with a dynamic environment in which to apply his academic skills but also invaluable training to become an effective manager.

Situation 2

As well as being intrigued by ancient and other cultures, Allen is especially fascinated by the richness and color of human relationships. This fact explains why he completed a Master's degree in Social Anthropology from National Tsing Hua University. With the advent of the new knowledge economy, humans and their knowledge (rather than pure capital) profoundly determine an enterprise's success. Skilled manpower is essential and Human Resources Management aims to retain employees at a company and effectively manage the knowledge that they create. Although different disciplines, Human Resources Management and Anthropology both focus on humans and culture. The latter adopts a global perspective and aims to integrate other societal viewpoints. Striving to understand human relationships, Allen is also interested in adopting different strategies and problem-solving measures to stimulate creativity and increase work productivity.

However, management theory and practices differ from anthropological ones. Notable examples include MBA theory and strategy, salary structure design and performance management, intellectual property law and employee law, organizational culture and leadership, and employer-employee relationships.

If able to secure employment at the Human Resources Department of National Central University, Allen believes that he will significantly contribute to related areas such as salary structure design, performance management, intellectual property law, organizational culture, leadership and employer-employee relationships.

Situation 3

Computers, telecommunications and related consumer products have markedly elevated living standards for quite some time. While some products entertain and offer convenience as well as comfort, others save time and reduce workload. Such diversified products have intrigued Tom since high school. This fascination explains why he completed his undergraduate studies in Electrical Engineering at National Tsing Hua University, one of Taiwan's premier institutes of higher learning. He also took a Master's degree in the same field from this university to acquire advanced academic training. While offering a unique workplace environment to put his academic skills into practice, DEF Corporation, a leading core logic and graphics supplier, can provide an excellent opportunity to foster his professional skills. Tom believes that his solid academic foundation and advanced research expertise will prove invaluable for any project team in which he is involved at DEF Corporation.

B.

These are only possible questions.

Answer Key
Expressing interest in a profession
表達工作相關興趣

What

What has Bob been preparing for several years to do?
Enter the challenging semiconductor industry

What is Allen especially fascinated by?
The richness and color of human relationships.

What does DEF Corporation offer Tom?
A unique workplace environment in which to put his academic skills into practice

What does Bob believe drives the intensely competitive global market?
Customers who demand the highest quality products

What are you determined to become professionally?
At what department at National Central University do you hope to secure employment?
What have you been preparing for several years to do?
What are you especially fascinated by?
What does DEF Corporation offer you?
What do you believe drives the intensely competitive global market?
What sort of background did your undergraduate studies in Electrical Engineering at National Chiao Tung University provide you with?
What company will offer invaluable training for you to become an effective manager?
What collaborative projects with industry did you participate in during your

graduate studies?

C.

These are only possible questions.

Which

Which industrial organizations were involved in the many collaborative projects
that Bob participated in during graduate school?
ITRI, AMAT and Chailease Finance

At which company is Tom seeking employment?
DEF Corporation

Which consumer products have markedly elevated living standards for quite
some time?
Computers, telecommunication products and related products

At which university did Allen receive a Master's degree in Social Anthropology?
National Tsing Hua University
Which organization is a leading supplier of pharmaceutical drugs and hospital
products?
Which industry have you been preparing to enter for several years?
Which industrial organizations were involved in the many collaborative projects
that you participated in during graduate school?
At which company are you seeking employment?
From which university did you receive a Master's degree in Social
Anthropology?

At which department at National Central University did you hope to secure employment?

Which line of work do you hope to find after completing your bachelor's degree?

Which strategies and problem-solving measures do you hope to adopt to stimulate creativity and increase work productivity?

Which profession are you interested in entering after you complete your undergraduate studies?

D.

These are only possible questions.

Why

Why did Bob complete a Master's degree in Social Anthropology from National Tsing Hua University?

Because he is intrigued by ancient and other cultures, and is especially fascinated by the richness and color of human relationships.

Why does Tom believe that he will be invaluable for any project team in which he is involved at DEF Corporation.

Because of his solid academic foundation and advanced research expertise

Why is Allen interested in adopting different strategies and problem-solving measures? To stimulate creativity and increase work productivity

Why is Bob determined to become a successful manager?

Because of his solid background in quality control, financial analysis, and industrial management at National Chiao Tung University

Why do you consider ABC Corporation to be a logical choice for your first employment upon graduation?

Why did you take a Master's degree in Electrical Engineering from National Tsing Hua University?

Why did you complete a Master's degree in Social Anthropology at National Tsing Hua University?

Why do you believe that you will be invaluable for any project team in which you are involved at DEF Corporation ?

Why are you interested in adopting different strategies and problem-solving measures?

Why do you believe that DEF Corporation offers a unique workplace in which to put your academic skills into practice?

Why have you decided to enter the biotechnology profession after completing your Bachelor's degree?

Why have you chosen DEF Corporation for employment in the biotech industry?

Why are you impressed by DEF Corporation's line of products and services?

E.

1. What is National Tsing Hua University?

2. What is Bob determined to become?

3. What is Bob striving to understand?

H.

1. C 2. B 3. A 4. B 5. C 6. B 7. A 8. B 9. C 10. B 11. B 12. C 13. A 14. C

15. B

I.

1. B 2. A 3. C 4. B 5. A 6. A 7. B 8. C 9. B 10. A 11. C 12. B 13. C 14. C

15. A 16. B 17. A 18. C 19. B 20. C 21. A 22. C 23. A 24. C 25. B 26. C

27. B

Answer Key
Describing the field or industry to which one's profession belongs
興趣相關產業描寫

A

Situation 1

With its recent entry into the World Trade Organization, Taiwan will encounter intense competition from global financial markets and must accelerate deregulation and globalization. As widely anticipated, the liberalization of interest rate derivatives, options, swaps, mortgage securities, and currency derivatives will occur in the near future. Developing expert capabilities in such areas is essential to match the rapid changes and innovation in Taiwan's financial market. Financial Engineering, an emerging field in Finance, addresses such issues and is the center of Matt's interest in joining ABC Company, which has actively implemented related practices.

Situation 2

Taiwan's electronics industry was not, until only a decade ago, globally competitive. Before that time, most corporations were not very profitable since they focused on assembling product components, while overseas firms dominated the manufacturing of vital components such as the CPU and the chipset. Taiwan's government then devoted itself to developing the electronics industry so that many Taiwanese corporations can now design complex chips. This ability has allowed local firms to generate considerable product revenues and capture a sizable share of the global market. An increasing number of Taiwanese companies have extended their product lines to telecommunications, especially wireless communications. Such products are widely anticipated to have a high added value in the near future. These exciting trends in the telecommunications industry in Taiwan have largely determined Jack's decision to undertake IC design research in telecommunications. Jack feels confident that he is moving in the right direction.

Situation 3

Computer applications have exploded with the emergence of computer graphics displays. Such displays allow users to present not only numbers and text, but also pictures and graphs that illustrate the implications of related figures. Doing so greatly adds to the quality of text material. Widely anticipated to become a consumer electronics product commonly found in households, the personal computer will be able to integrate graphics, audio and video features. Nevertheless, technological advances in semiconductor manufacturing technology have enabled the embedding of a graphics accelerator within the chipset (core-logic) into an integrated chip. Multimedia processes are directly sent to the integrated chip, reducing the overload of the processing recourse in the CPU. ABC Corporation, a leading core logic and graphic chips supplier, has positioned itself to be a leading manufacturer of system-on-a-chip (SoC). ABC's commitment to product excellence explains why Amy is eager to join the corporate family.

B.

These are only possible questions.

Which company has actively implemented environmentally friendly practices?

Which organization has Taiwan entered recently?

Which industry in Taiwan has rapidly expanded in recent years?

Which company are you interested in joining?

Which industry does your profession belong to?

Which country will encounter intense competition from global financial markets?

Which issues would you be interested in addressing if you are employed at DEF Corporation?

Which organization has Taiwan entered recently?

337

Which industry in Taiwan has rapidly expanded in recent years?

Which technologies are increasingly used in Taiwan's semiconductor industry?

Which areas of new development is Taiwan undergoing?

C.

These are only possible questions.

What are some of Taiwan's globally competitive industries?

What decisions have you made about your career direction?

What technological capabilities have Taiwanese companies developed in recent years?

What are you confident of?

What are some of the latest technological developments in your field?

What have an increasing number of Taiwanese companies extended their product lines to?

What are some of the exciting trends in the biotechnology industry in Taiwan?

What new biotechnology products are widely anticipated to be available in the near future?

What are some of Taiwan's globally competitive industries?

What decisions have you made concerning your career direction?

What technological capabilities have Taiwanese companies developed in recent years?

What companies have captured a sizable share of the global market?

D.

These are only possible questions.

Why are you eager to join ABC's corporate family?

Why are you so determined to succeed in the health care management field?

Why have you decided to enter the nursing profession?

Why is Taiwan's biotech industry increasingly competitive globally?

Why are an increasing number of multinational corporations investing in Taiwan's biotech industry?

Why are you confident of your ability to succeed in the highly competitive biotech industry?

Why has DEF Corporation positioned itself to be a leading manufacturing of semiconductor products?

Why does DEF Corporation's product have a wide consumer appeal to young people?

Why has Taiwan's biotech industry expanded rapidly in recent years?

E.

1. Why is Amy eager to join the corporate family?
2. Where does Jack feel confident that he is moving?
3. What will the personal computer be able to integrate in the future?

H.

1. B 2. B 3. B 4. A 5. C 6. B 7. B 8. A 9. C 10. B 11. B 12. C 13. C
14. A 15. B

I.

1. B 2. A 3. B 4. B 5. C 6. A 7. B 8. C 9. B 10. A 11. B 12. A
13. C 14. B 15. B 16. A 17. C 18. B 19. C 20. B 21. A 22. B 23. B
24. A 25. C 26. A 27. B

Unit Three

Answer Key
Describing participation in a project that reflects interest in a profession
描述所參與方案裡專業興趣的表現

A.

Situation 1

While working on his Bachelors degree in Chemistry from National Tsing Hua University, Sam developed a love for laboratory work and a strong interest in quality control. At his work in the Quality Assurance Department of ABC company, he focuses on statistical process control (SPC) and measurement systems analysis (MSA), and occasionally performs MASK inspection. As well known, an unstable or inaccurate measurement system causes errors in process control and judgment. Sam is especially concerned with determining whether a measurement system is stable, ensuring repeatability, reproducibility and matching of a measurement system, and criteria for assessment.

Situation 2

Electrical engineering has fascinated Mary from an early age, and she has taken related courses since university. Having nearly completed a Master's degree in Electronics Engineering from National Chiao Tung University, her research focuses on discrete signal process, digital control and VLSI. Graduate school has taught her innovative ways of solving problems logically and independently. With her strong interest in the impact on our lives by integrated circuit technologies, Mary believes that GHI Corporation would provide the ideal working environment for her to further pursue her professional interests. Becoming a member of the GHI family would also allow her to apply her strong research fundamentals to this exciting industrial field of integrated circuit design.

Situation 3

John has long been intrigued by science and technology. This interest culminated in his successful completion of a Master's degree in Electrical Engineering from

National Taiwan University, one of Taiwan's renowned universities. He then entered the hi-tech IC design industry, with a particular interest in logic design, communications and computer networks. While at graduate school, John was involved in a project in which he simulated an Ethernet protocol. His first assignment at JKL Corporation was to develop an Ethernet MAC controller. He is now developing a Serial ATA controller, a computer network product. John is glad that he has been able to apply his practical laboratory experience from graduate school to the highly competitive working environment that JKL Corporation offers.

B.

These are only possible questions.

What did you develop a love for while at National Tsing Hua University?

What major projects have you participated in as an engineer?

What specific tasks have you performed while conducting laboratory experiments?

What do you feel that your personal strengths are when participating in a project?

What do you feel that your personal limitations are when participating in a project?

What research skills would you like to develop further if you gain employment at DEF Corporation?

What experience do you have in participating in biotechnology projects?

What are you especially concerned with when participating in biotechnology projects?

What have you developed a strong interest in while participating in biotechnology projects?

C.

These are only possible questions.

How will you be able to apply the strong research fundamentals taught at National Chiao Tung University?

How did you become involved in this project?

How did you develop your interest in electrical engineering?

How did you become fascinated by biotechnology-related topics?

How did you learn innovative ways of solving problems logically and independently?

How has computer technology impacted our daily lives?

How can GHI Corporation provide the ideal working environment for you to further pursue your professional interests?

How much longer do you have to complete a Master's degree in Health Care Management?

How long has it been since you received your Bachelor's degree in Nursing?

D.

These are only possible questions.

Why have you long been intrigued by science and technology?

Why did you enter the hi-tech IC design industry to pursue a career as an engineer?

Why does your company offer such a highly competitive work environment?

Why did you develop a love for nursing while at university?

Why is your personality conducive to stressful work situations?

Why did you become involved in this project?

Why did you first become interested in participating in health care management?

E.

1. What was John's first assignment at JKL Corporation?

2. What does Mary believe that GHI Corporation would provide?

3. What was John particularly interested in when he entered the hi-tech IC design industry?

H.

1. B 2. C 3. C 4. A 5. C 6. B 7. C 8. B 9. A 10. B 11. C 12. B 13. A 14. B 15. A 16. C

I

1. B 2. C 3. A 4. B 5. B 6. A 7. C 8. A 9. B 10. A 11. B 12. A 13. B 14. C 15. A 16. A 17. C 18. A 19. C 20. B 21. A 22. C 23. B 24. A 25. C 26. B

Answer Key
Describing academic background and achievements relevant to employment
描述學歷背景及已獲成就

A.

Situation 1

Desiring to strengthen his theoretical and professional knowledge, Jerry acquired a Master's degree in Environmental Engineering from National Chiao Tung University. Following graduation, he worked in a consulting firm and participated in several projects. This work experience exposed him to a wide array of pollution control technologies and equipment. As evidence of his desire to continually improve his research skills, Jerry received certification as an "Air Pollution Control Equipment Technician" from the R.O.C. Environmental Protection Administration, following an intensive training course. The course addressed the formation and prevention of air pollutants and taught him training skills that will make him a valuable member of any research team, hopefully at ABC Company.

Situation 2

Joy received a Master's degree in Information Science from National Chiao Tung University, with a specialization in computer architecture. Despite her academic training, Joy is not particularly interested in hardware design. Instead, she prefers to create organizational and architectural designs and then write programs to simulate their effectiveness. She then proceeds to analyze the simulation results and modify the design to improve performance. IC design houses increasingly emphasize time to market for products to increase profits. However, in light of such requirements, implementing and optimizing the hardware are extremely difficult. Therefore, simulation and analysis are necessary to balance time to market with product quality. Joy is especially interested in this area of research.

Situation 3

Max received a Master's degree in Electronic Engineering from one of Taiwan's premier universities, National Taiwan University, in 1994. By providing him with a solid background in computer science, the departmental curricula allowed Max to absorb fundamental knowledge while obtaining practical laboratory experiences. At graduate school, he participated in a National Science Council-sponsored research project, aimed at developing a wireless Local Area Network. In addition to enhancing Max's communication skills by collaborating in a team, the research effort fostered his analytical and experimentation skills. This solid academic training challenged him to view bottlenecks in research as challenges rather than setbacks, thus increasing his patience and perseverance. Max believes that his solid academic training will give him a competitive edge in the workplace, hopefully at ABC Company.

B.

These are only possible answers.

At what university did you acquire a Master's degree in Environmental Engineering?

What motivated your desire to strengthen your theoretical and professional knowledge of Food Science?

What capacity did you work in at the consulting firm following the completion of your graduate studies?

What practical work experiences did you acquire at university?

What training do you hope to receive in the company at which you are seeking employment?

What have you done to enhance your research skills?

What projects did you actively engage in following the completion of your graduate studies?

What did your graduate school research focus on while you pursued a Ph.D. in

Computer Science?

What did you receive certification in while working in the semiconductor company?

C.

These are only possible questions.

Where did you receive a Master's degree in Information Science?

Where did you acquire specialized training in Radiology?

Where would you prefer to work in the electronics industry after completion of your graduate studies?

Where did you first work after acquiring a Bachelor's degree in Nursing at Yuan Pei University of Science and Technology?

Where did you receive a solid academic background in Nursing?

Where would you like to pursue a Master's degree if the opportunity arises?

Where did you gain a radiology certification?

Where did you receive your nursing training?

Where did you become familiar with the latest trends in biotechnology?

D.

These are only possible questions.

Which National Science Council-sponsored research projects did you participate in while pursuing a Master's degree in Food Science?

Which courses did you audit at university?

Which topic did you research during your postdoctorate work?

Which challenges did you encounter during your graduate school research?

Which skills were you able to enhance while collaborating with others in a research group?

Which of your personal strengths enabled you to get along with others in the research group?

Which qualities do you think are essential for a nursing professional to advance in a highly competitive environment?

Which of your achievements during university are you the most proud of?

Which setbacks did you encounter during your research, but were able to overcome eventually?

E.

What did the National Science Council-sponsored research project that Max participate in during graduate school focus on?
Developing a wireless Local Area Network

How does Max view bottlenecks in research?
As challenges rather than setbacks

What did the work experience that Jerry gained in a consulting firm expose him to?
A wide array of pollution control technologies and equipment

H.

1. B 2. C 3. B 4. A 5. C 6. C 7. B 8. A 9. B 10. C 11. B 12. C
13. A 14. B 15. C

I

1. A 2. C 3. B 4. B 5. A 6. B 7. C 8. B 9. C 10. C 11. B 12. A 13. A 14. B
15. B 16. A 17. C 18. B 19. A 20. B 21. A 22. B 23. C 24. B 25. C 26. A
27. B

Answer Key
Introducing research and professional experiences relevant to employment
介紹研究及工作經驗

A

Situation 1

Bill's studies at the Institute of Electronics Engineering at National Cheng Kung University provided him with a solid background knowledge of telecommunications and signal processing, as well as the desire to become a designer in this exciting field. After receiving his Master's degree and completing Taiwan's compulsory military service of nearly two years, he joined ABC Corporation to undertake signal processing-related research. Collaborative teamwork at ABC Corporation has stressed close cooperation among colleagues and minimization of design complexity, ultimately lowering product cost. Bill has excelled in logic design-related systems, such as Modelsim, Debussy, Mat lab and HDL. Moreover, his experience has sharpened his ability to analyze the merits and limitations of these methods, think logically, collect related information, and meet customer specifications, while using minimal resources. Bill is determined to devote himself to a career in telecommunications-related research so that he can continually refine the professional skills required to thrive in this highly competitive environment.

Situation 2

. During his six years as an engineer, Benson has actively engaged in several large public engineering projects, such as the Taiwan High Speed Railway, the Taipei Rapid Transit System, and National Highway Projects. Owing to the increasing governmental deficit and the trend to finance large public engineering construction projects, he has learned how to evaluate a project's financial plan. Given his strong analytical skills, Benson has focused on financial topics related to engineering, such as derivative pricing, fitting yield curves, and innovative financial product design.

Situation 3

As a statistician in the Sanitary and Health Care Center at Feng Chia University for two years and at the Industrial Technology Research Institute (ITRI) for the past six months, Harry has acquired much professional, hands-on knowledge of data analysis that has prepared him for a career in health-related research and knowledge management, on an international level. Collaborating with several companies on numerous projects, he has learned much about project management, leadership development and customer relations. During that period, he also audited courses in relevant areas, such as Financial Investment, Reliability Engineering and Human Relations. Harry's ability to develop knowledge-related skills and then apply them to management in a technological setting would make him invaluable as an engineer at ABC Company.

B.

These are only possible questions.

Why are you determined to devote yourself to a career in telecommunications-related research?

Why did you decide to work in the medical profession as a radiology technician?

Why did the Institute of Communications Engineering at National Chiao Tung University provide you with a solid background knowledge of telecommunications and signal processing?

Why did you join ABC Corporation after completing Taiwan's compulsory military service of nearly two years?

Why did the company that you worked for stress close cooperation among colleagues?

Why do you believe that you can thrive in the highly competitive environment of the semiconductor industry?

351

Why are you able to analyze the merits and limitations of conventional methods when selecting the most appropriate one?

Why are you able to still think logically in stressful work situations?

Why did the company that you worked for require that you collect marketing information and try your best to meet customer specifications?

C.

These are only possible questions.

How were you able to cope with the stress of working in the intensively competitive environment of your previous employment?

How did you learn from your previous work to evaluate a project's financial plan?

How did you actively engage in the projects that you participated in while working for an electronics company?

How were you able to strengthen your analytical skills in the company that you worked for?

How did you develop your interest in designing semiconductor products while working at DEF Corporation?

How did you become so determined to devote yourself to a career in nursing?

How were you able to secure a good position within the company in such a relatively short time?

How did you first learn of the company for which you are seeking employment?

How were you able to continually refine your professional skills in the company where you worked previously?

D.

These are only possible questions.

What important lessons have you learned while collaborating with several companies on numerous projects?

What university courses did you audit after work?

What position did you hold in the Sanitary and Health Care Center of Feng Chia University?

What company have you been working at for the past six months?

What career has your professional, hands-on knowledge of nursing prepared you for?

What have you learned about good customer relations in the healthcare management industry?

What expertise do you have in managing biotechnology projects?

E.

1. What are some of the financial topics related to engineering that Benson has focused on?

   Derivative pricing, fitting yield curves and innovative financial product design

2. What are some of the logic design-related systems that Bill has excelled in?

   Modelsim, Debussy, Matlab and HDL

3. Why has Benson learned how to evaluate a project's financial plan?

   Owing to the increasing governmental deficit and the trend to finance large public engineering construction projects

Answer Key
Introducing research and professional experiences relevant to employment
介紹研究及工作經驗

H.

1. B 2. A 3. A 4. B 5. C 6. C 7. C 8. A 9. C 10. B 11. B 12. C 13. A

14. B 15. C

I.

1. C 2. A 3. B 4. C 5. B 6. A 7. B 8. B 9. A 10. B 11. C 12. C 13. B

14. C 15. B 16. A 17. B 18. C 19. C 20. A 21. B 22. C 23. A 24. C

25. A 26. C

Answer Key
Describing extracurricular activities relevant to employment
描述與求職相關的課外活動

A.

Situation 1

While at National Taiwan University of Science and Technology, Alex served twice as a counselor in the Electrical Engineering Camp, which is sponsored by the Electrical Engineering Department. This camp helps high school students to grasp the basic concepts of Electrical Engineering and Electronics. Counselors thoroughly discuss the curriculum beforehand to arrange the details. Roundtable discussions held nightly during the camp address difficulties in instruction and review the following day's schedule. This activity developed Alex's collaborative, coordinating, organizational, and communicative skills. He believes that such experiences have greatly improved his work performance.

Situation 2

At university, Carey was involved with an environmental protection organization for which he attempted to understand how industry adversely impacts the environment, while considering industry to be an extension of science. This experience allowed him to develop a theoretical foundation to balance nature and science. Trying to grasp scientific knowledge in practical contexts is a good form of training. As well as broadening his horizons, these experiences gave Carey a framework for collaborating with others with various backgrounds, thus increasing his confidence in achieving goals by systematically applying knowledge and skills. Developing communication skills was one of the most rewarding experiences of his undergraduate years.

Situation 3

Realizing that the faculty and students of the Electrical Engineering Department should actively introduce its programs to recruit senior high school students, Jason worked with other classmates to organize an Electrical Engineering camp on the university campus. This camp informed students of the programs they can pursue after passing a rigorous nationwide entrance examination to enter the Department at National Cheng Kung University. In this camp, he was responsible for preparing curricula materials, teaching in the classroom, and helping students to complete experiments. He closely monitored the students and assisted them in finishing activities. These responsibilities enabled Jason to implement the knowledge that he had learned in the classroom and sharpen his presentation skills. Moreover, this experience strengthened and broadened his knowledge base, and further enhanced his ability to collaborate closely with peers. This unique opportunity proved to be one of the most rewarding experiences of Jason's undergraduate years.

B.

These are only possible questions.

What did you serve as in the Electrical Engineering Camp sponsored by your university department?

What extracurricular activities did you participate in during university?

What did the volunteer activities that you participated in during university help others to do?

What skills did you develop while participating in extracurricular activities at university?

What were some of your responsibilities in the extracurricular activities that you participated in during university?

What did you learn from your extracurricular activities during university that will be helpful in the future?

What personal traits did you realize that you have by participating in extracurricular activities during university?

What kind of relationships did you form in the extracurricular activities in which you participated during university?

C.

These are only possible questions.

Why did you become involved with an environmental protection organization in the university campus?

Why did you start participating in the student volunteer organization at your university?

Why did the extracurricular activities that you participated in during university heavily influence your decision to pursue a career in health care management

Why did your extracurricular activities during university strongly influence your interest in the nursing profession?

Why did you become involved in helping youth?

Why do you feel that participating in extracurricular activities is important?

Why did extracurricular activities make you aware of your social responsibilities?

Why do you feel that effective communications skills are essential in successful collaboration within a group?

D.

These are only possible questions.

Where did you volunteer your time in helping troubled youth?

Where did you become involved in helping youth?

Where did you acquire the unique leadership opportunity to help youth?

Where did you learn how to execute a comprehensive camp schedule when closely collaborating with others?

Where did you learn how to collaborate closely with others?

Where did you learn how to foster your communication skills?

Where did you come into contact with other youth volunteers?

Where did you learn how to develop your leadership skills?

E.

1.How did Jason's responsibilities in organizing an Electrical Engineering camp benefit him?

They helped him implement the knowledge that he had learned in the classroom and sharpen his presentation skills

2.What does Carey believe is a good form of training?

Trying to grasp scientific knowledge in practical contexts

3.What does Alex feel that his experiences as a counselor in the Electrical Engineering Camp greatly improved?

His work performance

H.

1. B 2. C 3. A 4. C 5. B 6. B 7. C 8. B 9. C 10. A 11. B 12. A 13. B
14. C 15. C

I.

1. B 2. C 3. A 4. A 5. C 6. C 7. B 8. A 9. C 10. A 11. C 12. A 13. B 14. A
15. A 16. B 17. C 18. B 19. C 20. A 21. B 22. C 23. A 24. B

Answer Key
Appendix A

Exercise 1
Answers

1. C 2. B 3. C 4. A 5. C 6. C 7. A 8. C 9. B 10. C

Exercise 2
Answers

1. B 2. C 3. B 4. C 5. A 6.C 7. B 8.C 9. C 10. A

Exercise 3
Answers

1. C 2. B 3. A 4. C 5. B 6. C 7. B 8. A 9. B 10. A

Exercise 4
Answers

1. B 2. C 3. A 4. C 5. B 6. C 7. A 8. C 9. B 10. C

Exercise 5
Answers

1. B 2. A 3. B 4. B 5. C 6. B 7. A 8. C 9. C

Exercise 6
Answers

1. C 2. A 3. C 4. A 5. B 6. C 7. B 8. A 9. C

Exercise 7
Answers

1. A 2. C 3. B 4. C 5. A 6. C 7. B 8. C 9. B

Exercise 8

Answers

1. A 2. C 3. B 4. B 5. C 6. A 7. B 8. C 9. B

Exercise 9

Answers

1. C 2. B 3. B 4. A 5. C 6. C 7. B 8. C 9. B 10. C

Exercise 10

Answers

1. B 2. A 3. B 4. C 5. B 6. C 7. B 8. C 9. B 10. C

Exercise 11

Answers

1. B 2. C 3. B 4. C 5. B 6. C 7. B 8. C 9. A

Exercise 12

Answers

1. B 2. A 3. C 4. A 5. B 6. C 7. A 8. C 9. B 10. A

Exercise 13

Answers

1. B 2. C 3. B 4. C 5. A 6. C 7. C 8. B 9. C

Exercise 14

Answers

1. C 2. A 3. C 4. B 5. C 6. B 7. A 8. C 9. B

Exercise 15

Answers

1. C 2. B 3. A 4. B 5. B 6. A 7. C 8. A 9. B 10. C

Exercise 16

Answers

1. B 2. C 3. A 4. B 5. C 6. C 7. C 8. B 9. A

Exercise 17

Answers

1. C 2. B 3. C 4. A 5. B 6. C 7. A 8. B 9. A 10. C

Exercise 18

Answers

1. B 2. C 3. A 4. B 5. C 6. B 7. C 8. B 9. C

Exercise 19

Answers

1. C 2. B 3. A 4. C 5. A 6. B 7. C 8. B 9. C

Exercise 20

Answers

1. B 2. A 3. B 4. C 5. B 6. A 7. C 8. A 9. B

Exercise 21

Answers

1. A 2. C 3. B 4. C 5. B 6. A 7. B 8. C 9. A

Exercise 22

Answers

1. C 2. A 3. B 4. C 5. B 6. A 7. C 8. B 9. A

Exercise 23

Answers

1. B 2. A 3. B 4. B 5. C 6. B 7. C 8. A 9. A

Exercise 24

Answers

1. B 2. C 3. B 4. A 5. B 6. C 7. A 8. B 9. A

Exercise 25

Answers

1. C 2. B 3. C 4. B 5. C 6. C 7. A 8. C 9. B

Exercise 26

Answers

1. B 2. B 3. C 4. B 5. C 6. A 7. B 8. A

Exercise 27

Answers

1. C 2. A 3. B 4. C 5. B 6. A 7. C 8. A

Exercise 28

Answers

1. C 2. A 3. C 4. A 5. B 6. C 7. A 8. B 9. B

Exercise 29

Answers

1. B 2. C 3. B 4. C 5. A 6. C 7. A 8. C 9. B

Exercise 30

Answers

1. B 2. A 3. C 4. B 5. A 6. B 7. A 8. B 9. C

Exercise 31

Answers

1. B 2. C 3. C 4. A 5. A 6. B 7. A 8. C 9. B

Exercise 32

Answers

1. C 2. B 3. C 4. B 5. C 6. B 7. A 8. B 9. C

Exercise 33

Answers

1. C 2. C 3. B 4. C 5. A 6. C 7. B 8. C 9. C

Exercise 34

Answers

1. B 2. A 3. C 4. B 5. B 6. C 7. A 8. B 9. A

Exercise 35

Answers

1. C 2. B 3. A 4. C 5. B 6. A 7. C 8. C 9. C

Exercise 36

Answers

1. B 2. C 3. B 4. C 5. B 6. A 7. B 8. A 9. B

Exercise 37

Answers

1. C 2. B 3. B 4. A 5. C 6. C 7. A 8. C

Exercise 38

Answers

1. B 2. C 3. B 4. A 5. C 6. A 7. B 8. A 9. B

Exercise 39

Answers

1. B 2. A 3. A 4. A 5. C 6. B 7. A 8. B 9. A

Exercise 40

Answers

1. B 2. A 3. C 4. B 5. A 6. C 7. A 8. C 9. C

About the Author

Born on his father's birthday, Ted Knoy received a Bachelor of Arts in History at Franklin College of Indiana (Franklin, Indiana) and a Master's in Public Administration at American International College (Springfield, Massachusetts). He is currently a Ph.D. student in Education at the University of East Anglia (Norwich, England). Having conducted research and independent study in New Zealand, Ukraine, South Africa, India, Nicaragua and Switzerland, he has lived in Taiwan since 1989 where he is a permanent resident.

Having taught technical writing in the graduate school programs of National Chiao Tung University (currently in the Institute of Information Management and Department of Communications Engineering) and National Tsing Hua University (currently in the Department of Computer Science) since 1989, Ted is a full-time instructor in the Foreign Languages Division at Yuan Pei University of Science and Technology. He is also the English editor of several technical and medical journals and publications in Taiwan.

Ted is the author of The Chinese Technical Writers' Series, which includes An English Style Approach for Chinese Technical Writers, English Oral Presentations for Chinese Technical Writers, A Correspondence Manual for Chinese Technical Writers, An Editing Workbook for Chinese Technical Writers, and Advanced Copyediting Practice for Chinese Technical Writers. He is also the author of Writing Effective Study Plans and Writing Effective Work Proposals, which are part of The Chinese Professional Writers' Series.

Ted created and coordinates the Chinese On-line Writing Lab (OWL) at http://mx.nthu.edu.tw/~tedknoy

Acknowledgments

Thanks to the following individuals for contributing to this book:

National Tsing Hua and National Chiao Tung Universities (Taiwan)

Jyh-Da Wei, Ming-Da Wu, Ing-Hong Liao, Yi-Min Kao, Professor Chuen-Tsai Sun, Professor Han-Lin Li, Professor Lee-Eeng Tong, Professor Shyan-Min Yuan, Professor Wen-Hua Chen, Zhih-Feng Liu, Dr. San-Ru Lin, Chou-I Chin, Min-Juen Dzhen, Min-xin Shen, Professor Duen-Ren Liu, Hung-Hui Chen, Hung-Je Ju, Ming-Sheng Yeh, En-Jie, Li, Chang-Chi Yu, Wan-Gye Yang, Pei-Fang, Yeh, Cheng-Chang Liang, Ya-Lan Yang, Ming-Wei Chang, Hsih-Tien Chen, Tai-Ing Yeh, Hu-Min Chu, Jung-Fa Tsai, Chang-Jui Fu, Kuo-Tzahn Chang, and Chiu-Hsia Hsieh.

Institute of Condensed Matter Physics at the Ukrainian Academy of Sciences and Institute of Physical Studies at Ivan Franck University(Ukraine)

Kyrylo Taburshchyk, Oleg Velychko, Maxym Dudka, Viktoria Blavats'ka, Roman Bigun, Oleh Klochan, Oleg Bovgyra, Ihoz Kajun, Tryna Kudyk, Roman Meruyk, Iryna Yaraphn, Iryna Hud, Oksama Mel'nyk, and Peter Pandiy

Silicon Integrated Systems Corporation, Hsinchu Science-based Industrial Park (Taiwan)

吳曉韻	鄔志賢	姜兆聲	游曜聲	邱美淑	劉銓	林平偉	朱俊威
曾若媚	韓承諺	蕭志成	陳方松	林宏洲	蔡璧禧	林柏廷	許資力
邱首凱	邱榮樑	葉國煒	呂忠晏	溫俊福	金慎遠	吳江龍	李鳳笙

林玫君　陳怡安　潘眞眞　李杏櫻　羅惠慈　孫蓮　　吳忠儒　賴東明

林志聰　翁育生　王志浩　陳仲一　林俊宏

Thanks also to Wang Min-Chia for illustrating this book. Thanks also to my technical writing students in the Department of Computer Science at National Tsing Hua University, Institute of Information Management, Department of Communication Engineering, and Department of Information Science at National Chiao Tung University, Institute of Physical Studies at Ivan Franck University (Lviv, Ukraine) and the Institute of Condensed Matter Physics of the Ukraine Academy of Sciences (Lviv, Ukraine). Robin Koerner and Seamus Harris are also appreciated for reviewing this workbook.

精通科技論文（報告）寫作之捷徑
An English Style Approach for Chinese Technical Writers （修訂版）

作者：柯泰德（Ted Knoy）

內容簡介

使用直接而流利的英文會話

讓您所寫的英文科技論文很容易被了解

提供不同形式的句型供您參考利用

比較中英句子結構之異同

利用介系詞片語將二個句子連接在一起

萬其超 / 李國鼎科技發展基金會秘書長

本書是多年實務經驗和專注力之結晶，因此是一本坊間少見而極具實用價值的書。

陳文華 / 國立清華大學工學院院長

中國人使用英文寫作時，語法上常會犯錯，本書提供了很好的實例示範，對於科技論文寫作有相當參考價值。

徐　章 / 工業技術研究院量測中心主任

這是一個讓初學英文寫作的人，能夠先由不犯寫作的錯誤開始再根據書中的步驟逐步學習提升寫作能力的好工具，此書的內容及解說方式使讀者也可以無師自通，藉由自修的方式學習進步，但是更重要的是它雖然是一本好書，當您學會了書中的許多技巧，如果您還想要更進步，那麼基本原則還是要常常練習，才能發揮書的精髓。

Kathleen Ford, English Editor,Proceedings(Life Science Divison), National Science Council

The Chinese Technical Writers Series is valuable for anyone involved with creating scientific documentation.

※若有任何英文文件修改問題，請直接與柯泰德先生聯絡： (03) 5724895

特　　　價　新台幣300元
劃　　　撥　19419482 清蔚科技股份有限公司
線上訂購　四方書網 www.4Book.com.tw
發 行 所　華香園出版社

作好英文會議簡報
English Oral Presentations for Chinese Technical Writers

作者：柯泰德（Ted Kony）

內容簡介

本書共分十二個單元，涵括產品開發、組織、部門、科技、及產業的介紹、科技背景、公司訪問、研究能力及論文之發表等，每一單元提供不同型態的科技口頭簡報範例，以進行英文口頭簡報的寫作及表達練習，是一本非常實用的著作。

李鍾熙／工業技術研究院化學工業研究所所長

一個成功的科技簡報，就是使演講流暢，用簡單直接的方法、清楚表達內容。本書提供一個創新的方法（途徑），給組織每一成員做為借鏡，得以自行準備口頭簡報。利用本書這套有系統的方法加以練習，將必然使您信心備增，簡報更加順利成功。

薛敬和／IUPAC台北國際高分子研討會執行長
國立清華大學教授

本書以個案方式介紹各英文會議簡報之執行方式，深入簡出，為邁入實用狀況的最佳參考書籍。

沙晉康／清華大學化學研究所所長
第十五屆國際雜環化學會議主席

本書介紹英文簡報的格式，值得國人參考。今天在學術或工商界與外國接觸來往均日益增多，我們應加強表達的技巧，尤其是英文的簡報應具有很高的專業水準。本書做為一個很好的範例。

張俊彥／國立交通大學電機資訊學院教授兼院長

針對中國學生協助他們寫好英文的國際論文參加國際會議如何以英語演講、內容切中要害特別推薦。

※若有任何英文文件修改問題，請直接與柯泰德先生聯絡：（03）5724895

特　　價　新台幣250元
劃　　撥　19419482 清蔚科技股份有限公司
線上訂購　四方書網 www.4Book.com.tw
發 行 所　工業技術研究院

英文信函參考手冊
A Correspondence Manual for Chinese Technical Writers

作者：柯泰德（Ted Knoy）

內容簡介

本書期望成為從事專業管理與科技之中國人，在國際場合上溝通交流時之參考指導書籍。本書所提供的書信範例（附磁碟片），可為您撰述信件時的參考範本。更實際的是，本書如同一「寫作計畫小組」，能因應特定場合（狀況）撰寫出所需要的信函。

李國鼎／總統府資政

我國科技人員在國際場合溝通表達之機會急遽增加，希望大家都來重視英文說寫之能力。

羅明哲／國立中興大學教務長

一份表達精準且適切的英文信函，在國際間的往來交流上，重要性不亞於研究成果的報告發表。本書介紹各類英文技術信函的特徵及寫作指引，所附範例中肯實用，為優良的學習及參考書籍。

廖俊臣／國立清華大學理學院院長

本書提供許多有關工業技術合作、技術轉移、工業資訊、人員訓練及互訪等接洽信函的例句和範例，頗為實用，極具參考價值。

于樹偉／工業安全衛生技術發展中心主任

國際間往來日益頻繁，以英文有效地溝通交流，是現今從事科技研究人員所需具備的重要技能。本書在寫作風格、文法結構與取材等方面，提供極佳的寫作參考與指引，所列舉的範例，皆經過作者細心的修訂與潤飾，必能切合讀者的實際需要。

※若有任何英文文件修改問題，請直接與柯泰德先生聯絡：（03）5724895

特　　價　新台幣250元
劃　　撥　19419482 清蔚科技股份有限公司
線上訂購　四方書網 www.4Book.com.tw
發 行 所　工業技術研究院

科技英文編修訓練手冊
An Editing Workbook for Chinese Technical Writers

作者：柯泰德（Ted Knoy）

內容簡介

要把科技英文寫的精確並不是件容易的事情。通常在投寄文稿發表前，作者都要前前後後修改草稿，在這樣繁複過程中甚至最後可能請專業的文件編修人士代勞雕琢使全文更為清楚明確。

本書由科技論文的寫作型式、方法型式、內容結構及內容品質著手，並以習題方式使學生透過反覆練習熟能生巧，能確實提昇科技英文之寫作及編修能力。

劉炯明 / 國立清華大學校長

「科技英文寫作」是一項非常重要的技巧。本書針對台灣科技研究人員在英文寫作發表這方面的訓練，書中以實用性練習對症下藥，期望科技英文寫作者熟能生巧，實在是一個很有用的教材。

彭旭明 / 國立台灣大學副校長

本書為科技英文寫作系列之四：以練習題為主，由反覆練習中提昇寫作反編輯能力。適合理、工、醫、農的學生及研究人員使用，特為推薦。

許千樹 / 國立交通大學研究發展處研發長

處於今日高科技時代，國人用到科技英文寫作之機會甚多，如何能以精練的手法寫出一篇好的科技論文，極為重要。本書針對國人寫作之缺點提供了各種清楚的編修範例，實用性高，極具參考價值。

陳文村 / 國立清華大學電機資訊學院院長

處在我國日益國際化、資訊化的社會裡，英文書寫是必備的能力，本書提供很多極具參考價值的範例。柯泰德先生在清大任教科技英文寫作多年，深受學生喜愛，本人樂於推薦此書。

※若有任何英文文件修改問題，請直接與柯泰德先生聯絡：（03）5724895

特　　價　新台幣350元
劃　　撥　19419482 清蔚科技股份有限公司
線上訂購　四方書網 www.4Book.com.tw
發 行 所　清蔚科技股份有限公司

科技英文編修訓練手冊【進階篇】
Advanced Copyediting Practice for Chinese Technical Writers

作者：柯泰德（Ted Knoy）

內容簡介

本書延續科技英文寫作系列之四「科技英文編修訓練手冊」之寫作指導原則，更進一步把重點放在如何讓作者想表達的意思更明顯，即明白寫作。把文章中曖昧不清全部去除，使閱讀您文章的讀者很容易的理解您作品的精髓。

本手冊同時國立清華大學資訊工程學系非同步遠距教學科技英文寫作課程指導範本。

張俊彥 / 國立交通大學校長暨中研院院士

　　對於國內理工學生及從事科技研究之人士而言，可說是一本相當有用的書籍，特向讀者推薦。

蔡仁堅 / 前新竹市長

　　科技不分國界，隨著進入公元兩千年的資訊時代，使用國際語言撰寫學術報告已是時勢所趨；今欣見柯泰德先生致力於編撰此著作，並彙集了許多實例詳加解說，相信對於科技英文的撰寫有著莫大的裨益，特予以推薦。

史欽泰 / 工研院院長

　　本書即以實用範例，針對國人寫作的缺點提供簡單、明白的寫作原則，非常適合科技研發人員使用。

張智星 / 國立清華大學資訊工程學系副教授、計算中心組長

　　本書是特別針對系上所開科技英文寫作非同步遠距教學而設計，範圍內容豐富，所列練習也非常實用，學生可以配合課程來使用，在時間上更有彈性的針對自己情況來練習，很有助益。

劉世東 / 長庚大學醫學院微生物免疫科主任

　　書中的例子及習題對閱讀者會有很大的助益。這是一本研究生必讀的書，也是一般研究者重要的參考書。

※若有任何英文文件修改問題，請直接與柯泰德先生聯絡：（03）5724895

特　　價　新台幣450元
劃　　撥　19419482 清蔚科技股份有限公司
線上訂購　四方書網 www.4Book.com.tw
發 行 所　清蔚科技股份有限公司

有效撰寫英文讀書計畫
Writing Effective Study Plans

作者：柯泰德（Ted Knoy）

內容簡介

本書指導準備出國進修的學生撰寫精簡切要的英文讀書計畫，內容包括：表達學習的領域及興趣、展現所具備之專業領域知識、敘述學歷背景及成就等。本書的每個單元皆提供視覺化的具體情境及相關寫作訓練，讓讀者進行實際的訊息運用練習。此外，書中的編修訓練並可加強「精確寫作」及「明白寫作」的技巧。本書適用於個人自修以及團體授課，能確實引導讀者寫出精簡而有效的英文讀書計畫。

本手冊同時為國立清華大學資訊工程學系非同步遠距教學科技英文寫作課程指導範本。

于樹偉 / 工業技術研究院主任

《有效撰寫讀書計畫》一書主旨在提供國人精深學習前的準備，包括：讀書計畫及推薦信函的建構、完成。藉由本書中視覺化訊息的互動及練習，國人可以更明確的掌握全篇的意涵，及更完整的表達心中的意念。這也是本書異於坊間同類書籍只著重在片斷記憶，不求理解最大之處。

王玫 / 工業研究技術院、化學工業研究所組長

《有效撰寫讀書計畫》主要是針對想要進階學習的讀者，由基本的自我學習經驗描述延伸至未來目標的設定，更進一步強調推薦信函的撰寫，藉由圖片式訊息互動，讓讀者主動聯想及運用寫作知識及技巧，避免一味的記憶零星的範例；如此一來，讀者可以更清楚表明個別的特質及快速掌握重點。

※若有任何英文文件修改問題，請直接與柯泰德先生聯絡：（03）5724895

特　　價　新台幣450元
劃　　撥　19419482 清蔚科技股份有限公司
線上訂購　四方書網 www.4Book.com.tw
發 行 所　清蔚科技股份有限公司

有效撰寫英文工作提案
Writing Effective Work Proposals

作者：柯泰德（Ted Knoy）

內容簡介

許多國人都是在工作方案完成時才開始撰寫相關英文提案，他們視撰寫提案為行政工作的一環，只是消極記錄已完成的事項，而不是積極的規劃掌控未來及現在正進行的工作。如果國人可以在撰寫英文提案時，事先仔細明辨工作計畫提案的背景及目標，不僅可以確保寫作進度、寫作結構的完整性，更可兼顧提案相關讀者的興趣強調。本書中詳細的步驟可指導工作提案寫作者達成此一目標。 書中的每個單元呈現三個視覺化的情境，提供國人英文工作提案寫作實質訊息，而相關附加的寫作練習讓讀者做實際的訊息運用。此外，本書也非常適合在課堂上使用，教師可以先描述單元情境而讓學生藉由書中練習循序完成具有良好架構的工作提案。書中內容包括：1.工作提案計畫（第一部分）：背景 2.工作提案計畫（第二部分）：行動 3.問題描述 4.假設描述 5.摘要撰寫（第一部分）： 簡介背景、目標及方法 6.摘要撰寫（第二部分）： 歸納希望的結果及其對特定領域的貢獻 7.綜合上述寫成精確工作提案。

唐傳義／國立清華大學資訊工程學系主任

本書重點放在如何在工作計畫一開始時便可以用英文來規劃整個工作提案，由工作提案的背景、行動、方法及預期的結果漸次教導國人如何寫出具有良好結構的英文工作提案。如此用英文明確界定工作提案的程序及工作目標更可以確保英文工作提案及工作計畫的即時完成。對工作效率而言也有助益。

在國人積極加入WTO之後的調整期，優良的英文工作提案寫作能力絕對是一項競爭力快速加分的工具。

※若有任何英文文件修改問題，請直接與柯泰德先生聯絡： （03）5724895

特	價	新台幣450元
劃	撥	19735365 葉忠賢
線上訂購		www.ycrc.com.tw
發 行 所		揚智文化事業股份有限公司

The Chinese
Online Writing Lab
【 柯泰德線上英文論文編修訓練服務 】
http://mx.nthu.edu.tw/~tedknoy

您有科技英文寫作上的困擾嗎？

您的文章在投稿時常被國外論文審核人員批評文法很爛嗎？以至於被退稿嗎？

您對論文段落的時式使用上常混淆不清嗎？

您在寫作論文時同一個動詞或名詞常常重複使用嗎？

您的這些煩惱現在均可透過柯泰德網路線上科技英文論文編修服務來替您加以解決。本服務項目分別含括如下：

1. 英文論文編輯與修改
2. 科技英文寫作開課訓練服務
3. 線上寫作家教
4. 免費寫作格式建議服務，及網頁問題討論區解答
5. 線上遠距教學（互動練習）

另外，為能廣為服務中國人士對論文寫作上之缺點，柯泰德亦同時著作下列參考書籍可供有志人士為寫作上之參考。

<1.精通科技論文（報告）寫作之捷徑
<2.做好英文會議簡報
<3.英文信函參考手冊
<4.科技英文編修訓練手冊
<5.科技英文編修訓練手冊（進階篇）
<6.有效撰寫英文讀書計畫

上部分亦可由柯泰德先生的首頁中下載得到。

如果您對本服務有興趣的話，可參考柯泰德先生的首頁標示。

柯泰德網路線上科技英文論文編修服務
地址：新竹市大學路50號8樓之三
TEL:03-5724895
FAX:03-5724938
網址：http://mx.nthu.edu.tw/~tedknoy
E-mail:tedaknoy@ms11.hinet.net

有效撰寫求職英文自傳

著　　者／柯泰德 (Ted Knoy)

出 版 者／揚智文化事業股份有限公司

發 行 人／葉忠賢

總 編 輯／閻富萍

登 記 證／局版北市業字第 1117 號

地　　址／台北縣深坑鄉北深路 3 段 260 號 8 樓

電　　話／（02）26647780

傳　　真／（02）26647633

郵政劃撥／19735365　戶名：葉忠賢

印　　刷／鼎易印刷事業股份有限公司

初版一刷／2003 年 4 月

初版二刷／2007 年 5 月

　ＩＳＢＮ　／957-818-495-6

定　　價／新台幣 450 元

E–mail　／ service@ycrc.com.tw

網　　址／ http://www.ycrc.com.tw

國家圖書館出版品預行編目資料

有效撰寫求職英文自傳 ＝ Writing Effective
Employment Application Statements /
柯泰德（Ted Knoy）著；王敏嘉插圖. --初版. --
臺北市：揚智文化，2003[民 92]
　　面；　公分. --（應用英文寫作系列；3）
ISBN　957-818-495-6（平裝）

1.英國語言 － 應用文

805.17　　　　　　　　　　　92003122